GHOST OF THE NILE

VERONICA SCOTT

Cover Art by Frauke Spanuth of Croco Designs

To my daughters Valerie and Elizabeth, and my best friend Daniel for all his encouragement and support through the years

Acknowledgment

Julie C and the E-book Formatting Fairies!

CHAPTER ONE

Periseneb had no idea how many years he'd been wandering in the gray lands of the Afterlife. Time had no meaning here. For time unending he'd done battle with monsters and demons, experiencing neither pain nor emotion, despite the horrific combat, until a startling moment when he felt pavement underfoot, not shifting gray sand. Raising his head with a rare flicker of curiosity, Periseneb found himself in a tunnel, walking toward an illuminated room. Radiance and warmth from a golden light beckoned him onward. He slowed and then stopped, fighting the tug of the summons bringing him here. Whatever was about to happen, he wouldn't go as a supplicant.

I was a warrior.

He straightened his shoulders.

One of Pharaoh's own guards.

He tightened the leather straps of his breastplate and drew his sword, intent on facing this new challenge as he'd lived, with pride.

Jaw set, eyes focused on the light ahead, Periseneb marched forward resolutely, braced by the discipline he'd learned in his life as a soldier.

He crossed the threshold into the chamber, his steps faltering at the sight of the deity waiting for him. But then, who had he expected? He was too lowly a shade for Isis or Osiris to bother with. Standing at attention, he saluted. "Lady Ma'at."

Calm smile on her face, the Great One, goddess of truth, nodded to him. Taller than he, dressed in a finely pleated red sheath, the goddess was imposing.

Her expertly painted face was accented by the towering red ostrich feather in her hair, and her expression could only be deemed welcoming. Eyebrows raised, eyes gleaming, she inspected him from head to toe as a commanding officer might.

He assessed the room with a glance, hope dying as quickly as it had sprung. Ma'at was alone. Neither of the other two judges, Anubis and Thoth, was present. Their chairs sat empty. The most dreaded occupant of the judging chamber was, thankfully, not paying any attention to him. As grotesque as the depictions of her hinted, the beast Ammit, Destroyer of Souls, slept snoring in a corner. Claws curled possessively, one hideous cheetah forepaw was draped over a gleaming human thigh bone. She snuffled, long pink tongue scraping the sharp crocodile teeth in her jaws, while her hippopotamus hind legs kicked in some dream. Repressing a shudder, Periseneb averted his eyes.

"I'm not here for my heart to be judged at long last, am I?" His voice sounded rusty to his ears.

"No indeed, Periseneb. The laws of the Afterlife haven't changed—you can't receive judgment, since none did you honor at the time of your death. No one performed even the tiniest ritual from the Book of the Dead on your behalf. You've no tomb, although your bones do lie in the soil of the Black Lands." Ma'at's voice was soft, her eyes misty with tears, apparently for him. "A paltry blessing, I know. I'm sorry."

He knew she was sincere. Truth was the only utterance Ma'at could make. He rammed his sword into its sheath and rolled his shoulders. "Why then am I here? I didn't seek this place out; I swear to you." Pride stiffened his spine. He wouldn't beg favors, not even when unexpectedly drawn into the presence of a gatekeeper, someone who could free his ka from ceaseless wandering…sentenced to defending the green serenity of the blessed duat, never to set foot there himself, banned for lack of proper ceremonies. The rule was harsh but just. No one deserved eternal life in the duat without proper judgment from the gods.

"Don't concern yourself about misunderstanding, warrior. I summoned you." The goddess walked to the ebony table where the scale for weighing the worthiness of human hearts stood ready. Idly, she tapped the balance beam and the arms swayed, cups twisting in the air on their thin gold chains.

Periseneb pushed away a rush of hot jealousy for the souls luckier than he, whose hearts had been weighed on the scales and obtained passage to the Afterlife for their owners. A tiny beacon of hope flickered in his mind. There had to be a reason Ma'at had picked him, of all the lost ones in the hinterlands, to meet with her.

"You recognize me as the embodiment of Truth?" She continued to toy with the scale, then picked up a slate and scanned the hieroglyphics before glancing at him, eyes gleaming under winged brows.

He nodded.

"Yet, I'm also a seeker of justice and balance, one who rights wrongs. I'm the goddess of second chances for the human race." She raised her elegant eyebrows. "Although such chances are few and far between."

Despite the warmth of the brightly lit room, a shiver worked its way down Periseneb's spine. "You wish to right the wrong of my murder? Bring my murderer to account for the crime?"

She shook her head, the golden beads in her wig chiming like little bells. "Your death is done, past, woven into the fabric of life in the upper world these two-hundred years and more."

He staggered, locking one hand on the edge of the table to steady himself. "So long?"

"Time here and time there run differently, warrior. Only the Nile remains unchanging." She moved to the black-and-gold chair, seating herself and leaning against the richly decorated back. "Yet, your death is connected in a way to events now." Ma'at nodded her head as if some decision had been reached. "I need a champion."

"To do what? How can a human accomplish something the gods or their servants can't?" Action sounded good, but he was wary after his time in the outer dark. She didn't invite him to sit—he didn't think he was brave enough to sit in the presence of a Great One—so he assumed parade rest stance. When in doubt, Periseneb's code was to rely on what the military had taught him.

"Matters are in flux in Egypt. A new pharaoh sits on the throne and he's repelled the forces of the god Qemtusheb, the great enemy of my King, Osiris. For a time." Ma'at raised one finger as if her listener might rejoice prematurely.

"Evil constantly seeks to re-enter the Black Lands, seize its richness and feed, grow stronger."

Taking little interest in the affairs of a pharaoh he'd never met, Periseneb spread his hands in a helpless gesture. "I can't fight the Hyksos god."

"Gods have agents. Pawns. Sometimes even the innocent commit acts advancing a Dark One's agenda, merely because the mortal mind lacks understanding of a god's agenda. Each of us on the other side of the scale must do our part to balance the evil." As her shoulders slumped as if with great weariness, Ma'at sighed. Then she straightened her back and smiled. "To business. I need a champion to go to the Nome of the Shield…"

"My home province," he said, knowing his voice was unsteady. Memories flooded into his mind, past the blocks he'd erected to keep away thoughts of home and family. No coward when it came to physical pain, he feared the agony any dream of his birthplace brought to his heart.

Apparently oblivious to his inner struggle, Ma'at nodded. "Events are in motion there. I wish to influence the outcome, but it isn't the kind of situation I can affect directly." She tapped the table with her stylus. "Nor can I be absent from my duties here for so long as this task may require."

He found it hard to imagine a goddess walking in his home province for any time at all. Shield Nome was dry, dusty, and far removed from Thebes and the known places of power. "What do you need done?"

Head tilted, smile on her ruby red lips, she said, "You to complete your interrupted journey home."

Disappointed, since he'd been thinking of battles with demons or other epic deeds, he said, "That's all? Show up two-hundred years late and say, here I am? Who would know me now? Who would care? I have no place there, Great One." His voice cracked a little on the last sentence and he clamped his lips closed, taking a deep breath. Thinking about the simple dreams he'd cherished as a man hurt like a knife to the heart. All gone, turned to dust.

Leaving the chair, she walked to him and the scent of her blue lotus perfume was calming. "Complete the journey and act as your heart dictates." She tapped his chest with her index finger and he felt his heart thump loudly. "Do what you believe best represents truth…what represents me. I request no more, and will accept no less."

He swallowed hard. "Forgive me for asking, Great One, but…"

"What reward is there for you?" Smiling, she reached to pluck the feather from her turquoise-and-malachite encrusted gold headband. "Spend one month in the upper world, complete my task, and your reward shall be eternity in the paradise of the duat. I'll convey you there myself." Hand over her heart, she said, "I swear by my own symbol. Lord Osiris, ruler of the gods, has agreed to this plan and the reward."

He stepped back. Surprising himself, he hesitated, even as he questioned what could possibly be making him pause. This was an unprecedented offer and she could change her mind just as suddenly. He chose his words with great care, wary of the tiny frown gathering on her forehead. "Reward isn't the issue, Great One. Returning to my home now after all these years wandering the fringes of the Afterlife is hard to contemplate. I—there were people who mattered to me. There was a woman…"

"All gone," she said, not unkindly. "I can't discuss their fates with you." She studied him for a moment. "Don't you wish for completion? Don't you wish for entry to the duat and eternal Afterlife? I've never met a human who didn't, save for one who married a god instead."

He shut his eyes for a moment. *Why do I hesitate? Give the goddess one month's service and then spend eternity in the Afterlife. Simple. After so many years, my home will be much changed. I won't know anyone and they won't know me. As an anonymous wanderer, how hard could a month there be?* Reopening his eyes, he met her gaze. "I'll do it."

"Good." She touched his bare shoulder with the feather. "But my task must be completed and the order of the universe restored, or you'll return to the gray wastes. Such was the condition set by Osiris. Thirty days is the time limit."

Having decided, he didn't hesitate. "I'll take the risk."

At first, he felt only the soft brushing of the fronds, which tickled, but then his entire shoulder throbbed and he grabbed at it with his other hand. Glancing down, he realized she'd branded him—four tiny red feathers had been tattooed on his shoulder in the shape of her cartouche. The ink blazed for a second, fiery scarlet-tinged light, before fading, leaving a residue of flat paintings on his skin. Wondering, rubbing his tingling shoulder, he stared into the deep black pools of her eyes. A shiver spiraled through his limbs.

Ma'at glanced away. "You may call upon me four times while you're in the Nome of the Shield if you need to do so. There will be no penalty."

He nodded without fully understanding her comment. *What would I need her intervention to accomplish?* "How will I know when the task is done?"

"You'll have no doubts, my champion." She touched the quill to his forehead, a light tap.

Periseneb felt a breeze springing up and he grew chilled, falling to his knees in front of Ma'at as the wind gathered strength. She stood strong as ever, her dress not even ruffled by the wind battering him. Buffeted by the gusts, he screwed his eyes shut against the force and swayed. His return journey to the upper world had apparently begun.

"Are you sure we're following the path of our own cows, not his?" Neithamun pulled her shawl closer, unhappy to be trespassing on her contentious neighbor's land. She stumbled in the loose dirt and clutched at her companion's arm.

Supporting her weight for a moment while she regained her balance, the gangly cowherd nodded. "You climbed through the damaged fences with me, my lady. And see the tracks in front of us?"

Neithamun squinted at the dusty path. "How do smudged marks in the dirt answer my question?"

The boy knelt beside the churned up ground. "Old Henut is the queen of the herd and her left front hoof has an overgrowth. See, here's her mark on the trail, clearly."

"Good eye." Reassured, Neithamun followed the boy along the cows' meandering path. "It's no wonder the poor beasts wanted to roam over here once the fence was damaged. The green fodder is so lush! I wish we had half the amount on our land this year."

"Henut knows the best places all right. The other cows follow her, bossy as she is." Sounding proud of his wayward charges, Mentu puffed out his chest.

"The patties are fresh, not long since the herd wandered by. We'll find them and get them home again before Lord Haqaptah's bullies even know we've been here."

"You seem quite confident," she said, leaving the trail to avoid stepping in the evidence her cows had left.

"Cook read the goose entrails last night before she cooked dinner, and she said things were highly favorable to us right now." Brows drawn together as he mimicked the woman's serious tones, Mentu's expression was grave. "And I've had dreams," he said, deepening his voice to add weight to his own pronouncement. "Extremely favorable dreams. The omens are positive."

"Well, I can't argue with omens." Deliberately, Neithamun kept her voice light and cheery. She'd had dreams too, but not the kind she wanted to share with anyone, especially her happy-go-lucky cowherd. The most frequent one featured a woman standing in the distance, swathed in black robes, face concealed in shadows. Last night the woman had come unusually close, the dream terrifyingly hard to wake from, which sent her to the temple, on her knees until dawn, praying to the gods for help. Surely such a powerful dream meant the female inhabiting the nightmare was the portent of a disaster more dire than missing cows.

Mentu was supplying details of his own prophetic experience, something about hyenas and a lion, as she reached the top of the ridge. Neithamun found her wayward cows happily grazing in a lush patch of greenery. "We have to gather them as fast as we can and get off this cursed estate," she said. Breaking a switch from a nearby bush, she trailed Mentu down the slope.

"If I drive Henut home, the others will follow," he said.

Neithamun stood well clear while Mentu persuaded the stubborn lead cow to abandon her newfound, lush grazing, but eventually he got the animal moving leisurely in the right direction. Casting anxious glances in the direction of her neighbor's dwelling off in the distance, Neithamun chased the laggards, calling to them and swishing the branch. Until she reached the safety of her own land, her nerves would remain taut as a bowstring.

But as Mentu and the cow he was leading reached the hilltop, five guardsmen came running over the rise, blocking their path.

"What's this? Stealing cattle is a serious offense." The leader skidded to a stop, hands on his hips, jaw jutting, eyes narrowed.

"These are my cows," Neithamun answered, wishing she wasn't short of breath. "I'll thank you to get out of our way, and we'll leave as fast as the cows can be driven."

"Without souring their milk," Mentu added, reliably conscious of his responsibility as the chief herdsman.

Although she was trespassing and surrounded by five leering mercenaries, Neithamun wasn't particularly afraid until the tallest of Lord Haqaptah's servants grabbed her arm as she brushed past him. The one-eyed, badly scarred man stroked her cheek with his free hand.

"Set's teeth, how dare you lay hands on me?" Jerking back, she aimed a kick at his shins. The men circling her laughed. "Let me pass," she said, clutching the acacia branch she was using to drive the small herd of wayward black and white cattle. "These are my cows, bearing my brand and I have the right to take them home."

Braceletting her wrist with one hand, the ringleader rubbed his jaw and glanced at the others. "Not so fast, trespasser."

"Pharaoh's law entitles me to pursue my own animals when the herd escapes the fences," she said. "I demand you release me and allow me to take my cattle to their field." She wished she was safe at home, but wasn't this exactly why she'd insisted on accompanying her young cowherd? It was her duty to retrieve her roaming animals, and to protect Mentu.

The man released her with a mocking laugh. "We haven't checked the brands. For all we know, the marks might be counterfeit, drawn with charcoal perhaps? Maybe these belong to our master. A hussy brave enough to stroll onto another's property might not hesitate to commit other crimes." He leered at her. "It's well known how desperate times have gotten for you."

"You jackal spawn probably stole the cows in the first place," shouted Mentu, kicking dirt onto the shins of the nearest man. "You know the animals are ours, none other in the province have the ruddy hue to their spots."

One of the men grabbed the cowherd by the neck and held him off the ground. "You need to be taught manners." The boy flailed uselessly, trying to defend himself, his face purpling.

Neithamun launched herself at the pair, beating the aggressor about the head and shoulders with the small stick, while the other men guffawed and made rude remarks. Ignoring them, she scolded the person abusing her servant. "Let him go, you're strangling him." Throwing the ineffective branch aside, she clawed at the man's fingers, kicking him in the leg for good measure as he choked Mentu.

Arm snaking around her waist, the ring leader lifted her away. "Such fire, wasted on rescuing a mere cowherd. Come on, give me a kiss, to pay forfeit for trespassing. The soft lips of a noblewoman against mine will be a novel experience, one to boast of in my cups."

She tried to hit him, but a second man caught her arm. The first assailant got a better grip on her, his hands fondling her breasts. Neithamun tried to slam her head into his face, but he laughed as he nuzzled her neck, his stubble scraping her skin.

A sword interposed itself between the ruffian and Neithamun. Thinking for an instant she was seeing things in her panic, she nevertheless stood motionless, to avoid harm from the blade's sharp edge.

"First, you'll release the lady, and then you'll apologize." A deep voice, from someone standing to the side and behind her, issued the orders.

"We meant no harm." The man let her go immediately, retreating from the blade and whoever was wielding it. Hands raised to ward off an attack, Haqaptah's hired bully said, "Only a bit of harmless fun between neighbors."

Not recognizing the voice, astonished anyone on this estate would rescue her, she spun on her heel to see this new player. The man was a stranger to her. Tall and broad shouldered with straight black hair, longer than the norm, framing a handsome face, the new arrival was well muscled and carried himself balanced for combat, like a soldier.

"My impression is the lady believed otherwise. Your ill-advised horseplay seemed to upset her." The tall warrior who'd intervened shook his head, flicking a glance in her direction from dark brown eyes. "We need to defer to her sensibilities."

Neithamun straightened her dress with an angry swipe of her hand and ran to Mentu, sprawled in the dirt, coughing, with large bruises in the shape of his assailant's fingers forming on his neck. She fell to her knees, putting an arm behind his back to brace him, glaring at the five men. "Shame on you, picking on a boy."

"You're on Lord Haqaptah's land," retorted the boldest mercenary, with a nervous sideways glance at the stranger who'd intervened.

"Which doesn't give you any right to molest her," said the huge soldier who'd come from nowhere to rescue them. "Now, unless you're planning to help drive her cattle home, I suggest you move along about your own business." He waved the sword towards the east.

Several of Haqaptah's guards fingered knives at their belts, muttering and exchanging glances.

Neithamun tensed, tugging Mentu to his feet. If there was to be a fight, he had to be ready.

"I wouldn't advise you to try what you're thinking," the soldier said, grinning. He rubbed his jaw, as if pondering his own admonition. "Perhaps I shouldn't try to talk you out of your folly. It's been a long time since I had a good skirmish. My sword is thirsty."

The leader spat in the dust. "I've no time for sparring with wandering mercenaries. If you know what's good for you, stranger, you'll lose no time leaving my master's lands." He pointed at Neithamun. "This isn't over, merely deferred. Get your scrawny cattle off my lord's land before your pest-ridden beasts give his herd some disease. Your bad luck might be contagious."

She didn't deign to reply but took Mentu's hand and both moved to form the cows into a herd again, urging them to walk placidly down the narrow trail. Spoiled milk was the least of her worries at the moment, but she refused to give Haqaptah's men the satisfaction of seeing how frightened she still was. She wasn't running away like she'd been in the wrong. Half expecting the guards to follow her with taunts, she risked a glance over her shoulder and observed how the newcomer was standing between her enemies and the path she'd taken. *Who is he? Where did he come from? At least he doesn't seem to be a new member of Haqaptah's growing army of mercenaries. Yet.*

Periseneb lingered as the girl and her cattle moved away, watching as the five men took the opposite direction, muttering among themselves and glancing at him once or twice. When he was sure the ruffians had gone, he sheathed the sword, taking a moment to draw a deep breath of the fresh air. Ma'at had plunged him into the middle of a problem and his head was spinning. He'd reacted instinctively to protect the underdog in the standoff, soldier's reflexes coming to the fore. He'd felt something else as well, a thrum of power in his veins, hot and hungry to kill. His deadly nature as a ghost seeking to take over?

Something to watch out for, while here in life. Once he loosed the anger of the much reviled *akh* he truly was, could he control the destructive urges? Reclaim mortal form? Resolving to be on guard against his own dangerous status, he turned to follow those he'd rescued.

Time to learn more about where the goddess had sent him and why. Why did she place him in this spot, at this moment? Some sort of answer must rest with the woman and boy, so he trotted after them.

Swatting a grazing cow lightly on the haunches to get the placid animal moving again, he slowed to a walk beside the young woman. "Are you all right?" he asked.

She smiled at him hesitantly, color in her cheeks. "Fine, thanks to you, stranger. I owe you much gratitude for coming to our aid. I hope you'll have no cause to regret the kindness in coming days. Lord Haqaptah won't be pleased you interfered."

Haqaptah? The name rasped on his nerves, bringing a vision of the overly proud, arrogant noble of his day. *A descendant surely. Makes sense the family would still be in the area.* "I'm passing through, not planning to stay long. My path probably won't cross this unpleasant noble's." He gave her a little bow. "I'm Periseneb, late of Pharaoh's army, attaining the rank of leader of one hundred, now honorably discharged."

"Were you in the battle for Thebes? Did you see service against the Hyksos?" the boy asked. Mimicking the slash of a sword with his stick, startling the nearest cow into moving somewhat more rapidly for a moment, he said, "I wish I was old enough to be a soldier."

Periseneb kept his face straight. *So young, so eager.* "I saw combat in many places, yes." True enough as far as it went.

The girl made a shushing motion with her hand. "Hush, Mentu, it's not polite to interrogate him." Apparently recalling she'd not introduced herself, she said, "I'm Neithamun, of Heron Marsh. This belligerent one is my chief cowherd."

"*Lady* Neithamun." The boy's reprimand was stern.

She laughed, gesturing at her plain blue cotton dress and rude sandals. "Yes, although our visitor probably won't believe such a lofty claim."

"I've heard of the great estate of Heron Marsh." He stared toward the horizon, mixed emotions over her status churning in his gut. In his time, a daughter of the house wouldn't lower herself to herding cows. Why was she allowed or encouraged to do so?

Neithamun laughed again, but he thought he heard a bitter tone. Spine straight, chin held high, she said, "Not such a great estate these days, but we do our best. Land rich and deben poor. Are you from this area then?"

"I've some familiarity with the area."

"Then you must know my family and Haqaptah's have been rivals for a long time. He covets my land." She shrugged. "Things are a little difficult right now."

Mentu snorted and Neithamun scowled at him before turning to Periseneb. "You're welcome to spend the night under my roof, traveler. Dinner will be simple but filling. You can continue your journey tomorrow."

Marveling at how simple it was to insert himself into the estate, hoping his task for the goddess would also prove to be easily accomplished, he said, "Very kind of you. I accept the offer. I'm in no particular rush, having no set destination."

Whistling as if he'd no cares in the world, Mentu chased after a cow wandering from the small herd. Neithamun and Periseneb walked silently behind the other cattle. He was content just to be in the outer world again, breathing fresh air, watching birds fly across the blue sky, in the company of other people. He'd forgotten how it felt to be alive, to enjoy the simple pleasures. The vivid colors of the upper world were pleasing to his eyes. His troubled ka felt lighter already after the unrelieved gloom and grayness of the deserts fringing the Afterlife.

The path topped a ridge and he halted in mid-step, staring ahead. He drew a shaky breath at the sight of the two story, sprawling house of Heron Marsh, outlined in red by the setting sun. *Unchanged,* was his first thought, but as he performed a more critical appraisal, heart pounding, shielding his eyes against the sun's rays, he saw new outbuildings, a large addition to the shrine next to the garden and other revisions since his time.

"The house is impressive." Neithamun stood beside him as the cows picked their way down the hillside, snatching mouthfuls of grass as they plodded homeward. "From a distance. When we get closer, you'll see the many repairs needed, fallow fields, and empty grain bins." She grimaced as if in physical pain. After a moment, she continued along the path.

Periseneb took a few steps to catch up, his stride equal to several of hers. "What's happened? Why has the estate fallen upon hard times?"

"The demise of Heron Marsh is a long story." Neithamun shook her head. "Poor choices by my ancestors is as good an answer as any." Pausing for a moment, as if hesitant to continue, she said, "Some people will tell you there's a curse or the family offended the gods."

Startled, Periseneb missed a step. "How?"

Shoving her hair off her face, the lady laughed. "No, you mistake me, I don't believe such stories. I'm a practical person. I have to be, to keep the estate going. But if you stay any length of time in the area, you'll hear talk of curses and the like."

"I may be here for a few weeks, a month perhaps."

"Mentu, take the cows to the barn." Neithamun slapped the rump of the black-and-white spotted animal nearest to her. "Your sisters will be waiting to do the milking." Touching his arm with one hand, she issued an invitation to Periseneb. "Let's go to the house and get you settled in a guest room. Dinner will be at sunset. We've become unfashionably informal here, I'm afraid. We all dine together."

"All?" He wasn't prepared to be plunged into a gathering of people after so much time alone in the Afterlife. Yet, he'd no time to waste either, being on the goddess's timetable, with his ka at stake.

"The servants, the workers, and me." She smiled apologetically. "Too much trouble for the cook to prepare a separate dinner for me every night. And I eat what the rest have."

"You're the only family member in residence?" His surprise became shock as he absorbed the dilapidated state of the great house's façade, the spotty whitewash, the withered greenery, and the cracked steps. Even the huge doors, now standing open on rusty hinges, were warped. Keeping a mental version of a scribe's tally of all the things requiring attention, he stood aside to let her precede him.

Neithamun paused on the threshold. "I'm the only family member, period. The entire bloodline has dwindled to one person…me."

Speechless, he walked after her into the entry hall. The house was as rundown inside as it had been outside. The murals were faded and chipped, the tile floor scuffed and marred. His hostess led him to the central hall as a servant came to greet them. The room was scrupulously clean and the floor swept, which made the overall dilapidation all the more glaring.

"Please show our guest, Periseneb of—I'm sorry, in all the unpleasantness with Haqaptah's men, I forgot to ask where you're from."

Here. Biting his lip, he barely kept himself from giving voice to the telltale word. "I'm a wanderer, but born in this province."

"Well then, Wanderer of the Shield Province, welcome, and the maid will show you to a room." Neithamun frowned. "The big room, Meritka. No other will have a bed frame strong enough, I fear."

As the servant nodded in acknowledgment of the request, the lady of the estate walked away, saying over her shoulder, "I'll see you at dinner."

Neithamun hurried to her own rooms, the dust of the day on her skin making her feel coated in grime. *And this is how he first met me, like a common worker in the fields. No wonder he seemed so surprised to learn I was the lady of the estate.*

Her maid Menwe was waiting at the entrance to the suite. "We've poured the water for your bath, my lady."

"Good. I got covered in dust when Mentu and I tracked the missing cows." Stopping in front of the gazelle-footed, gilded table where her makeup box and hairbrushes waited, she grimaced in the mirror. "And my hair is a wild tangle, I see."

"You refuse to wear wigs, so of course your hair becomes a bird's nest." Menwe helped her unfasten the tabs on the dress and carried the garment to the basket for soiled clothing. "Who is he, my lady?"

Strolling toward the far doorway, which led to her private pool, Neithamun smiled. "Who?"

"The man who escorted you home, of course. Don't play coy with me," the maid said, with the familiarity of one who'd known Neithamun since childhood. "I want to hear all the details. I caught a glimpse of him when you came into the house. So handsome."

Neithamun tested the water with one toe and then descended the three steps into her pool, humming a little tune of contentment. It wasn't full enough to swim, but she immersed herself for a moment, relishing the cool liquid on her overheated skin. Rising, she smoothed her dripping hair away from her face. "Mentu and I were surrounded by Haqaptah's thugs and this man Periseneb appeared out of nowhere and made them leave us alone."

"Out of nowhere?" Menwe held out the basin filled with the natron and salt solution. "Do you think the gods sent him?"

Lathering her hair with the cleansing mixture, Neithamun said, "Of course not, don't be foolish. He's a soldier returning home from the wars. Says he's from somewhere in this nome. I don't remember exactly." Ducking to rinse her hair, she pondered her own words. *Where did he come from? We were in the middle of Haqaptah's lands, not near any road.* Goose bumps pebbled her skin as she stood. "He was probably lost," she said, as much to herself as to Menwe. "Have we any scrubbing sand?"

The maid handed over a small bowl full of glittering crystals. "Are you going to wear a wig tonight? And paint your face?" Her voice was eager.

Briefly tempted, Neithamun shook her head as she rinsed away the sand and the remaining suds from her hair. "It's pleasant to have a guest, but there's no need for me to make a special fuss."

Although she brought towels as Neithamun left the pool, Menwe made it clear she wasn't abandoning the argument. "When was the last time a handsome man came anywhere near Heron Marsh? And you won't daub a bit of kohl on your eyes? Make your lips redder? At least tell me you'll wear perfume!"

Wrapped in the towel, Neithamun toyed with the lid of her special blue glass perfume bottle for a moment, considering. Allowing the towel to fall, she dabbed a bit of the precious scent between her breasts. "All right, since you insist, this much I'll agree to do. But no more fuss!" Catching up her comb, she dragged it through her unruly hair as she walked to the bed. Eyeing the clean linen sheath, plain and simple, as were all her garments these days, she stifled her urge to indulge in self-criticism. "He'll be gone in the morning, so don't be weaving any wistful scribes' tales about him. He probably has two wives and many children waiting, wherever his home may be. And I'm not about to cast lures to a stranger because he's handsome." *And gallant. And blessed with a deep voice.*

Periseneb followed the elderly maid out of the hall, going to the left, into the corridor leading to sleeping quarters for family and visitors. He remembered the layout of the house as if he'd been there yesterday. Even the faint smell of the beeswax and cleaning fluid made from salt, potash and natron, sweetened with some spice, were the same. *Imagine what my father would think of me spending the night in a guest room.* Periseneb suppressed a grin. *Probably be horrified at my effrontery. I hope his shade rests easy or he'll be here to yank me from the bed.*

The door to the room was stuck and he hastened to assist the old woman in opening it, adding yet another thing to his mental list of needed repairs.

"I'll have a maid come in and clean for you." Running a finger over the nearest table, leaving a track in the dust, the servant sniffed. "We don't get much company these days, so the room hasn't been used since the Master died."

"When did he pass into the Afterlife?" Periseneb walked over to test the bed's webbing, concerned whether it would hold his weight.

"Four years ago, but things were going downhill even before his final illness. Nothing is like it used to be when I was young, I tell you plainly. It used to be an honor to serve at Heron Marsh; we were the envy of all in the nome, but now the gods avert their eyes from us." She cleaned her grimy finger on her overskirt. "There's no water for a bath, if you desire one. Sorry."

"No water?" He was astounded and disappointed. A bath and a shave were treats he'd been anticipating after all the years of wandering. Not that his beard had grown in the Afterlife, but the familiar ritual would have been soothing.

"We haul all the water by hand nowadays and we're done for the day. We filled Lady Neithamun's pool not half an hour ago, for her bath, not knowing you'd be arriving."

"Don't fret over it on my account." He had a momentary image of his curvy hostess stepping nude from her bath and firmly pushed the vision away. However long it had been since he'd had a woman, Lady Neithamun was untouchable. And to even think of lying with another in Sitre's house was to insult her memory. Or so he told himself, closing his eyes for a moment. His head whirled.

"Dinner in the great hall at sunset. I'll send a girl to show you the way." The elderly retainer batted ineffectually at a clump of dust with her toe and shuffled out, leaving the door ajar behind her.

Taking off his blue cloak, multicolored leather breastplate and the sword, laying them on the long black and gold table, Periseneb took a deep breath, stretching side to side and swinging his arms. He couldn't remember when he hadn't been wearing those, wandering the Afterlife. These were the garments he'd died in, struck down from behind by some coward. Thank the goddess for sending him to the upper world without visible wounds and bloodstains.

Gingerly, he sat on the edge of the bed. The wood creaked, but seemed sturdy enough. The lattice work under the mattress stretched a bit under his weight. Seized by a sudden desire to make sure he remained himself, had his own face, he searched the room in vain for a mirror. The bareness of the chamber distracted him from his worry over whether the goddess had restored his ka to his own body, not some borrowed set of bones. *Surely there was more furniture here? And, come to think of it, where were the gilded statues of Sekhmet in the entryway? The eye of Ra set with turquoise and coral in the hall? Has she been selling possessions to make ends meet?* The condition of the estate bothered him, lacing his already unsettled mood with an edge of anger. *But can this be the task Ma'at sent me to do? Repair broken fences and collect missing cattle?* Running his fingers through his hair, he said, "Surely not."

"Beg pardon, sir?"

Realizing he'd spoken aloud, Periseneb beckoned to the young girl peeking at him from the edge of the door. "It's all right, I won't bite, come in and do your cleaning."

She bobbed a little curtsey and stared at him. "The household's sitting down to dinner, sir. I'm to tell you where to go and then I'll clean the room."

He didn't want this child to go hungry so he could have a dust-free bedroom. He'd slept in far worse conditions. "What about you?"

"My mother will save me a portion. She works for the cook, so I'm assured of food. Do you need a guide to the dining hall?"

He shook his head, crossing back to the table. *No need for a sword at dinner.* "I'm sure I can find it." He touched the dagger at his belt and then unfastened the golden Pharaoh's Own badge from the leather strap of his breastplate and hooked it into his plain brown tunic. "I'll get out of your way."

Having no trouble remembering where the great hall was, a few moments later Periseneb paused at the entry. Neithamun, dressed in another plain blue tunic and skirt, sat in the large, ornately inlaid chair at the head of a long table. Her petite frame was dwarfed by the imposing seat, but she sat like a queen, back spear-straight. A place was empty next to her, presumably being saved for him as the honored guest. The rest of the room was full of women of all ages, children, elderly greybeards, a few teenage boys like Mentu, and almost no able-bodied, grown men. Only a few were mixed in the crowd of diners.

Disoriented, expecting against all odds to see familiar faces in the assembled residents of Heron Marsh, he tarried on the threshold. Neithamun beckoned to him as a large platter of roasted quail was set in front of her. As he walked toward her, she stood and the room fell silent. She addressed her companions in a pleasing voice, pitched to carry to all corners of the room, yet melodious. "This is Periseneb, recently discharged from Pharaoh's Own regiment, traveling home. He's our honored guest tonight, having assisted Mentu and me in retrieving our lost cattle."

The assembled residents of Heron Marsh gawked at him as he walked to sit next to his hostess. He heard whispers as people talked furtively with their neighbors.

The room was unbearably stuffy, yet there were no fan bearers. A servant poured him a mug of beer, and dinner resumed with a hum of conversation.

With surprise, he realized he was thirsty and took a long, satisfying swallow of the beer. At least something on this estate was still as good as he remembered it. "Where are your workers, my lady?"

She gave him a puzzled look and waved a hand at the assembled diners. "All around you."

Wiping his lips, he glanced at the tables. "But surely you can't farm without field hands? Where are the men? Your overseer?"

Forehead wrinkled in a frown, Neithamun sipped her beverage before answering. "You ask many questions."

He reached for a fat quail and dropped the meat on his plate. "I didn't mean to be rude. I'm surprised. I've some familiarity with the running of a great estate, supervising the fields, managing the livestock, and I'm puzzled how the tasks can be done without staff. I meant no disrespect."

She nibbled at her quail leg for a moment, as if trying to decide how much to share with him. "Quite a few of the men left to join Pharaoh Nat-re-Akhte's army, when he was battling the Usurper for the throne. Life in a conquering army was more appealing than working fields, the rewards much richer." Dimples appeared in her cheeks for a moment as she gave him a small grin. "I'm sure you, of all people, can understand their motivation."

Nodding to acknowledge her small victory, he said, "All the able-bodied men enlisted?"

Setting the drumstick aside, she reached for her beer. "I can't pay any wages right now, so the work is for room and board only. Lord Haqaptah hired away some of my other workers who couldn't support their families adequately. As for the overseer, he died under unusual circumstances." A frown flashed across her face. "I can't afford another, so I fill the role."

Not sure what to say, Periseneb worked on his dinner for a few minutes. Food tasted amazing to him, the spices and flavors exquisite on his tongue after two hundred years as a shade. He would have eaten even more if he hadn't begun to suspect his hostess and a few of the older women at the head table were holding back to leave more for him. Deciding another of the many tasks he needed to tackle would be hunting game for the table, he drank more beer. If Neithamun was the only family member left, he had to admire her for trying to run the estate all by herself, but it was a monumental task. One person, man or woman, no matter how determined, was doomed to fail. Taking a handful of nuts from a duck-shaped bowl, he cracked them and picked out the sweetmeats, placing the best pieces on her plate in a neat line. "Forgive me, Lady Neithamun, are you widowed? And, if not, how is it no one has offered for your hand? With Heron Marsh as your dowry—"

"I'll not be married for my property." She glared at him. "I'm well aware I'm past the usual age of marriage. I'm not a widow."

Berating himself for speaking too plainly in his dogged determination to get all the facts, he apologized. "Forgive me, I wasn't trying to be insulting. I've grown unaccustomed to speaking in any courtly manner."

She nibbled on the nuts, but after washing the tidbits down with beer, she apparently decided to forgive him. Leaning on her elbow, picking seeds from a roll, she said, "The estate has great debts. My father, may Osiris bless and keep him, wasn't a good manager. He wanted to spend his days in contemplation, meditation, and studying the ancient texts. Anything but farming." Her smile was a bit crooked. "His older brother would have inherited the land and the responsibilities, but died of an illness when I was young. And my other uncle went off to the war and was killed in some nameless skirmish. So then my grandfather forced my father to step in."

Periseneb remembered her earlier comment, about people thinking the estate was under a curse. Now he could understand why. The loss of three healthy men in one generation was a heavy toll.

Having begun sharing her family's tale, Neithamun continued, as if it might be a relief to unburden herself. "The estate also owes taxes in arrears, which wasn't a problem until the new pharaoh sent a new nomarch to be in charge of the province. One Tiy-Ineb-Menhet, if you please, a person with no ties to this province, but a close connection with Pharaoh. The old nomarch was a boyhood friend of my father's and told his scribes to ignore the mounting debt. But the new person travels to our town soon and has sent an official scroll to tell me he intends to collect the current and the delinquent taxes on Settlement Day, one month hence. Have I now shared enough information for you?"

Periseneb's head was spinning, trying to take it all in, while sorting out which part Ma'at had sent him here to fix. Or was she expecting him to resolve all of it? Settlement Day occurring in a month made him suspicious. Why did the gods always have to be so mysterious? "But what happened to create such a dilemma? In my day, I mean, as far as I was aware, Heron Marsh was more than self-sufficient, one of the richest estates in the entire nome, hundreds of workers."

Neithamun frowned, tilting her head. She pushed the pile of seeds and the bread aside. "You're sadly out of date on your news, soldier. The estate has been drifting downward for a hundred years at least. Then there were the five years of drought. My family borrowed deben from Lord Haqaptah's family, thinking the loan would be easily repaid, on favorable terms. We have a distant family connection, after all. When the Nile did flood generously again, our canals and reservoirs failed to fill. During the drought, Lord Haqaptah dammed and diverted some of the canals. It makes his land more fertile, but the life-giving waters no longer reach our fields."

Anger blazing through his heart, Periseneb set his mug on the table with a thump. "That's illegal. What's he planning to answer when the gods ask him if he interfered with the flow of the Nile?"

"By the time the gods ask him anything, my estate's story will be finished, I fear. As for legalities, Haqaptah was the old nomarch's nephew by marriage, so he flouted the law with impunity." She leaned closer and lowered her voice. "The rumor is he paid substantial bribes to many. He was hoping to be named as nomarch after the old one died in the war with no son left to inherit the position, but the new pharaoh preferred his own man."

"As would I, no doubt." Periseneb was amused. "This province is so far from Thebes, Pharaoh needs a man he can trust."

"Oh, I forgot you served in Pharaoh's Own regiment." Neithamun's eyes were wide, her face glowing as she glanced at his badge. "You'll have to tell me what he's like. What his queen is like." She fanned herself. "Now I'm as bad as Mentu was earlier, interrogating you, but I would so enjoy hearing about life at court."

Fortunately for Periseneb, another young servant came rushing into the chamber, heading for the head table. Watching the child approach, guilt pricked at him. The pharaoh he could tell her about firsthand was dead these two centuries, and he didn't want to lie, especially not in the service of Ma'at herself, embodiment of Truth. Neithamun didn't notice his lack of response, focused as she was on the lad running towards the head table.

Flushed and out of breath, the newcomer skidded to a stop, grabbing at the corner of the table to steady himself. "My lady, there's a guest at the front gate. He insists on seeing you immediately and he said he wants to talk to the soldier as well."

The expression on Neithamun's face hinted at wariness, her eyes narrowed as she bit her lip. "Who makes all these demands?"

Eyes wide, the boy answered as if there could only be one name to utter. "Lord Haqaptah, my lady. He came in his chariot, with another chariot full of armed men."

There was consternation in the hall, as the youth's clear voice carried.

Neithamun rose. Periseneb restrained her with a gentle touch. "Let me arm myself with more than a dagger before we go out to them."

She shook his hand off impatiently. "He'll hardly be here to attack me in my own home. Our disagreements haven't come to violence. We've a family connection, I told you." As she walked toward the door, she raised her voice to address her staff. "Remain calm and finish your dinner, please. I'll handle whatever our neighbor wants, no need to panic." She waved a hand at Periseneb, walking by her side. "And our guest has bested five of Haqaptah's finest today already, so we're in no danger."

There was good natured laughter and the crowd settled back into their dining. He and Neithamun reached the long hall leading to the front entry and her shoulders sagged as her steps slowed. Hands fisted, she lowered her head and took a deep breath. "I loathe dealing with him. He's oily and deceitful."

"I'd rather have my sword handy, but I'll stand with you, my lady. I'll make it clear that he and his men insult you at their peril."

She brushed ineffectually at the wrinkles in her skirt. "I appreciate your support, especially as this is none of your concern."

"You welcomed me into your home. I owe you the duty of a good guest."

"Thank you." She walked onto the wide steps of the entrance, Periseneb right behind her. There were not two but three chariots drawn up in the yard, armed men standing all around. The noble intruder Neithamun had come outside to see had his back to them, staring in the direction of the fallow fields, but as her light footsteps sounded on the stone, he wheeled.

Set's teeth. Adrenaline coursed through Periseneb and slammed his heart. He half drew his dagger, staring at the hated face of an enemy from his own time. He took a step forward and Neithamun laid a restraining hand on his arm, staring at him in dismay.

"Quite a ferocious attack dog you've hired, Neity," said the present day Haqaptah.

The voice was different, higher pitched, and now that he took a moment to control his breathing, Periseneb could see the man's face was thinner, the jawline a bit more angular. The eyes were the same, deep-set and dark brown, under bushy brows. *Yet* this *isn't the man I knew.* Angry at himself for the momentary loss of control, despite all his good intentions earlier about not giving in to the easily roused fury of an akh, he sheathed his dagger. "When the lady met your men earlier today, their behavior was unruly, my lord."

Hands on his hips, having made no move toward his own weapon, Haqaptah looked him up and down. "Yes, and I've come to make sure she's fine and render appropriate apologies, if it's any of your business."

"This is Periseneb, of Pharaoh's Own Regiment, travelling in the area. He happened to be in the vicinity when your men accosted me while my herdsman and I retrieved our cattle." Neithamun descended one stair, but then remained, forcing Haqaptah to raise his head to her. "He's here as my guest tonight, not my employee."

"Well, I could use another man of his caliber on my estate," Haqaptah said enthusiastically. "We're on the frontier of Egypt after all, never know when the Hyksos may attack again. A former member of Pharaoh's Own Regiment is worth ten ordinary soldiers." Haqaptah extended his hand to Periseneb. "What do you say? I pay a good wage and my table is renowned. Won't get much to eat here, I'm afraid. Place is going to rack and ruin."

Periseneb felt Neithamun go quiet beside him, but she didn't speak. He stared at the noble, taking note of the phony smile, which didn't match the shrewd eyes or the aggressive stance. He shook his head, ignoring the outstretched hand. "I'm only in the area for a month, and the lady has been kind enough to offer me her hospitality. I'm not in need of a job. If I were, Heron Marsh would be my choice."

He watched Haqaptah's face flush in anger. "Was there anything else you wanted, my lord?"

"You'll regret spurning my offer, soldier. And you—" He pointed at Neithamun. "Keep your scrawny cattle off my land or I'll have my men slaughter them and burn the carcasses, understood?"

Not waiting for an answer, Haqaptah strode away and jumped into his chariot, all his guards hastily clambering into their vehicles. The column took off in a choking cloud of dust and disappeared down the long road.

Neithamun retreated a step, breathing deeply, head bowed. Periseneb circled her shoulders with his arm. "Are you all right?"

"He infuriates me. I loathe being in debt to him. Thank you for your gallantry, but you may have cause to regret making an enemy of him. You should have accepted his offer." Stepping away from his loose embrace, she shook her head.

Hand on his belt knife, Periseneb stared into the dusky haze where Haqaptah and his men had driven. "I'm happy to have him as an enemy."

Neithamun laughed, ascending the stairs. "Did you mean what you told him? Are you staying?"

"I only speak the truth," he said, following her. "I'm not sure how much help I can be in a single month. The troubles you've described have been building for a long time."

"I can't pay you. I told you, no one is getting paid currently. All deben the estate brings in is going toward the taxes and the interest on the debts."

He let the deepest truth escape his lips. "I don't care about payment. I care about Heron Marsh."

"Why?" She searched his face, her eyes wide and puzzled. "What are we to you?"

Apparently the task the goddess has set for me, although I don't begin to understand why. He tried to recover from his too revealing remark about the estate, summoning a cheerful grin. "A challenge, my lady. I relish a challenge."

They reached the doorway, where two servants waited with torches to light their way to the dining hall. Periseneb stood aside to allow her to precede him into the great house.

"I admit relief, having someone to help through this last push to the deadline," Neithamun said. "Perhaps the gods heard our prayers." She smiled as she said it and walked away.

Toss and turn though he might, Periseneb couldn't sleep, which didn't surprise him, not after two-hundred years as a shade. Obviously, his body was out of tune with the world above, where the sun rose and set and a man needed sleep. Rising from his bed, he belted on his kilt and stalked barefoot into the deserted hall. Taking a torch from its receptacle outside his door, he wandered through the main part of the house, taking note of the lack of a night watchman. He found himself heading for the records room. There was something he wanted to see, something he had to see, to anchor himself in what was actually going on here.

The door to the library was unlocked. He slipped inside, carefully placing the torch in the holder beside the door and watching for a minute to be sure it would burn steadily. One spark in this room and the entire house would burn down. The vast collection was much as Periseneb remembered it, shelves of papyrus scrolls and even stone tablets, holding the records of the estate going back to the original landholder many generations ago, well before Periseneb's birth. A long black enameled table with legs in the shape of golden herons dominated the center of the room. Two black and gold stools with faux leopard skin ornamentation painted on the seats were drawn up to the table on one side, while the elaborate chair of the master sat at the end. Endless shelves full of tightly rolled papyri stretched away on both sides on the room.

He lingered beside the table, eyeing the baskets and boxes on the nearby shelf. Struck by an impulse, he went to his knees beside a container he remembered from his time. He stroked his hand across the inlaid top, with its depiction of lions and gazelles. Unbidden, memories flooded his mind, of how his father would open this chest as a reward when Periseneb had done especially well with his scribing. The two of them had spent many long hours in this library, playing senet together, not talking much, but able to find common ground. He swallowed hard, telling himself the burning in his eyes was from the smoke of the torch.

Carefully raising the lid, he peered inside. The box was divided into three compartments, each holding a different game. There was the senet board, with throwing sticks and pawns. Next was a more playful set of hounds and jackals, set upright in their carved malachite board, waiting for someone to set them loose to chase each other through the spaces. What he sought tonight was in the compartment underneath. Setting aside the two modern games, he lifted out the carved stone of the mehen game.

As a boy, he'd been forbidden to play with this, since it was ancient even in his day. His father had told him once mehen had been a mere game in the time of the first pharaohs, but had come to be regarded as symbolic of life itself, and therefore not to be taken lightly. The board was in the form of a tightly coiled snake, with the head at the center. Made of carved red stone, the body of the snake had sixty spaces cut into its coils, leading to the head with its ivory fangs and gleaming turquoise eyes. He fished in the bottom of the chest for the bag holding the spheres used to play the game. Rolling the smooth, colorful stones in his hand, he picked the green malachite ball to represent himself—green was his favorite color—and let the others fall from his hand into the leather sack.

Board in hand, he rose and paced along the nearest shelves, searching for one where he could hide his find. Moving a section of papyrus scrolls, he made a big enough space to set the mehen board. He counted thirty spaces from the center, and with deliberation, let the malachite sphere slip into the thirtieth space.

"If you truly represent the struggle between good and evil, Great One Mehen," he said, addressing the snake god for whom the game was named, "Then I pray my coming here is for good—mine and Heron Marsh's. Help me count the days, and by so doing, keep my purpose in mind."

Hastily, he covered the game board with the scrolls, creating the illusion that the shelf was undisturbed. Returning to the game box, he set all the other items neatly inside and closed the lid.

Those tasks accomplished, he felt compelled to satisfy the original purpose that had brought him to the library. Lighting a small oil lamp and walking along the shelves, he breathed in the scent of aged papyrus and ink. Periodically pulling out a scroll, he unrolled each far enough to find the date. Eventually he got to the section he sought, the estate's records of two-hundred years past, and wrapped his hand around the proper record, carrying the stiff cylinder to the long table in the center of the room. Moving aside inkwells, quills and blank papyrus, he spread out the scroll, anchoring it at the top with the oil lamp before cautiously unrolling the brittle record. His finger traced along the line of hieroglyphics until he came to the entry he sought.

Born this day, male child Periseneb, son of Merneseneb, Overseer of Heron Marsh estate, and his wife Siptah. Died this day, Siptah. Closing his eyes for a moment, he wondered what his father's fate had been, how long he'd lived, whether he'd spared a thought for the son who'd gone off seeking fame and fortune in Pharaoh's army.

"What are you doing here?" Eyes narrowed and frowning, Neithamun was standing in the doorway.

He let the scroll roll itself up while he took a deep breath, and faced her calmly. "I couldn't sleep."

"So, you came to read the old records?" Her voice had a tinge of skepticism. She walked to the table and held down the bottom edge of the scroll to see the date. "Records from hundreds of years ago?"

He nodded. "I'm sorry; I know I should have asked permission first."

Neithamun's regard was steady, her face giving no hint of her intentions while she considered his answer. After a moment, she inclined her head in acceptance of his apology. "No harm done, Heron Marsh has no deep secrets to uncover. I was merely surprised. Did you find anything interesting?"

"Not particularly. Births, deaths, harvest tallies." Smoothly, he took the papyrus and stuffed it into the correct basket. "What brings you here so late?"

"I have to enter the corn tallies." She set her lamp on the stone floor and extracted a set of scrolls from the masses of similar records on the shelf.

Moving to help her with the basket, he said, "You should be resting for tomorrow, my lady, not doing common scribe's work."

"Haven't you realized if I don't do whatever the task at hand may be, it doesn't get done? Tomorrow will bring new jobs, so I have to finish today's before I can sleep." Stepping to the desk, she shook the dry inkwell and started mixing fresh ink from the waiting bottles of carbon, beeswax, gelatin, sap and water. As she poured the ink onto the wooden palette, she stifled a yawn. "The estate can't afford a scribe these days."

No overseer, no scribes—she works herself to the bone to keep this place running. "I'd be happy to enter the figures for you, if you'd entrust the task to me."

Neithamun looked at him, eyes wide. "You'd lower yourself to do scribe's work? You, one of Pharaoh's Own Regiment?"

"Retired from duty," he said with a smile. "I have the skills, might as well use them." *Because my father insisted I learn all the million details I'd need to know to follow in his footsteps as the overseer of this place, before I rebelled and ran away to seek fortune and glory. Life certainly would have turned out differently if I'd stayed.* Hooking an ebony and wicker stool with his foot so he could drag it to the table, he plucked a quill from the wooden block and checked the tip. "I owe you for your hospitality."

"Let's do it together then, and get the task done in half the time." She handed him the tablets where the day's tally had been scratched out in the fields. "You read the figures off to me and I'll scribe."

He found he was enjoying the quiet domesticity of working with Neithamun, but all too soon the task was done. Torch in hand, he escorted her to her rooms. Yawning hugely, she thanked him again and disappeared behind the painted door. Trying not to compare the living woman to the memories he held of another woman from this same house, two centuries gone, he sought his own chamber and this time managed to sleep.

CHAPTER TWO

In the morning, he rose with the dawn, grabbing a meat roll and a handful of dates from the communal table and heading off to walk the estate. Happy as he was to be in the world of the living again, the tour began first to depress and then anger him. Broken fences, unplanted fields, and drooping crops all spoke to the difficulties the estate was facing. He believed Neithamun was doing her best, given the limited resources, but the losing battle she was waging was all too obvious to him.

But when he topped the ridge and faced the cracked expanse of dirt and scrub grass where the marsh that gave the place its name used to be, he stopped in his tracks and swore. By the look of it, the marsh had been gone for years. Now he had the explanation why the nearest fields were fallow, since the estate had relied on the wetlands for irrigation.

He came down the hillside and walked a short way out onto the baked earth of the marsh, spinning in a slow circle to see the scope of the devastation. A few spindly trees struggling for survival in a cluster were the extent of greenery. Periseneb shut his eyes for a long moment, remembering the marsh as it was in his time—cool, green and thickly surrounded by trees, a refuge for the stately herons, cranes and ibis, stocked with fish, redolent with lotus and lilies, an amazing year-round haven in the hot, dry nome.

Cool water splashed his ankles and he inhaled the perfume of abundant lotus flowers. The cry of a startled bird sounded and he opened his eyes to find himself standing at the edge of the marsh as he remembered it. "By the gods, what sorcery is this?" He stared in disbelief, reached a cupped hand to the water's surface, and tasted the sweet, crystalline liquid cautiously. A fish jumped nearby to catch a careless flying insect and a white ibis swooped in to snare the fish, just missing and winging away with a harsh cry of disappointment. Periseneb glanced behind him. Sure enough, there were his tracks in the dusty hillside, leading to the water's edge. "Am I going mad? This cannot be here!" He bent to pluck a single blue lotus and as the stem broke, releasing the fragrant flower, the marsh disappeared, leaving him standing on the hot, cracked lakebed.

Holding a blue lotus.

His tattoo burned on his shoulder.

Periseneb felt a wave of vertigo, as if the ground moved under his feet. Hastily, he retraced his steps, ascending the slope, tucking the amazing lotus into his belt. Making his way to the great house, he went in search of the mistress of Heron Marsh. He found her at the grain silos to the rear of the house.

"We need to talk," he said, striding over to her.

"I'm busy at the moment," she answered, raising her dust-covered hands for him to see. "We're getting ready for the primary harvest in a few weeks' time, pitiful as it will be, we must gather every grain." She pointed at his belt, eyes wide. "Where did you find the lotus?"

Plucking the bloom from his belt, he handed it to her with a flourish and a bow, imitating courtiers he'd observed in those long ago days at his pharaoh's side. "For you, my lady."

Holding the large blossom in her hands like a fragile treasure, she inhaled a deep breath of the heady fragrance. "There haven't been any lotuses anywhere in this area for years, not in my lifetime, certainly." Her face reflected her delight. "I should go put this in water."

He walked through the house with her, matching his stride to her shorter one. "Water is the subject I want to discuss."

"The estate is parched. We haul all the water daily from the one canal that does get replenished annually when the Nile overflows its banks," she told him, sniffing at the lotus. "It takes half my people all day to bring enough water for the house, the livestock, and crops."

"Yes, one of your servants told me the story last night." He took a deep breath, reminding himself it would do no one any good for him to allow his anger to show. "I've been all over the property today and I have a list—an imposing list—of things needing to be done, repaired, and set to rights. I think water is the top priority."

Neithamun's response was calm. "I don't disagree, which is why I have so many people hauling it daily. How do you propose to solve the problem? I can't appeal to the nomarch to have Haqaptah's illegal dam removed until the end of the month when he makes his procession to our village. The Nile doesn't flood again for months, even if the judgment goes in my favor and Haqaptah removes the barriers." She sighed. "I've no way to enforce a judgment, even if the nomarch rules for Heron Marsh." She caught a passing servant girl by the arm. "Bring me a small urn with water, for the flower."

"At once, my lady." The girl's eyes widened as she peered more closely at the lotus. "Is this magic?"

Neithamun offered her the bloom to sniff. "Maybe. Perhaps our luck has changed a little. I'll be in the library; bring the urn there. And some beer, two clean mugs."

The girl hastened off toward the kitchen.

As they entered the library, Periseneb and Neithamun exchanged glances, both smiling. He found the memories of their time together the night before pleasant, even if scribe work was tedious by its very nature.

She sat in the big chair, as was proper for the lady of the estate and waved him to the closest stool. The servant girl brought in the requested urn, alabaster with a pattern of fish incised around the base, water sloshing at the bottom. She promised to fetch the beer next and departed as the lady of the house set the long-stemmed lotus in the vase.

"Now, talk to me about water," she invited Periseneb, tracing the delicate petals of the flower with one fingertip.

He drew a blank slate toward him from the pile on the table. Choosing a stylus, he said, "How much do you owe at the end of the month?"

Mouth in a thin line, she hesitated. "The taxes or to Haqaptah?"

"Both."

She named two astoundingly high figures. Periseneb whistled though his clenched teeth as he wrote them down. "A pharaoh's ransom."

"I told you the interest was staggering," she said. "I know I must seem unnervingly calm about this to you, but I've lived on the edge of disaster my whole life. And the alternative to making good on the debt is so awful, I can't contemplate it or I'll go mad."

He could barely utter the words. "The estate would be forfeit."

"Yes." Her eyes were hooded, sad. "The nomarch would have to fight it out with Haqaptah for who took the land and the house. The people would go with the land."

"And you? Where would you go?"

Neithamun put on a brave smile, but he noticed how her hand trembled. "I don't know. I've no other relatives to take me in, no skills beyond running an estate, which isn't a job anyone would hire me to perform. Throw myself on the nomarch's mercy perhaps? I won't accept charity or anything else from Haqaptah, distant relative or not."

Periseneb assumed the nomarch's idea of charity might be to hand her over to Haqaptah with her estate, but he bit his tongue. "What's your plan for satisfying these debts? The crops ready to be harvested appear to be only enough to feed the estate itself."

She sat back in the chair. "You've a shrewd eye, soldier. Did you hike the fields from boundary to boundary?"

"East to west." He nodded. "Let me guess, you plan to sell the bulls to the temple of Amun and reduce your debts from the proceeds?"

Her eyes widened a little. "Exactly. Heron Marsh cattle are much prized, for the sweetness of the milk, which makes excellent cheese, as well as for the tenderness of the meat, beautifully marbled with fat. Nine tenths of my efforts have gone to preserving the breeding stock, especially the bulls. It's said the goddess Hathor herself—"

"Gave your ancestor the original bull and three cows to start his herd, in repayment for a mysterious service he rendered her. Yes, I know the story," he said, pleased by her astonished look. "The bulls of Heron Marsh are much renowned."

"And sought after by temples throughout the nome," she said with pride. "I'm expecting the priests of Amun from the great temple in the capital to arrive in two weeks, to make their customary purchase. Our major income derives from that single transaction every year. Our bulls are the only ones qualified to satisfy Amun's demands and we charge accordingly."

"But based on what I've seen, even if you auctioned most of the herd, you'll barely clear the sums owed, leaving you nothing to invest in improvements for the future. If you can't solve the water problems, next year may be as bad again or worse. And you'll have little breeding stock. Then what?"

"I have to deal with the problems I can handle, one at a time, beginning with the most pressing." Frowning, she picked up the tablet to glance at the figures before allowing the clay to clatter to the table's polished surface. Eyes closed, she rubbed her forehead. "So many people depend on me."

"All right, I've no desire to distress you," he said. "Let me see what can be done about the water first." Teasing, he added, "I'll adopt your one thing at a time approach for now."

"There's nothing to be done," she said. "Haqaptah has built his own series of canals and dams, I told you."

"I'm going to reconnoiter his water management for myself tomorrow."

She set her hand on his forearm, eyes widening in alarm. "Please, don't anger him. Dealing with his visits is one of my worst nightmares. I know you want to help, gods only know why I'm so blessed, but stirring up a hornet's nest—"

Patting her hand reassuringly, he said, "I promise, soldier's oath, he won't even know I've been on his property."

But the next day, even though Periseneb accomplished his aim of infiltrating the neighboring estate undetected, observing the illegal waterways the noble had constructed, and evading squads of workers and overseers with laughable ease as he left the land, Periseneb had to admit Neithamun was right. There was nothing to be done about the professional, sturdy job Haqaptah had executed in diverting the life giving waters of the Nile from their traditional path. A path which, over the centuries, had shared the annual inundation with the greedy noble's lands and

Heron Marsh. As it was, his crops were lush, his cattle fat, while only one canal on Neithamun's estate contained any water at all.

Retreating to the hillside overlooking the parched plain where the marsh had been, Periseneb sat under the remaining trees, munched on a hard roll and dried meat the cook had given him, and considered the options. "It would take many men and much time to take apart or block those canals," he said out loud. "Certainly, I can't do anything about it in a month, by myself." Unless he unleashed the akh's power. Ghosts were known to revel in destruction, in destroying things the living cared for. The idea repulsed him, going against his own fundamental nature, and fearing he wouldn't be able to rein it in, fearing what other damage he might cause. He wasn't here to make matters worse. Returning to his orderly assessment of the situation, he pondered. "The new nomarch is likely to accept the situation as it is, no matter what Neithamun's rights are, because she can't afford to enforce a judgment. If I were a new governor trying to get control of the province, I wouldn't take on the more powerful landowner."

He closed his eyes to block the view of the dry marsh, which made him uneasy and angry at the same time. Yesterday, he'd brought the area to life somehow for a brief moment—the lotus blooming in Neithamun's bedroom was proof. He suspected whatever miracle had allowed him to accomplish the feat wouldn't be repeatable. "It was temporary," he said, not sure if he was apologizing to the land, opening his eyes to stare at the dry, cracked expanse where marsh should be. The water had been so cool and refreshing yesterday for that brief moment.

Something tickled his memory.

Scrambling to his feet, trying not to be too excited about what might not be useful at all, Periseneb oriented himself and set off to the south at an economical trot, heading for the furthest reaches of the estate, chasing a remembrance from his boyhood. When he arrived at his destination, the site was disappointing. Trees grew in a rough circle around a sunken basin of land where he remembered a pond, fed by a cold spring. He'd swum there, first with his boyhood friends, playing rowdy games after the day's chores were complete, and then once or twice with Sitre. His excursions with her had been made by the light of the moon, and involved more heady indulgences than swimming—but he wasn't going to revisit *those* memories.

Disappointed, but unwilling to admit defeat, he walked into the center of the pond area. Maybe the spring had exhausted itself, dried up? Spinning slowly, he realized the rocks and ledges surrounding the location weren't exactly as he remembered from boyhood. Certainly he and his companions had dived from the far side of the pond into deep water, but if he tried the stunt today, assuming there was water, he'd break his neck. The rocks were disarranged, jumbled. Had there'd been an earthquake in the last two-hundred years, blocking the spring's channel below the ground? Could the water be lingering there, deep in the earth?

Squatting, he drew his belt knife and dug a small hole in the center of the pond where weeds sprouted. The ground was moist in a few places, but no welcome puddles grew when he scooped the plants out of the soil. Disappointed, he stood, cleaning his knife on a broad leaf. Certain water must be lurking in this location, he considered his options. Without water from some source, there was no real solution to Neithamun's problems. Selling her cattle would buy her one year's grace perhaps, but next year would bring the same challenges. "She'll never get ahead of the game. Haqaptah will try something else. And I won't be here to help, goddess willing." Struck by inspiration, he dropped the leaf, and rolled up the sleeve of his tunic, revealing the entwined feathers inked on his shoulder. Rubbing his fingers over the imprint, he said, "How does one summon a goddess?" *With a sacrifice ordinarily, but perhaps these symbols give me a more direct connection?*

He sheathed his knife and stood tall, gazing into the sky. "I stand here as a voice for truth, Lady Ma'at, attempting to restore the balance you desire, to undo the chaos which prevents the Nile from flowing freely in this place. I humbly request thy help." Next moment he felt a sharp pain in his shoulder and a red glow spread from the tattoos, bathing him in scarlet light. An actual red feather floated away from his arm, drifting lazily in the air. He reached to catch the plume, but a stray breeze caused it to elude his fingers. Landing quill down in the ground, the scarlet vanes along the spine quivered. Overhead, there was a boom of thunder and a flash of light. Staggering, Periseneb blinked, eyes watering.

Ma'at stood before him where the ostrich plumage had been. Clad in a scarlet dress decorated with golden ribbons, coral and turquoise bracelets on her wrists, she was regal. "Excellent, my warrior, you've wasted no time. I see you understand the situation to some extent, even though the entire scroll of problems has yet to reveal itself to you. What assistance do you require from me?"

He swallowed hard and shifted into parade rest stance, relying on his military discipline to handle the shock of a goddess coming at his request. "I remember a pond here, fed by a cold spring from deep within the ground, my lady. I would see the spring restored, enabling the people of my ancestral home to irrigate the fields and water the beasts more easily while I work to solve the issues."

Eyebrows raised, Ma'at gazed at her surroundings. "I'm hardly a goddess of the Nile or of water. You might need help from my sister Anuket or the Crocodile God Sobek himself perhaps."

Wondering what sort of help Ma'at had anticipated he'd ask for during this assignment, he said, "I wasn't aware the Great One Sobek concerns himself with any water but the Nile. We've no special ties to him in this province, unfortunately. A small temple in the city, but nothing of note."

"Anuket then." Ma'at nodded. A magical *was* scepter appeared in her hand, taller than Periseneb.

Carved from cedar, forked at the base, the staff was topped with the curving stylized head of an animal he didn't recognize. Details of the beast's features were accented in gleaming gold. Power flared from the *was* in bursts of white light, and there was humming as if thousands of invisible bees were hard at work. Eyes closed, Ma'at thumped the forked end of the staff on the ground three times. "I call upon you, sister Anuket, send your gazelles to bring forth the hidden water in this place. My warrior requires the blessing to carry out his tasks."

Thunder boomed directly overhead, but Periseneb stuck to his post, facing the goddess he served. He was already dead. If lightning struck him, he couldn't die again.

Could he?

"Behold," she said, raising the staff. The formerly indistinctly carved animal head had now become a recognizable gazelle, horns and all. Ma'at pointed the scepter at the jumbled rocks behind him. Periseneb whirled as the sound of clattering hooves came like beats on a drum. A herd of tawny gazelles with golden horns was pouring over the stones, leaping and cavorting with unmatchable grace as they flowed past him, each one disappearing as soon as it reached the far banks of the dry pond, literally leaping from the ground into thin air. The dust slowly settled after the last beast had made the run. Coughing, Periseneb tried to see through the murky cloud. There was a woman with skin the color of rich ebony standing on top of the small rock cliff. Her red dress was form-fitting and accented with intricate beading at the hem and neckline in a style he'd never seen before. Crowned with an amazing headdress of multicolored plumage, she nodded to him, waved a languid hand at Ma'at, and was gone. A stream of water gushed forth from the rocks where she'd been standing.

He wheeled. "Thank you—" But Ma'at too had departed. He glanced at his shoulder, where now only three feathers swirled in the intricate tattoo. *I've barely begun and already I've used one fourth of my promised assistance.* Enjoying the cold water lapping at his ankles as the spring continued to feed the growing pond, he felt a sense of accomplishment, mixed with pure happiness. *This was worth it.*

He wanted to surprise Neithamun. During the return trip to the main house, he was anticipating the expression on her face when she saw the pond and realized a partial solution had been found. To preserve the element of surprise, he didn't tell her why he wished her to abandon her duties and take a ride in the donkey cart with him. Persuading her proved more difficult than he'd expected. Neithamun was supervising the brewing of new batches of beer when he arrived at the house.

Hands on her hips, flour dusting her apron, the mistress of Heron Marsh stared at him. "I can't go off on a moment's notice, soldier. For what purpose?" A worried frown on her face, she said, "Oh no, are the cows wandering into Haqaptah's fields again? I suspected his men of breaching the fence last time."

"No, calm yourself, my lady, nothing so dire." Periseneb laughed. "What I plan to show you will be good news."

"Oh, go with him," said the listening cook, giving Neithamun a friendly nudge with her ample hip. "We've set the bread to baking, which takes hours as you know, so there's plenty of time before we have to crumble it and strain it into the water. I've been making beer for more years than you've been alive. I know the right mixture of dates and spices to make our special estate brew. Or, don't you trust me?" The cook winked at Periseneb as Neithamun rushed to reassure her.

Hugging the older woman, Neithamun said, "I don't know what we'd do without you, Khensa. All right, since you both think I need to see whatever marvel Periseneb has found, I'll go. Let me change into a fresh tunic and stronger sandals."

Removing the apron and folding the cloth neatly first, she left the kitchen to change. Despite the heat from the ovens, Periseneb lingered for a moment to grab a freshly baked roll. Tossing the bread from hand to hand, he noticed the cook glaring at him. "I took only one," he said, laughing. "Plenty left for the beer making."

Frowning, she shook her head. "I don't know what game you're playing here, soldier. Maybe you're simply a good hearted man who wants to help, which I know is what Lady Neithamun believes. Some good luck for Heron Marsh at last."

He leaned against the table. "And you?"

"I'm not sure yet." She surveyed him from head to toe. "The scales are still balancing in my mind. But I warn you, if you hurt her, if you're a drifter with an eye for using our misfortune to better your state by using her, I swear you'll regret it. My sister is a priestess of Hathor in the capital city and I'll gladly pay to have the goddess curse you."

"Yet, you encourage your lady to accompany me," he said.

Khensa shook her wooden ladle at him. "Lady Neithamun's had a hard life, stuck with trying to save this estate. She deserves time away from her duties. She's had little chance for anything of her own, much less the company of a man. I think she's a bit dazzled by you, all good looking and one of Pharaoh's heroes besides." She pulled a new bowl of bread dough toward her and began kneading, trying and failing to suppress a smile. "Come to that, I'm a bit dazzled by you, old lady that I am."

Hand over his heart, Periseneb bowed to her. "I promise, by any Great One you care to name, I've no intention of doing anything but helping Heron Marsh and its lady through this crisis, if such be possible. And then I'm moving on, to my final destination."

Eyes narrowed, Khensa didn't seem appeased. "Which is?"

"Not set as yet," he answered truthfully. If he couldn't manage to solve the issues Ma'at wanted him to fix, he'd be dumped in the gray wastes forever.

"What's not set?" Neithamun stood on the threshold, attired in a pretty light blue dress with white papyrus flowers embroidered along the hem.

"The dinner menu," the cook said grumpily, stalking off to check the ovens.

"I hope she wasn't too rude to you," Neithamun told Periseneb as they walked toward the barn. "Sometimes Khensa behaves as if she was the lady of the estate, with all of us as her incompetent underlings."

"Not at all. She and I understand each other quite well," he answered.

"She's one of the older servants, has known me since I was a baby, so it's hard to overawe her," Neithamun said with raised eyebrows. Her dimples flashed.

Harnessing the cranky donkey to the small cart took only a few moments, after which Periseneb drove them away from the house, heading south.

"You're probably more used to handling a spirited team and a chariot," Neithamun said.

"I've driven them, yes, although at times I was assigned to infantry duty." Flicking the donkey on its gray rump with the reins, he attempted to discourage the animal's constant attempts to browse. "I think even foot soldiers could march faster than your donkey moves."

"We have a chariot, if it hasn't rotted away, but no horses. The teams were sold off long ago, even before I was left in charge. I know we couldn't afford to keep them, but I think it's a pity. I suppose using a donkey to pull such a vehicle would be strange. Quite the amusing idea." Laughing, she clutched his arm as the cart bumped over a small ridge. The donkey seemed to choose the most challenging route as a matter of course.

Her hand felt good on his skin, soft and cool. The swell of her breast brushed his arm before she managed to sit upright again as the track smoothed out. Trying to distract himself from his companion's charms, Periseneb asked, "Why in the name of the Nile would an estate such as this one keep a chariot?"

"My late uncle was a charioteer for Pharaoh." Giving him an appraising glance, she said, "Might you have known him? Granted, he'd have been older than you—"

"Pharaoh's army is huge. A man rarely knows any but his own immediate comrades and officers." He didn't want to discuss the military in any detail.

There was silence between them for a few moments as the donkey plodded along.

"I'm sorry if I've called forth unpleasant memories," she said, running her fingers through her hair and allowing the small breeze to cool her head.

"No, nothing serious. My comrades ribbed me unmercifully for resigning from the army, seeking this provincial way of life, leaving Thebes." He bit his lip, afraid to say too much. His well-intentioned friends had predicted he'd soon flee to the army again, that he'd find estate life dull. Now he wondered what had become of those men, his brothers at arms, closer ties forged in the heat of combat than those bound by birth. Gone to their well-deserved rest in the Afterlife, no doubt, properly honored and buried by wives, children, and grandchildren. He flipped the reins, making the donkey move a little faster, although it brayed in protest. Anger burned in his gut again, fury at whoever had struck him down in his prime, depriving him of so much.

"Well, I for one am grateful you did return to our nome." She stretched, clearly enjoying the beautiful day.

Periseneb tried to ignore the way her tunic outlined her ample figure. "We'll be there soon."

"No rush. Now you've extracted me from my duties, I'm quite happy to play lady of leisure. It's something I never get to do." She gazed at the sky and laughed in sheer pleasure. "The servants and farm workers mean well, but it's been such a treat to talk to you about other things than the corn tally and the beer recipe."

"I'm no better born than they are, my lady, just a common man."

"Why do you constantly talk yourself down? Becoming a member of Pharaoh's Own is quite an accomplishment for a warrior, won on merit and fighting skills. Not only were you accepted into an elite regiment, you can scribe, you've traveled outside the boundaries of this dusty nome, and seen something of the world—I'd say whatever your birth, you've clearly bettered your station in life. Shai, the god of Fate must have felt kindly to you at birth."

If she only knew. "The surprise I have for you is over this next rise," he said, leaving her remarks unanswered.

Neithamun was silent as the donkey toiled up the small ridge and then trotted toward the pond. Periseneb glanced at her, but was unable to read her expression. Her lack of reaction disappointed him and made him curious. He drew the donkey to a halt at the edge of the new pond, short of the muddy area, and lifted Neithamun to the ground, forcing himself to release her. He was a little startled to find himself reacting so strongly to her proximity. The lady of the estate was petite but pleasing to the eyes, yet his focus was on other things. Wasn't it?

She strolled a few feet while he stayed with the cart. Bending with cupped hands, she brought a mouthful of the water to her lips and drank. Shaking the droplets from her fingers, she turned on her heel to stare at him.

"Who are you? Are you a god? A sorcerer?"

Not expecting this reaction, alarmed by her questions, which struck too close to the truth, he opened his mouth to answer, but she kept on talking.

"First the lotus where none have grown in a century and now this pond where none has been for nigh onto two centuries, according to the estate records." She gestured at the serene water. "I'm grateful, but honestly, I'm also a little frightened. What's going to happen next?"

Dropping the reins, he reached her side in a few quick strides, catching her hands as she backed away a step. "I'm no more than I've said, a simple soldier who wants to help. You've no need to be frightened of me. I can't explain the lotus any more than you can, but I stumbled over this pond when I was doing my north to south walk of the estate. If you say it's been dry for two hundred years, then I believe you. My only thought was happiness that there'd be ample water, closer than the canal."

Eyebrows drawn together in a frown, she said, "But how did the pond get here?"

"An earthquake perhaps?" *Certainly the pounding of the magical gazelle herd caused ground tremors.* "I've known a big temblor to drain a lake as often as a new one is created."

She considered. "Perhaps. There was some shaking a few days ago." Having accepted the prosaic solution he offered, she tugged to free her hands.

Instantly, he let her go.

Kilting her skirt, Neithamun waded knee deep into the water. "Better than the Afterlife! So delightfully cold."

Beset by memories of the stolen moments he'd enjoyed at this very pond with another woman, Periseneb stayed out of the water, ignoring her unspoken invitation. "Tomorrow, we can organize the servants to haul the water from here instead of the canal."

Going further toward the center, she splashed water at him in a glittering arc of droplets. "Can you allow me to continue being an impractical lady of leisure for a bit longer, please?"

Concerned about the stability of the pond's floor, he reached out. "Best not go further."

With a scream, she disappeared under the water, either having stepped into a deeper section without realizing, or the ground might have collapsed under her. Periseneb ran into the pond and then dove into the area she'd been wading in. The bottom was disturbed, mud silting the water and obscuring his view, but he touched cloth and got a firm grip, pulling her to him as he surfaced. She was gasping, clinging to him, making it a challenge for him to swim, strong as he was, but he got them both to the shore. Staggering, he carried her to the cart and set her on the flat tailgate.

Crying and retching, she kept her arms wrapped tightly around his neck. He held her close, rocking her a little. "I know it must have been frightening, but you're fine, I give you my word." He stroked her shiny black hair and rubbed her back.

"I don't know what happened, suddenly the bottom fell away under my feet. I felt as if someone grabbed my ankle." She rested her head on his shoulder. "I'm so fortunate you were here."

From Sitre, he'd have suspected artifice, an invitation to take things further. Neithamun had shown herself to be a straightforward person and probably meant nothing more than simple gratitude. Either way, he had to rein in his own reactions to holding her before she became embarrassed or frightened. "We'd better get you to the house." He lifted her to the seat and then swung up next to her. "You'll have to warn the workers not to wade too far into the pond. It's a tempting menace right now."

Pausing in her efforts to restore her hair to a state of order, she said, "Where will you be?"

"I'm going into town tomorrow, if you'll let me borrow the cart."

"Of course, but what errand takes you there?" Neithamun blushed. "I'm sorry, it's none of my business, soldier. Forget I asked."

"No, you have the right, you're my hostess and I'm borrowing your cart. I want to see what the situation is in the area, how the townspeople talk about Haqaptah. See if he's playing any unpleasant tricks on people other than you."

"Oh, such a possibility never crossed my mind." She abandoned her hair. "I mean, he wants Heron Marsh for the land. It's an old family rivalry stemming back several centuries. Why would he bother anyone else?"

"He must have other neighbors," Periseneb said. "It might bolster your case with the nomarch if there are claimants against him besides yours. A pattern of unsavory behavior to present as evidence."

She stared at him as if he was an oracle. "Why didn't the idea ever cross my mind before today?"

"You've been understandably wrapped up in the struggle to keep your own estate viable, don't criticize yourself. I'll nose around the taverns, talk to people a fine lady like you might not want to consult. Nor would they talk to you, most likely." The mere idea of Neithamun trying to obtain information from the ruffians in town left him bemused. "I also want to see if I can find out why he's got so many armed guards."

"What do you mean?"

"Yesterday, when I was scouting his land, I counted quite a few able-bodied men fulfilling no function beyond carrying weapons and watching his borders." Periseneb shook his head. "Not effectively. The majority of his troops are badly trained, mercenaries no doubt. I was able to sneak in and out undetected. Why is he maintaining his own small army?"

"I didn't know he was."

"Are there raids on the province? Nomads? Hyksos?" Periseneb tossed out the most likely reasons, if Haqaptah had no secret agenda.

"Not since the war ended and Pharaoh drove the enemy from Egypt," she said. "I know the nomarch defeated the last major attempt to infiltrate Shield

Nome after the war, and it's been quiet ever since. We've never had problems with the wandering herdsmen raiding us, not even for forage for their animals." She laughed. "Raiders would find meager pickings on my land."

"Well then, all the more reason for me to try to get to the bottom of the situation." Periseneb wasn't sure what exactly Ma'at had sent him to rectify, but for the price to be his immortal ka's entry into the Afterlife, the stakes had to be higher than retrieving lost cows and paying Heron Marsh's taxes. He hoped there might be some answers to be found in town. He chirruped to the donkey to move faster and the estate house was soon in view.

"Would you mind taking some trade goods to town for me tomorrow? We've the estate's special beer and several dozen lengths of fine weaving. You'd only be required to drop them off," she said hastily, as if afraid he'd object. "There's a merchant who agreed to sell such things on my behalf, for a small fee. His wife's sister is one of my weavers."

"Certainly. But if there's deben to be made by selling, shouldn't we—I mean the estate—be sending a team of people to market regularly?"

Neithamun grimaced as if in momentary pain. "We used to, but then the last two times, my people were beaten and robbed on the long drive home. We were lucky no one was killed and we didn't lose the donkey."

"Who would do such a thing? Are there many such incidents these days?"

She shrugged. "Some. There are quite a few beggars and drifters and itinerant workers. After the Usurper Pharaoh and the Hyksos were defeated by Pharaoh, several estates were forfeit, their people displaced. But the fact this was done to my workers twice in a row, as they drove along the road skirting Haqaptah's lands, makes me suspicious. He doesn't want me to accumulate any deben that might go toward paying the loan or the back taxes. And the thugs wore masks, which is odd, unless the intent was to prevent my servants from recognizing someone."

Periseneb evaluated the details. His gut told him she was right—these incidents were more of Haqaptah's intimidation techniques. "And I'm guessing there's no one to complain to?"

"Right." She nodded. "No official in this part of the nome investigates such things. The city guards merely protect the local officials and the temples, keeping order in the streets and inns. The headman of the town owes his position to

Haqaptah. As reluctant as I am to meet the new nomarch over my own tax issues, I hope he implements some independent administrative structure loyal to a higher authority again."

"I'll be happy to take a load of goods with me. And then let his mercenaries try to separate the purse from my belt." Periseneb rested one hand on the carved hilt of his knife. "Not so easy as terrorizing poor servants."

CHAPTER THREE

Something Neithamun had said about the feud with Haqaptah going back in time between the families set him thinking. The more Periseneb considered the fact, the more he felt there might be some connection to his own task for Ma'at. He'd asked the cook, oh so casually, who was the oldest servant remaining on the estate, working his question in among other topics. She'd directed him to a woman named Benerib. "You'll get little sense from her. Dreams in the sun, she does, and waits for her ka to be ready for the Afterlife. She must be more than one hundred years old." Wiping her hands on her apron, Khensa went to a shelf at the rear of the kitchen, beckoning him to follow. She selected a clay jar, removing the stopper, and taking a deep sniff of the contents. Then she took a small bowl and ladled a generous serving of honeyed figs from the jar. "Here, my special recipe. Benerib loves these, greedy as a child she is. I don't know what you want of her, but with these as your greeting, you're more likely to get her to talk. Don't expect much sense."

Taking the treat with a murmured word of thanks, he left the house in search of the old woman. Asking people he met in the yard, he was directed to where the elder sat in the shade of a willow tree, a cat purring on her lap.

Clearing his throat to get her attention, he bowed. "Old mother, I'm told you've been in service in this house for a hundred years."

She laughed, peering at him from rheumy eyes. "Not quite that long, but yes, I've been a body servant to all the women of the family, including young Neity. I started running errands at the age of five, holding combs and wigs and pins and ironing linen, and I don't know what all else over the years. Until I got too old and bent. My hands don't work well anymore." She showed him her gnarled fingers. "Do I know you? Are you a noble of the house, home after the war?"

Wondering which war she was thinking of, in her age-addled mind, he seated himself next to her. "No, I'm Periseneb, a guest, only here to help Lady Neithamun until the tax collection day. I've brought you something."

Shooing the cat off her lap, she accepted his offering and popped one of the figs into her mouth. Eyes closed in contentment, she said, "Many years since I had a suitor bring me treats." She giggled like a girl. "And never one as handsome as you are. Although, never doubt I had my share of attention from men when I was younger." She broke into song, her voice quavering, a poem of love and seduction, incongruous coming from one so advanced in years.

He kept his voice gentle, reining in his impatience. "Your tune is lovely, old one, but—"

"Oh yes, I had many men chasing my skirts, let me tell you." Benerib swayed in her chair and began enumerating the swains of her youth.

Remembering the cook's warning about getting anything sensible from such an elderly person, Periseneb felt the akh's power pushing at him, feeding on his barely suppressed frustration. Benerib was his only chance to learn things about the family history which would never appear in the dusty scribes' records. "Have another fig?" When she reached for the treat, he clasped his hand around her wrist and let a small amount of the pent up anger leach from him where their skin touched.

Benerib gasped, clutching at her chest, and slumped against the back of the chair. The cat, which had been purring as it twined around her ankles, hissed and spat at Periseneb before scurrying away. Dismayed at the effect he'd wrought, he prayed he hadn't killed her. One so old didn't deserve to die at the hands of an akh.

A moment later, opening one rheumy eye, she peered at him flirtatiously. "What is it you want to ask?"

With a huge sigh of relief, he offered her the figs, taking great care not to touch her again in his unsettled emotional state. "I'm curious about the family that owns Heron Marsh. Not this generation or even the generation before. Older times. Have you any tales of a great great aunt? Sitre by name?"

Both of Benerib's eyes popped open and she slapped her knee as she sat up. "Oh, that one! She was a handful right enough, sir. Not at all like our Neity. Oh no, Sitre was mean, through and through. My mother used to tell me tales about her."

He was surprised by the harsh characterization of the woman he'd known. Searching for a kinder description, he asked, "Headstrong perhaps?" Certainly many had labelled her thus in his time, with a degree of understatement. No one told Sitre what to do or denied any impulse she took into her head. Spoiled from birth by indulgent parents is what the servants in *his* time had said.

The elderly woman he was questioning cackled. "As a child, my mother was one of Lady Sitre's attendants. Mind you, only for the last few years of the harridan's life. The noblewoman must have been nigh onto the age I am now. Nothing ever pleased her. Threw her mirror at my mother, she did, or was it a cosmetics box? Maybe both! Mother said she didn't move fast enough to please the high and mighty lady. None of the maids did. Bitter, nasty woman, according to my mother." Falling silent, Benerib plucked another fig from the bowl and chewed noisily with her few remaining teeth. "Afraid to die, Sitre was. Tried all sorts of nostrums and spells to live forever. Most superstitious woman anyone ever met. Might even have dabbled in black magic in her last years, or so it was whispered. She never spoke of her fears, at least not in my mother's hearing, but plainly the lady was terrified of what awaited her at the Judging of her heart."

Discomfited by this description of the apparent harridan Sitre had evolved into before her death, Periseneb waited. Nothing could persuade him to repeat the mistake he'd made earlier, touching her with the strong negative emotions of the akh uppermost in his heart. He pondered what Benerib had revealed thus far. True, Sitre had thrown some tantrums even in his day, whenever her will was thwarted in any regard. This third-hand account was the closest he was going to come to anyone who'd met the woman he'd once hoped to marry. As he handed the old woman the water skin, keeping his fingers well clear of hers, he prayed silently that Benerib had more to share.

She took a long drink and wiped her lips. "Where was I?"

Hoping she hadn't retreated into senile dreams again, he gave her a prompt. "You were telling me how your mother was a servant to Lady Sitre—"

"Oh, yes, after she was widowed. She'd married Lord Haqaptah. Well, the one in that day, not the one plaguing us."

Periseneb's heart thumped hard in his chest and he rocked on his heels. "She—she married Haqaptah?" Well, what had he expected? He never showed up to claim her, so of course she'd married someone else.

"Aye." Lips working as she chewed, Benerib calculated and made some tallies on her fingers. "Sitre was the great great grandaunt of the current Haqaptah. She never got over her bitterness at not inheriting this estate either, let me tell you. My mother talked of it often. Cursed, the servants used to whisper, all Sitre's schemes and efforts going for naught. Any more figs?"

A shiver ran down his spine at her words, surprising him. Curses shouldn't concern him—he was a ghost himself, after all. Rolling his shoulders to dispel whatever momentary twinge the idea of a curse had given him, he held the bowl closer to her. "As many as you want, old one."

"You must have flirted with the cook," Benerib said, tilting her head to see him more closely. "She never gives anyone so many of her special figs."

"The cook and I have come to an understanding," he answered. "Why didn't Sitre or her sons inherit Heron Marsh?"

The elderly woman leaned close, as if to prevent anyone else who might be interested in centuries' old gossip from overhearing. "Her father took a young third wife, who gave him male heirs. His first wife only produced Sitre, the second wife was barren, but his third choice was blessed." She nodded. "Good, sturdy sons. Of course, over time, the line died out till there's only my Lady Neithamun left. All properly laid in their tombs now, the ancestors are. Gone to the Afterlife. Some say the family is cursed, maybe even by Sitre. She never got over being displaced from what she regarded as her own here." Benerib patted her chair as if it represented the land and possessions Sitre had coveted. "She didn't want the Haqaptah estate, but made her sons and then her grandsons promise they'd get their hands on the Heron Marsh land. And now, in this time of upheaval and change, her descendants might, if my poor lady Neity can't pay her debts and her taxes." Picking a stray bit of the sticky fig from her teeth, his informant chuckled. "Sitre consoled herself by taking lovers well into her eighth decade, my mother said. No sitting and mourning for her."

Periseneb had an uncomfortable mental picture of the beautiful girl he'd known reduced to the status of a crone with six teeth, like his elderly confidant. "Why was she living here when she died? Is she buried in this family's tombs?"

"Heard her sons' wives couldn't stand her, were afraid of her, so she was driven from the Haqaptah estate. Her relatives here took her in, not that their charity was rewarded with any appreciation." Hand trembling with age, the old woman reached for another fig. "Some say she killed the overseer."

Astounded, he uttered his father's name. "Merneseneb?"

Benerib frowned, fig poised against her lips. Eyebrows raised, she gave him a blank stare. "Who? Our overseer was a man by the name of—of, well I can't recall. Short, squat, one squinty eye."

"Never mind the name, old mother. How came he to die?"

"Tomb robbing. Some of the men said he'd been complaining he wasn't paid for his services. The estate is close to forfeit," Benerib said, sniffling. Tears fell onto her downy cheeks. "Never dreamed I'd live to see the day we'd be evicted from our homes."

"By the gods, let's hope you'll have many more years under your own roof, safe and snug." He risked patting her shoulder as she dried her eyes with a corner of her shawl. "But how could a woman dead these hundred years and more kill Neithamun's overseer?"

"He was found in the entryway to her tomb, his neck broken and face frozen in a horrible grimace. Some of her possessions were in a sack by his side, looted from the outer chamber of her resting place. It's said she walks the estate sometimes," Benerib said, as calmly as if she was talking about Mentu or one of the other residents of Heron Marsh.

"Sitre is an akh? A ghost?" The idea made him nauseous, despite the fact he himself was in no better state. What would happen if one ghost encountered another?

Benerib shrugged. "I've not seen her, but others speak of it, in whispers."

There were no more tidbits of information to be gleaned from Benerib. She shared more recent gossip, which, of course, Periseneb had no interest in. He sat with her a few more moments to be polite before taking his leave and strolling away. She'd given him much to ponder, but he was driven to know more. Briefly, he considered asking the Great One Ma'at, but she'd already made clear in the Chamber of Judging that she wasn't going to share the details of anyone else's fate with him. No, he was on his own to discover what he could, and he knew where to do the searching. But first the trip into the small local city to see what he could learn there about the present-day Haqaptah.

"I'm a weaver of sorts myself, gathering all these strands," he said to himself as he walked past the room where the estate's craftswomen were busily at work. "I wish I had a better grasp on what result Ma'at desires."

Neithamun was late to the scribe work that evening, and when she arrived in the library, her face was drawn, with shadows under her eyes. She moved like one exhausted.

Alarmed, Periseneb guided her to the master's chair and took the daily tallies from her hand. "Are you all right?"

"Harvest is hard labor, surely you know that. We're reaping the early blooming crop before the heat can destroy the corn."

"I'll do the tallying. You sit and relax." Periseneb spread the sheets and the correct scroll in front of him on the ebony table, and began entering the numbers. He could always make quick work of even long columns of information, but he found himself going slower and slower, as things failed to add up. Setting the papyrus aside, he rose and fetched another from the storage basket. Reading it where he stood, he returned to the table. "These figures are way off."

Neithamun raised her head from her arms, having been drowsing. "What are you talking about?"

"Even with your shortage of labor, the record shows a planting of several hundred square cubits during Peret, the growing season. Yet your field tallies show only a small harvest to date. Has there been a plague of locusts?"

She took a deep breath, as if preparing to face an unpleasant discussion. "No locusts. Actually, the corn prospered this year and grew well, despite the need to water by hand. But how many times must I tell you, I have very few people left to do the harvest? And accomplish all the other tasks?"

"Are you going to leave corn in the fields to rot?" Horrified at this lapse in good agricultural practices, he allowed his tone to sharpen and sound accusatory.

She bit her lip, plainly annoyed. "If I'd received a prophecy last year about how well the damned stuff was going to grow, despite everything indicating otherwise, I'd have planted less land. Yes, corn is going to rot. Put that on the lengthening tally sheet against me, why don't you?" She rubbed her left shoulder and winced.

He thought he heard unshed tears in her voice. "I'm keeping no such record, I promise. I only want to help. Are you in pain?"

Neithamun nodded. "I was trying to harvest as fast as I could this afternoon, believe me. I don't like waste any more than you, but my people and I are only human."

"If you'll allow me, I can alleviate some of the knots in your shoulders. The military physicians have a specialized technique. Men often overuse their joints in training."

Eyebrows raised, she said, "I suppose it can't hurt. I felt as if I was in a battle with the corn stalks today." She loosened the tie at the neck of her dress and allowed the fabric to slide perilously close to the tops of her breasts before gathering the cotton in her hand to stop its flow. "Show me."

Moving to stand behind her, he swallowed hard, feeling his own response to her bare flesh. "There are special oils which would also help, warming the muscles to loosen the coils. When I go to town, I'll see if the physician there has any." He rubbed her upper back and shoulders, startled at how tense she was. Kneading the large knot in her left shoulder, he felt her stir under his touch, murmuring her pleasure at the relief from pain. She rolled her head in a leisurely circle, exposing the soft skin of her graceful neck. Not sure this was such a good idea after all, he fought the urge to drop a kiss at the spot where her graceful neck met her shoulders. The view she was affording him of the pillowy tops of her breasts, was testing his self control. Despite his best intentions, his hands slowed, temptation affecting him.

A basket of clay tablets fell from their place on the nearest library shelf, striking the floor with a noise that echoed through the room, even as the tablets shattered into a million pieces.

Neithamun screamed, hand to her mouth.

Startled, Periseneb retreated, half drawing his belt knife, searching the gloom beyond the circle of light from the oil lamp. Was someone in the room with them? The heavy basket had fallen as if shoved. Grabbing the lamp, he approached the fallen container. Cold air like that of a tomb assaulted him and his nostrils clogged with the scent of a perfume he'd not smelled in two hundred years.

Neithamun touched his arm and he jumped. "What is it? What caused the basket to fall like that?" Not waiting for an answer, she knelt to sweep the many fragments into a pile with her bare hands.

The sensation of cold and the perfume were gone. He blinked, wondering if he'd imagined them. "Leave the mess for someone else to clean tomorrow," he said, reaching to pull her to her feet. "I think it's time you turn in. We've finished the tallies."

Normally, Neithamun never left a task to someone else to complete, but tonight she put up no argument, abandoning the broken clay without protest. He escorted her to her chambers, pausing for a moment before he opened the door for her. "I'll delay my trip to town for a day or two. I think I should work the harvest with you. Saving as much of the crop as we can is a higher priority than my checking on conditions in Khemjekhu."

Yawning, Neithamun gave him a sleepy smile. "I'd be grateful for the help."

"All right, I'll report to the field at dawn. See you then." He slid the painted panel aside. "Sweet dreams, my lady."

Neithamun lingered for a moment as if tempted to say more, and then stepped into her chambers with a softly whispered, "Good night."

He shut the door behind her and walked to the library, preoccupied with concerns. Everything there was as they'd left it, no more damage. Uneasy at the sight of the basket on the floor and the broken tablets, Periseneb picked up the mess himself, depositing the debris outside the library, a neat pile in the hallway. Then he pulled out the mehen board, moving the malachite marker that represented him one day closer to the center. He counted the remaining squares, although the steadily diminishing number was ever present in his head. Could he spare a day or even two for the harvest? Should he? Rotting corn couldn't possibly be what the goddess Ma'at cared about. This was exactly why he'd resorted to counting the passage of days on the mehen board, to keep himself intent on the reasons he was here, versus the tempting concerns of the estate and the lady. "But Neithamun will work herself to death over this cursed crop if I don't help," he said out loud. And surely Ma'at had some reason to wish Heron Marsh and its mistress well, or else why did she send him to this exact spot? Satisfied with his reasoning, Periseneb restored the coiled snake board to its hiding place and left the library.

Neithamun had planned to be in the fields before anyone else, but apparently the massage Periseneb had given her had near-magical qualities, because she slept in well past dawn. She hadn't done that since she was a carefree child. As she hurried to dress, she realized her back and shoulders were pain-free, ready for another day of hard work. When she arrived at the field, she found a number of people already harvesting ears of corn, but her gaze was drawn to Periseneb as if he was the only one in the field. He moved like he'd harvested grain or corn all his life, smooth and sure. Runners were constantly taking his baskets to be emptied into the central repository as he proceeded along the rows.

Neithamun walked over to check the level and was astonished at how much had been accumulated so early in the day.

"He's been working at that pace since Ra sailed his sun boat into the sky," Amenemopet, her senior harvester said, as she dumped a basket full of corn into the bin. Admiration was plain in the woman's voice, and in her gaze as she looked over her shoulder at the warrior. "No one can keep up with him. We might clear the entire field after all, if he can maintain the pace." Hands on her hips, Amenemopet nudged the woman next to her and made some low-voiced comment about Periseneb's stamina that set them both to laughing as they strolled to the next area of the field ready to be harvested.

Neithamun felt her cheeks flush, realizing she'd been staring at him. He was bare chested, wearing only the short kilt of a field hand, which barely covered a plain linen loin cloth. The play of muscles in his arms and back as he cut the ears from the stalks with his sickle was enticing to watch. Each movement was economical, easy and assured.

"Not too hard on the eyes, eh?" Menwi was standing behind her, taking the day off from her usual indoor tasks to help harvest. "Handsome, strong—"

Neithamun bent to collect an empty basket. "You talk too much." As she moved into the field to follow Periseneb, she found herself hoping he might repeat the amazingly effective massage for her again after dinner. She felt a pulse of desire between her thighs at the thought of his strong hands on her. If she hadn't been so tired last night, and if the stupid basket of tablets hadn't fallen, breaking the mood, might he have wanted to take things further than a mere shoulder massage?

Neithamun wasn't sure what she would have said, if he'd asked for more intimacy. Her attraction to him on many levels was nearly impossible to resist, but he said himself he wasn't staying at Heron Marsh. "And I know nothing about him," she muttered, earning a sideways look from Menwe. Biting her lip, Neithamun tried to stop thinking about Periseneb and concentrate on the field work

She and Menwe both trailed him as he harvested. One person couldn't hope to collect the amount of corn he was cutting, especially since Neithamun kept stealing distracted glances at the scars he bore. There was one thin line along his ribs, as if a spear had cut a close path in battle, and several puckered slashes that had to be from swords. She knew he was unquestionably a mighty warrior, to have achieved the honor of joining Pharaoh's Own, but looking at the proof of that bravery on his body was daunting, worrisome. She wondered how much the wounds had hurt and who had cared for him while he recovered.

Menwe pressed a waterskin into her hands, startling her. "Drink," she said, "And then deliver the remainder to him. He must need refreshment, as hard as he's working."

Feeling a little shy and annoyed with herself for being diffident when, after all, she was the lady of the estate, Neithamun did as her friend ordered. Timing her approach to Periseneb as he finished a stroke with the sickle, she tapped him on the shoulder. "Water?"

Turning on his heel, he put the sickle in his belt, giving her a smile. Wiping his forehead with the back of his hand, he said, "Just in time, for I was growing sadly parched."

"You've harvested so many rows already—I'm amazed." Neithamun handed him the waterskin and watched as he drank.

Periseneb needed the cool water, but he enjoyed Neithamun's company even more. He didn't know if she realized it, but she'd been humming a little song as she gathered the corn ears. It was pleasant to hear her voice and know she was close at hand.

He'd deliberately opened his mind to the surging power of the akh today, feeding it with anger at the potential waste of perfectly good food. He found it almost frightening how the strength grew and fed on dark emotion. He hoped the sheer physical nature of the work would help him channel the flood of energy, rather than being subsumed in the fire. Staying on a knife edge between giving in to the urges of the ghost and behaving as the man he'd once been was stressful. As long as he kept his body in the smooth rhythm of the harvest, the ghost's temptations stayed harnessed.

Turning to give the waterskin to Neithamun, he froze. "Don't move," he said, fear for her coursing through his veins.

"What?" Her eyes opened wide and she turned her head fearfully, searching for the cause of his distress.

"Stop!" He feared she was going to take a step. "You have a black cobra directly behind you."

The snake was about as long as he was tall, with a mottled gray-and-black back and a creamy white belly. It must have slithered out from between the rows of corn, where it would have been feasting on mice and other small prey. Hood flared, the cobra's head was raised several feet above the ground, body swaying slightly on the coiled tail. Tongue flickering, the creature was still deliberating whether to strike. If it sunk its fangs into Neithamun, she'd be dead by sunset, and there was nothing anyone could do to save her, not even him.

Next moment, Periseneb realized the snake wasn't paying any attention to Neithamun, although she stood closer to it. The reptile's big eyes were focused on him. Snakes were the sacred creatures of the goddess Renenutet. Did it recognize his unearthly nature?

Slowly, barely moving, he reached to draw Neithamun away from the snake and toward him. White-faced, she obeyed his silent command, moving ever so cautiously in response to the pressure he exerted on her arm, never turning her head. Once he'd gotten her safely behind him, he released her. The snake hissed again, still watching his every move.

He went down on one knee, ignoring Neithamun's gasped protest. Searching his mind for what to say to the snake, he was acutely conscious of the audience he had. Not only was the lady of the estate listening, but all her workers. He couldn't reveal his own nature, but he had to appease the goddess who ruled these serpents. Hoping she wasn't minded to take revenge for the many gigantic snakes he'd killed in the desert of the Afterlife, he lowered his head as if bowing to Pharaoh. "We honor your efforts, Great One Renenutet, and the way in which you preserve the harvest by sending your servants to destroy the pests of the field. We pray you'll allow us to continue our work unmolested this day. I'll personally make sacrifice of the finest meat and wine tonight at the temple in your honor."

The snake swayed, lowering itself to the ground, and slithered toward him. Periseneb forced himself to remain stock still as the massive serpent paused a few inches from him, raising its head once more to study his face, hood flaring with a suddenness that made his heart pound. The cobra's huge eyes with their round black pupils fixed on him. He saw golden flecks in the snake's eyes, a sure sign of the goddess's presence.

"I swear by Ma'at to atone for past actions, and to honor you as I've promised." He prayed silently for his patron goddess to protect him, and for Renenutet to accept his apology. It had been his appointed task as an unjudged shade to kill the giant snakes that passed through the gray desert, but he had a suspicion Renenutet didn't approve, nonetheless.

The snake leaned closer, until he could feel the touch of its tongue on his forehead, featherlight.

Then the cobra folded its hood and slithered away, going deeper into the corn field.

Shakily, he rose to his feet. Neithamun threw herself into his arms. "I was so frightened for you! I feared the snake was going to strike at your face. How did you know what to say to the goddess?"

He shrugged. "Instinct and half remembered old prayers from when I was a child. Are you all right?"

"I'll be fine. How can I ever thank you for saving me again?"

"I'm just glad I was here." Hugging her for a moment, he gently disengaged her arms from his waist. "We must make the sacrifice I've promised."

"Yes, of course, tonight before dinner. We'll go to the family temple and perform the rites together." She was practically babbling in her relief.

Periseneb raised his head, looking at the crowd of workers who'd gathered in the row of corn.

"I've never known a cobra to behave in such a manner," said Amenemopet. She was frowning, eyes narrowed as she stared at Periseneb. "Usually a serpent strikes at once, or flees."

"We were blessed by Renenutet," he answered, raising his voice for everyone to hear. "The goddess approves of the hard work you're all doing to save the crop. Her goal is ever to provide for a bounteous harvest, and Heron Marsh is making sure the efforts of her creatures don't go to waste. Give praise to the Great One."

There was a ragged cheer for Renenutet and he was relieved to see people smiling. Amenemopet's brow remained furrowed, but as everyone else returned to their assigned rows with renewed enthusiasm, she merely cautioned the group to be alert for the snake, or its burrow mates.

Periseneb escorted Neithamun to the center of the field and insisted she sit in the shade for a time before she resumed her gathering. "I'll miss your company and your song," he said, "But you're pale and a bit shaky. Rest, and come help me when you're feeling more yourself. There'll be plenty of corn to glean, I promise."

Fingers to her lips, she blushed. "Was I singing?"

"In a lovely voice," he said, giving her a half bow. "You have hidden talents, mistress of Heron Marsh. I look forward to discovering more during the remainder of my stay here." Realizing too late he'd allowed himself to voice some of what he was really thinking about his beautiful hostess, he turned on his heel and walked into the corn, drawing the sickle and summoning the anger of the akh to fuel his efforts. Regret that he wasn't a mortal man provided no small spark to the fire.

Two mornings later, the corn harvest complete for now, he rose early and strolled outside to harness the donkey to the cart. He grabbed a generous portion of fruit and rolls on the way, although his stomach was still content after last night's dinner. Being in the upper world was a joy, yet his body hadn't adjusted to the need for sleep and food. He enjoyed the tastes and sensations of food, but felt no special hunger. Sleep seemed like a waste of time with his ever-looming deadline, especially having sacrificed two days to wielding a sickle as he'd done many a time in his youth.

As he walked to the fenced enclosure, he forced himself to eat, hungry or not, knowing a warrior must keep replenishing his strength. The cart waited for him, already loaded with the trade goods the evening before. It was a small enough pile of baskets and woven containers, but every spare deben would increase Neithamun's chances of keeping the estate.

When he went to catch the braying donkey, the animal kicked its heels and trotted to the far side of the enclosure, as if daring him to catch it. Periseneb's gaze fell upon the chariot she'd spoken of, covered with heavy cloth, parked next to the rear of the small shelter. Leaving the donkey to savor its temporary victory, he walked to the vehicle and threw the covering aside to examine it. The wooden wheels had rotted where the rims rested on the ground, but the axles appeared sound and the basket of the vehicle itself was in good condition, the leather in need of oiling and cleaning. Some of the wicker might need reweaving. Curious to see what emblem the noble had carried, Periseneb walked to the front of the chariot and rubbed away the grime on the electrum plate. Not surprisingly, the cartouche was that of the Heron Marsh estate itself.

Straightening, Periseneb dusted his hands. *If we ever get to the point where we could afford to keep a team of horses, it wouldn't be hard to refurbish this.* He had a momentary vision of himself, driving a laughing Neithamun in the restored, gleaming chariot, as fast as the horses could gallop. She wouldn't be frightened of the speed. No, she'd laugh and toss her hair and want him to drive faster. Neithamun had courage and spirit.

"What am I thinking about?" he muttered, drawing the covering over the dilapidated chariot. "I won't be here long enough to see the things I'm daydreaming of. If anyone takes her for a drive, it won't be me."

Annoyed, he made short work of his second attempt at catching and harnessing the donkey, and was soon on his way into town. Khemjekhu had been a small, dusty village in his day, with a temple to Horus, and another to a local god. There was a tiny harbor on the Nile, where fishing boats and the occasional merchant vessel put in. He found the town had grown over the centuries, although as he drove through the surprisingly busy streets, he recognized the major landmarks. There was a temple to Isis now, next to the one consecrated to Horus, with Ra's on the other side. He heard the priestesses of Isis chanting morning paeans to their goddess as he drove by. The central square was bustling. It was market day, a good omen for him, since he wanted to catch up with the gossip and observe the local populace. First, he had to dispose of the trade goods. Neithamun had given him directions to the merchant who'd taken the commission to sell Heron Marsh's extra beer and cloth.

There, he encountered his first setback. The tradesman greeted him with the friendliness of a born salesperson, but as soon as Periseneb explained his errand, the man paled and retreated. One hand raised as if to ward off a demon, he said, "No, no there's been a misunderstanding. I can't handle any more goods. I can barely sell a deben's worth of my own these days. Take your cart and go."

Periseneb eyed the man's busy stall, with numerous people shopping. Several women were waiting to haggle over goods they'd already selected. "Business appears to be good."

The man edged further away. "I can't help you."

This reaction was so odd, Periseneb felt sure it had something to do with his quest for Ma'at. He followed the merchant into the shade of the awning, moving toward the threshold where the shop area adjoined a home. A woman interposed herself between the two men. "Go wait on the priestess from the temple of Isis, my husband," she said, patting his arm. "I'll take care of this matter."

Eyes wide, the man grabbed at her sleeve. "You know we can't—"

Nodding, she gave him a gentle shove. "It'll be all right, don't worry so."

Periseneb watched the husband stumble away, moving toward a priestess holding a length of fine linen, embroidered with lotuses. The priestess was eyeing him intensely, making him uncomfortable to be the object of her attention, so he turned to the wife. "Are you the sister of the weaver at Heron Marsh?"

She nodded. "We can't talk long. His men blanket the town today, watching."

"Haqaptah's men?"

"Yes. Please don't get us in trouble. I know I promised my sister we'd sell the cloth and beer for her mistress, but it's impossible." Wringing her hands, she lowered her voice. "His thugs paid my husband a distressing visit, threatened to burn our shop if we sold Heron Marsh goods. They gave him a black eye for good measure. Please go now."

"What am I to do with a cartful of beer and cloth?" he said.

"Sell them yourself, if you dare. The space at the western edge of the square is for one time vendors." She drew her shawl closely around herself and walked away from him without a second glance.

Deciding she'd actually made a good suggestion for furthering his mission of assessing the mood in town, he led the donkey to the designated area and spread his wares on the tail of his cart. He shouted enticements at the passers-by like the other merchants. He soon had customers for the beer, but he noticed all of them were travelers, or from the ships currently in the harbor. Local people averted their eyes and hurried past.

Haqaptah's mercenaries patrolled the marketplace, wandering through the area in pairs, making crude jokes and harassing the merchants—especially any woman unlucky enough to be selling wares today—helping themselves to fruit and anything else that caught their eye. As the men progressed, they came to a beggar, seated off to the side, his begging bowl nearly empty. Two of the thugs evidently felt there was amusement to be had.

"We don't tolerate your kind here," said the first man, kicking over the beggar's bowl. "Lord Haqaptah doesn't encourage thieves and vagrants in his town."

"The gods allow one such as me to pray for sustenance and petition passersby," the man answered, his voice shaky. "The laws apply to any village in the Black Lands, although yours has shown scant charity today." He glanced at the moldy loaf lying broken in the dirt, after spilling from his bowl. "I'm no thief, merely a disabled soldier, one who served his Pharaoh well. Now, I'm reduced to existing on the generosity of the townspeople and nobles such as your patron." He reached for a cane.

One of the mercenaries grabbed the wooden staff, holding it out of reach above his head. "Beg for this, old man. Come on, let's hear your best groveling."

"And no more lies," said the other. "No stories about being a soldier. Even if you were, you probably fought for the wrong side, not the one our master favors."

Using the shop wall behind him as a crutch, the man attempted to rise. "Please, I must have my staff to walk."

Periseneb had seen enough. Anger rose in his heart at the discourtesy being shown to a former soldier. Marching over to the trio, he snatched the cane from the unready mercenary and handed it to the beggar. "Here."

The man staggered for a moment and Periseneb extended a hand to help him balance. The beggar's grip was surprisingly strong. His face, shadowed under the robe's hood, seemed younger than Periseneb had expected. Even as his skepticism was rising, the other stepped away with murmured thanks, the robe fell free of his leg and Periseneb saw terrible scars. This man had unquestionably seen serious combat and was fortunate to have lived. "Come to my cart," he said to the beggar, "And I'll share some beer and bread, to replace what the dogs have now stolen."

"You're very kind." Awkwardly, the ex-soldier bent to retrieve a small sack. "I'll take that offer. Blessings upon you, sir."

The mercenaries swaggered to block Periseneb's path. "You should stay out of this. You're in enough trouble, refusing our master's offer of a job and staying at Heron Marsh, helping her. Lord Haqaptah doesn't encourage interference with his dictates. And he's adamant about no beggars."

"He'd better hope the Queen of the Gods never arrives on his doorstep as a beggar then. Remember the legend of the seven scorpions? And what happened to the rich woman who refused to help the poor supplicant?" Periseneb laughed at their expressions. It was a well-known scribes' tale in his time, and now too, judging by their reaction. The Great One Isis had paid a visit in disguise to an arrogant noblewoman, and the human suffered greatly for her for lack of charity.

"This scruffy thief isn't a god in disguise," said the first mercenary, but his voice was a little uncertain. He backed away a step.

Emboldened by Periseneb having coming to his aid, the beggar laughed until he coughed and shook a finger at Haqaptah's man. "One never knows for sure though."

Periseneb retrieved the bowl as the two mercenaries moved off. Handing the chipped and poorly made dish to the beggar, who tucked it into his sack, he escorted the man across the market to his own cart. He had to move slowly, as the beggar limped. "Thank you for interceding," the man said, as he hobbled behind Periseneb. "This village is more unfriendly than any I've ever been in, I think."

Periseneb glanced across the market, noticing again how people would look away rather than catch his eye. He grunted in disgust. "Afraid of the local bully and his hired thugs."

"But you're not?"

Periseneb rolled his shoulders. "I'm a soldier of Pharaoh, as you can see from my falcon badge. Retired, but in possession of my skills and my honor." He stepped ahead to draw a mug of beer for the beggar, handing it to the man as he reached the cart and leaned on the side. "What will you do next?"

Handing Periseneb the empty mug a moment later, the beggar bent to rub his damaged leg. "I'll move on from this place and thank the gods to see the last of it. I don't envy you who must remain here."

"Probably wise to travel elsewhere in the nome. I wish you well." Periseneb thrust bread and a piece of dried meat into the edge of the man's pack.

"Life, prosperity, health to you also." The beggar hobbled away with a wave of his hand, heading in the direction of the waterfront.

Periseneb settled in to observe the townspeople again and try to make at least a bit of deben for Neithamun. He wished he could have spared something other than food for the beggar, but the coin wasn't his to give away. Heron Marsh was nigh unto a charity case itself.

The afternoon wore on. The cloth wasn't selling, save for a length bought by a tipsy sailor for the dancer accompanying him, but the beer supply was nearly gone. Periseneb was considering his options when someone tapped him on the shoulder.

"I'd like to see some of the linens, please." The priestess of Isis, who'd been in the shop, was standing beside the cart.

"Aren't you concerned about Haqaptah's men?" He pointed with his chin to the two beefy mercenaries who'd taken a position across the square, where they could keep an eye on him and intimidate any local foolish enough to want to pay deben into the Heron Marsh coffers.

Standing straight, she gave them a glare. "Not in the least. Haqaptah hasn't begun preying on the temples. Yet. He has a modicum of respect—or fear—left in him. The Great One Isis won't tolerate depredations on what belongs to her. I do wish the new nomarch had made it a priority to visit this town sooner in his reign. We're on the edge of the Black Lands, after all, which makes us important."

He decided he liked her, although he hadn't lost his wariness as to why she'd sought him out. "Beer? No charge for one who serves the goddess."

"I'll have a mug. I've heard much of the famous special recipe from Heron Marsh but never tasted it." The priestess accepted a serving from him, tipping a few drops to the ground to honor the Great One Isis. She drank deeply, licking her lips in pleasure and raising the cup to her lips a second time to catch the last droplets. "This certainly lives up to the claims of those who have drunk it." Handing him the cup, she said, "I'd better be going. Even if Haqaptah's paid jackals don't dare challenge me, I don't wish to provoke them unduly."

Reaching into the cart for his wares, he stopped in surprise at her readiness to leave. "Did you want to see the cloth?"

"No, I needed an excuse to stop and talk. I was curious about you." She eyed him from head to toe. "When we were in the merchant alley earlier, I smelled the scent of the Nile lotus. You've seen my goddess, haven't you? Are you ushabti? Did Isis send you? Is she intervening in matters here?"

Her questions struck uncomfortably close to home, yet he was able to give her a truthful answer without hesitation. "I've never seen Isis and I'm not one of her servants. Just a retired soldier."

She studied him for a moment, eyes narrowed, then shook her head. "No. There's something. I *have* seen the Great One Isis, in the temple at Thebes before I was posted here. To my eyes, you have something about you that isn't quite…human."

Periseneb swallowed hard, glad others didn't possess the mystical intuition this priestess apparently possessed. He realized he was rubbing his shoulder where the tattoo rode. Annoyed, he lowered his hand.

"I won't press you," she promised. "Clearly, I'm not meant to know or Isis would have told me." She held out her hand. "I'm Hernebti."

Bowing his head as he lightly clasped her hand, he gave her his name. "Periseneb, late of Pharaoh's army."

Head tilted to one side, glossy black wig framing her face in graceful curls, Hernebti said. "The nomarch's arrival in a few weeks is going to bring all aspects of the situation to a boil, isn't it?"

"I believe so."

"I'll tell my temple guards to be extra vigilant." She walked away.

Periseneb gazed after her for a moment. Had he told her too much?

"So pretty," said a shy little voice from right beside him. "I wish my mother had a dress like this."

He glanced down to find a raggedly-dressed girl fingering the closest length of linen, which he'd half spread over the cart tail, intending to show Hernebti the best work. Colorful birds and papyrus flowers embroidered by the estate's skillful women practically glowed in the sunlight.

"Don't touch!" A painfully thin woman hurried to pull the child away. Behind her came a weary man with the bearing of a soldier, hand on his belt knife as he assessed Periseneb from shrewd eyes, taking his measure as a possible opponent.

"The child was doing no harm," Periseneb said. "I'm selling fabric cheap today, special prices."

The man shook his head. "No matter how special the price, peddler, we've no use for fancy clothing."

"You look thirsty, would you care for some beer? No charge," he added hastily. "I'm reduced to the dregs and I want to pack and head home soon."

The woman licked her lips and gave the man a glance. "It's warm today and we've a long way to walk."

He hesitated, shifting the small bag of foodstuffs he carried. "We haven't fallen to accepting charity, wife."

"It would help me out," Periseneb said with utter truth.

"All right then." The other nodded once.

As Periseneb poured the last of the beer into mugs, he asked, "From around here?"

"Do we look like we're from here?" the other man said truculently. "Passing through. And I'll be glad to leave this place behind. I've seen how miserable the territory to the east is, but at least we didn't have self-appointed bullies running things."

As the adults drank deeply, Periseneb brought out the last of the fruit and rolls he'd carried for himself, offering them to the child, whose face was pinched with hunger. Eagerly, she tore into the meager snack. He frowned, hating the idea of a child in the Black Lands not having enough to eat. "Forgive me, I've no desire to offend, but you seem to have fallen on hard times," he said to the girl's father.

"No fault of our own," the woman answered. "We'd better be going, Amethu." Her eyes had gone wide as she glanced over his shoulder and her voice had a slight tremor. Defensive instincts pricking him in warning, Periseneb had no doubt what—or who—must be upsetting her.

Next moment, the gruff voice of Haqaptah's mercenary confirmed his suspicions. "I told you riffraff to clear out days ago, move along somewhere else."

Hand on his belt knife, the husband moved smoothly to maneuver his wife and child behind him. Periseneb took a position at his elbow, drawing a swift glance from the man and a nod.

"Customers, sampling my wares," Periseneb said. "Too bad you're too late. I've sold out."

"No one was talking to you." All bluster and self-importance, standing tall, frowning, the mercenary pointed a stubby finger at him. "Although you'd be well advised to move along too, before I run out of patience."

"Who set you in charge of the public market?" Periseneb stepped forward, hands on his hips.

The other man laughed. "Lord Haqaptah, that's all you need to know. Be gone by sunset, all of you, or suffer the consequences." He swaggered away, his two subordinates in his wake.

"We'll be going now. Thanks for the beer." The man took the little girl's hand. "Come along, it's quite a hike to the camp."

Periseneb nodded and watched them until the trio was safely out of sight on the far side of the square. Reflecting on his day in town, he packed the beer jugs in straw, strapping them in place, and rolled the cloth into neat bundles. He had a pretty clear picture of how Haqaptah dominated the local populace through intimidation. Half the town was probably in debt to the noble as well. Jingling the deben in the leather pouch at his belt, he decided to continue with his original plan, spend some time in the harbor taverns and listen to the talk there before returning to Heron Marsh. Might as well be thorough. Leaving the donkey and cart with a local merchant willing to bear the responsibility for a half-deben, Periseneb made his way dockside.

Other than a few of his men drinking in a rowdy bar, Haqaptah seemed to have no presence at the harbor. The talk was all of shipping conditions on the Nile, the most recent sandstorm, and speculation about what the new nomarch might do when he eventually came to town. Sipping his inferior beer, Periseneb concluded that his assessment of the situation made sense. The port was separate from the village. Even the taverns and merchants catering to the shipping trade were more aligned with the river than the land. If Haqaptah officially came to power, which Periseneb suspected was what the noble desired, he couldn't do much more than impose taxes on the Nile trade. There were other towns and other harbors, maybe not as convenient as Khemjekhu had come to be in the last two centuries, but well enough.

No, Haqaptah couldn't hope to wield much influence here.

Retrieving his patient donkey and the cart, Periseneb drove out of town, heading along the river road toward Heron Marsh. The sun was setting, Ra the Sun God making his daily journey through the heavens. There was no other traffic. Periseneb had a prickling between his shoulder blades as the donkey, eager to get home to its barn, picked up the pace with no need for encouragement. One-handed, he slid his sword from its place of concealment under the seat. A few moments later, as the road curved, he found the path ahead blocked by Haqaptah's men. He recognized the three from the town and several of the thugs who'd been harassing Neithamun the day he'd arrived.

No masks. No effort to conceal their identities. They plan to kill me. He drew the protesting donkey to a halt. There was no way to turn the cart, the road being bracketed by low hills. Two chariots blocked the road ahead, drawn across the track. The cart would come to grief if he tried to drive past them on the rough terrain beside the road. The trap was well devised.

Idly, he wondered if Ma'at would allow him to be killed. He guessed she would, if he was stupid or unlucky enough to die in combat. Determined to control his own fate, he shook his head. What kind of an elite soldier called on the goddess of truth to rescue him from a band of mercenaries? And he would not unleash the akh unless as a last resort. He feared he couldn't recover human form if he ever gave in to the allure of raging as a ghost. "Only the foolish seek to challenge a member of Pharaoh's Own Guard," he said, raising his voice, assessing the group of men facing him.

"Ten of us, one of you." The man who'd been the ringleader in town gestured with his belt knife. "You could give us the deben you collected today and be on your way."

Not for a moment did he believe the paltry amount of deben he'd collected was the reason for this ambush. He shook his head. Raising his sword, he jumped from the cart. "Come, try to take it." He beckoned with the fingers of his free hand as if inviting them. Unless there were more of them sneaking up from behind, he might actually stand a chance of surviving the ambush. He whacked the donkey on the rump with the flat of the sword and the offended animal bolted straight at the men, who scattered. Running behind the cart, Periseneb slashed at the legs of the two closest thieves as they scrambled to get out of the way of the irate donkey and the plunging cart. His targets fell, badly wounded.

Placing his back to the chariots as the donkey ran on, Periseneb defended himself against three assailants who got in each other's way in their eagerness to cut him down. With one blow, he half-severed the neck of the closest, who knocked the others off their feet as he fell, blood spewing profusely into the road. Sensing a threat from behind, Periseneb ducked and sidestepped as someone tried to tackle him. The attacker's knife scored his shoulder, but in the grip of fighting frenzy, he barely felt the pain. He plunged his own knife into the man's shoulder as the mercenary fell and then smoothly stepped forward to engage the next opponent.

Sword to sword, he battled in the dusty road. Haqaptah's mercenary had some skills, but nowhere near enough expertise to defeat one of Pharaoh's crack troops, especially not a warrior honed by centuries of fighting uncanny hazards in the underworld deserts. Periseneb realized he was toying with his opponent. Chiding himself because he couldn't afford the luxury of taunting a lesser man when so many other combatants were waiting to challenge him, he launched an offensive. He drove the other back, reducing the mercenary to desperately defending himself from the slashing blows Periseneb was landing on his shield and sword. Periseneb could tell the other's arms were weakening, his shield dipping lower and lower, but just as he was going in to finish the battle, a new adversary attacked him from the rear. It was a classic move, and he cursed the fact he had no shield brother to watch his back. The assailant had his arm around Periseneb's neck, cutting off the air, and attempted to stab him with a knife in the other hand. Sensing a chance at victory, the rest of the mercenaries circled like a pack of hyenas.

Periseneb had no choice but to drop his sword in order to deal with the man choking him from behind. Spinning, he used his opponent as a human shield for a moment, before getting a good enough grip on the surprised man to throw him to the ground, kicking him in the ribs to gain a moment to retreat to a better position.

But the remaining guards, some of whom hadn't engaged in the fight at all and so were still fresh and untired, ringed him.

He spat, rolled his shoulders and clenched his fists. "By the Great One Horus, you're not going to find it easy to take me. You jackals will pay dearly."

"Be that as it may, you'll be the loser here," said the nearest man with a sneer.

Periseneb launched himself at the bold speaker, trying to wrest his sword away from him, even as the others were closing in, yelling insults and curses.

Suddenly, an arrow blossomed in the neck of the man he was grappling with. The other's eyes opened wide and he fell away from Periseneb, crumpling on the road.

Sword in hand, Periseneb tried to fight off the others, but his knee gave way under him. He hadn't even realized he'd sustained a wound there. Half kneeling, blackness closing in, he shook his head, trying to refocus on the combat. He felt the power of the akh swelling but was too weak to focus. Dimly, he was aware of more men swarming the scene and more arrows whizzing past him. The sword fell from his hand and he collapsed.

CHAPTER FOUR

It was night when he woke, lying on a thin blanket beside a campfire. The small child he'd befriended earlier in the day was sitting next to him, studying him with a serious look on her face. As soon as she realized he was awake, she scrambled to her feet and ran, calling for her mother.

Hand to his aching forehead, Periseneb attempted to sit. He realized his shoulder and knee had been expertly bandaged. Searching for his weapons, he discovered that he lay in the middle of an encampment. Men, a few women, and several children were gathering on the other side of the small fire, staring at him.

"Thank you for coming to my aid," he said, addressing the remark to the crowd at large.

One man stepped away from his fellows, and walked toward Periseneb. He wasn't surprised to see it was Amethu, the person he'd met in the market. The man spoke a quiet word to the others, who dispersed.

"We were returning from the hunt and came upon you battling Haqaptah's thugs," said his host. "No one fights as well as one of Pharaoh's Own, but you were badly outnumbered."

"Indeed. I owe you. You had no duty to intervene, but I'm grateful."

Amethu shrugged. "I couldn't stand by and let them prevail. After I killed the man fighting with you, we launched our arrows to injure, not kill, but to drive them away."

Periseneb checked the surroundings, not recognizing the area. "Where are we?"

"My camp, well off the road, tucked away in the hills. Don't worry, guards are posted, but the mercenaries aren't likely to search for us—or you—in the dark. You killed or injured so many, it'll take Haqaptah awhile to recover." The man's tone was admiring. "We'll be long gone by then."

A woman came to them carrying several platters—freshly cooked meat, which smelled delicious to Periseneb—and some fruit. His stomach growled. The little girl followed, carrying two mugs, her face full of pride at being allowed to help.

"Thank you," he said to the child, as he accepted the mug she held out with a shy, unsmiling glance.

"It won't be as good as the beer you shared with us earlier today." His host laughed. "But it'll clear a parched throat."

Periseneb realized he was starving, for the first time since his parole from the Afterlife, but he hesitated. "I don't want to eat someone else's portion."

"Rations have been slim, you're right, but today we had good hunting." Spearing a juicy portion with his knife, Amethu dropped the meat on the plate, handing it to Periseneb. "The Great Ones favored us. Everyone else has eaten their fill, so have no concern."

"A warrior has to eat, especially one who has fought such a hard battle," the woman said, resting her hand on her husband's shoulder.

"Do I have you to thank for the expert wound care?" Periseneb asked, raising his mug to salute her. "You must let me repay you. I scarce feel any discomfort."

She shook her head. "The Great One Hathor gave me a small healing gift when I was born. It's my duty and my honor to have assisted you." Taking the child's hand, she said, "Come, we'll let your father keep our guest company at dinner. I'm sure he'd rather not be gawked at."

"Who are you?" Periseneb asked as he cut into the meat, dripping with juices, and prepared to eat. "You haven't the garb or attitude of nomads, but I remember you said you weren't from this area?"

Shaking his head, his host grimaced. "It's a long tale, but as there's no other entertainment in our poor camp, I'll spin it for you. We're from Hethshur, in the eastern portion of the Nome?" He asked the question as if expecting Periseneb to recognize the name.

Chewing, he shook his head. Swallowing, he said. "Sorry, I'm not familiar with the east."

"No matter. When the war against the Usurper Pharaoh and the Hyksos broke out, the lord of our estate took all the able bodied men and marched to fight." Stirring the fire and adding a few small pieces of wood, Amethu said, "You'll not like to hear this since it would have made us your enemies, but my master was sworn to support the Usurper, although then, of course, we didn't call her such."

"So, your noble gave his allegiance to the losing side?"

Nodding, his host reached to take a crispy tidbit of the meat, chewing reflectively for a moment before swallowing. He lifted his mug. "And paid dearly for the error of his ways. Died in the final battle. We—the few of us left here—survived the battle somehow and surrendered when it was done. Your Pharaoh is a surprisingly merciful man."

Not my Pharaoh. Periseneb repressed a grin, thinking of the man he'd truly served. Fair, yes. Merciful, no. "What course of justice did the Great One follow?"

"Gave us the chance to swear by the goddess Ma'at we'd never take up arms against him again. We were allowed to go home, told to work diligently to restore the granaries and the treasuries of Egypt…so that Pharaoh could better defend the Black Lands against the Hyksos in the future, should the enemy attempt to retake what they'd lost."

"Unheard of generosity indeed." Periseneb glanced across the fire, to where the others were sitting. "Yet, you're here, far from home, camped in the wilderness."

His host was silent for a moment. "When we reached our homes, there was utter devastation, as if the Lake of Fire had come to the surface. The Hyksos attacked the village during their retreat from Egypt, and burned it to the ground. The bastards killed everyone or carried them off to be sold into slavery. My wife and our child, and a few of the other women, were lucky enough to find safe hiding places when the attack started. Most…did not." Swallowing hard, Amethu took another swig of beer, his knuckles clenched tight on the handle. "The estate was ruined, fields sown with salt by the enemy, apparently for spite. Fruit trees hacked down for firewood. Cattle taken for the enemy soldiers to eat. We tried to scratch a living in the ruins, but it was impossible."

Sympathetic, but hardly surprised—wars inevitably took a harsh toll on the noncombatants—Periseneb understood Amethu's choice. "So you left, hoping for something better elsewhere?"

He nodded. "I couldn't let my family, my people, starve. We were afraid the Hyksos might regroup and invade again. Their rulers still covet Egypt. My few men and I could never fight off an organized attack. Word was this area was fairly untouched by the war, work to be had for ex-soldiers. Of course, when we arrived, we learned the employment was serving as Haqaptah's attack dogs, bullying his neighbors, preparing no doubt for his attempt to come to full power." Brow furrowed, the man gave Periseneb a hard look. "I have pride and honor as a soldier, even if I was defeated in battle. No shame lies there. I couldn't take deben for doing such tasks as Haqaptah demanded, not even to feed my family."

Acknowledging the point as a fair one, Periseneb nodded. "What are your plans now?"

Amethu gazed at the stars for a moment, as if hoping to find an answer there. "Find an abandoned oasis in the Red Lands perhaps, one large enough to support our small number, but insignificant enough not to tempt anyone else. Cling to life there."

"Which is no life," Periseneb said, reaching a swift decision. These men had honor and he needed allies. "I would offer you something else, at least for the next month, maybe longer if the gods be kind."

Lowering his gaze from the heavens, the other man studied him with a grave expression. "Word is your lady is about to lose her estate, if that's the sanctuary you offer. Haqaptah is intent on taking it away from her. The judgment of the nomarch rests on the blade of a sword, free to fall to either side."

"True. I can't dispute the truth of what you say. Yet Neithamun has a chance, maybe better than a chance if she had help for the next few weeks. There's no deben to be paid, but you could have a roof over your heads, food, and a chance to rest. Haqaptah has shown his unwillingness to attack her lands openly. If I had seasoned men such as yourselves to help me keep watch—" Periseneb paused and took a sip of the weak beer, surprised yet again by the force of the passion he felt over the fate of Heron Marsh. *And Neithamun.* Drawing a deep breath, he said, "We've crops ready to harvest, but not enough hands. I'd like to get a second planting in the fallow ground if at all possible. Your women and children could help there. I've found a new source of water, but we need to dig a canal to channel it. You and your men could assist me."

"Clearly a cause you believe in, soldier, judging by the daunting list of tasks." Amethu's tone was mild. "Yet, you yourself are newly come to this part of the Nome, or so it's said. Maybe it's the woman you believe in?"

"I can't deny the truth in your words. But Heron Marsh could be an opportunity for your people as well, maybe a permanent home, if the Great Ones favor her cause." Periseneb studied the other man's face. "Are you afraid to run afoul of Haqaptah?"

Shaking his head, the man said, "No. As you say, he doesn't want the estate destroyed before he can claim it, and the woman with her land. My understanding is he may ask the nomarch to give her to him as well."

Clenching his fist, anger stirring in his gut at the mere suggestion, Periseneb took a deep breath. "All the more reason to help her."

"In the morning we'll go with you then. If the situation doesn't work out, we'll keep moving, into the wastes of the Red Lands."

She'd kept herself busy all day, while wondering how Periseneb was faring in town. She wished she could have gone with him, but she was needed at the estate to keep activities humming. Neithamun found her mind constantly wandering to the handsome warrior. She missed his quiet voice and helping hand as the day's labors went on in various areas of the estate. Missed his sound advice. Pausing for a moment as she left the kitchen after tasting the most recent batch of beer, she shook her head. How had she come to lean on this stranger so unquestioningly, so fast? The cook constantly reminded her they knew next to nothing about Periseneb, but Neithamun felt it couldn't be mere coincidence he'd arrived so soon after she'd prayed yet again in the family temple for help with her impossible task of preserving the estate.

Considering the question of her reliance on Periseneb as she untangled yarn skeins in the weaving room later, she reached the same conclusion yet again. He'd been sent to help her—it couldn't be a coincidence he appeared out of nowhere to rescue Mentu and her from the mercenaries. In his time at the estate so far, he'd said and done only things which would benefit her cause. And then there was the fact that he wore the golden falcon badge, emblem of Pharaoh's trust in matters of life and death. How could she have doubt, if Pharaoh himself had declared Periseneb worthy?

Just because the events reminded her of a scribe's tale where the handsome stranger appeared to the maiden to rescue her, and sweep her off to be his wife, didn't mean the comparison had to reach the same happy conclusion. This might be too good to be true. Comparing her life to a scribe's tale brought her good mood to a halt. Hadn't Periseneb been most emphatic he was only staying a month?

"But a man can change his mind," she said out loud, earning herself sideways glances from the nearby weavers. She blushed as several of the women tittered and whispered to each other.

Eager to hear the tale of Periseneb's day, she took extra care with her hair after her bath before opening the baskets where she kept her clothes. For once, she was unhappy with the choices. Emptying them all in an unusual fit of annoyance, she stood in the pile of garments for a moment, disappointed. There wasn't much she could do about her dresses, all serviceable cotton meant to withstand the hard work the estate demanded. Moving to the table and opening her long disused cosmetics box on a sudden whim, she decided to apply a thin layer of kohl to accent her eyes. Picking up the elegant carved bone applicator next, she stained her lips. Pleased with the effect, and how well her hair was coiffed, she chose the least utilitarian dress and accented her appearance with her one remaining pair of carnelian and turquoise earrings. Sniffing the perfume of the still-blooming, miraculous lotus before leaving her rooms, she strolled to the evening meal with a lighter heart than usual, daydreaming about what he might bring her from the market.

But, as dinner was served in the main chamber, Periseneb's chair beside hers remained empty.

Worry dampened her appetite. Pushing away the platter of vegetables and stew, she felt the bite of anger, fairly or unfairly, directed at Periseneb for his absence when she'd been so eager to hear how his day went and recite the events of hers. Sipping her beer, she tried not to give in to jealous anxieties. *Did he linger in the taverns? Is he watching dancers while drinking? While he knows I'm waiting?*

She tossed her head, scolding herself. But she did feel foolish, having made extra effort for the benefit of a man who wasn't even present to admire the effect.

"He'll be home soon, my lady," said the wizened weaver to her left, patting her hand. "Not to worry. He won't have abandoned us."

"I don't know what you're talking about." Neithamun realized her tone was sharper than she'd intended. Picking apart her bread, she tried again, consciously lowering her voice and forcing her lips to curve in an awkward attempt at simulating good cheer. "I'm merely curious what's kept him so late in town."

She heard sounds in the hall and rose, relief sweeping over her like a cool breeze. Mentu broke into the room, shouting, "My lady, the donkey came home without Periseneb!"

"What?" The roll fell from her hand and she felt a wave of vertigo pass through her. She braced herself with one hand on the chair's carved frame. Could Haqaptah's thugs have attacked him on the road?

"The side of the cart is broken and the beer jugs are missing," Mentu said, breathing hard. "But even worse, his weapons are gone."

"Show me." She ran through the house on the boy's heels into the yard, where one of Mentu's younger sisters held the bridle of the exhausted, trembling donkey. A weaver stood by with a torch to light the scene. The cart was indeed a mess, with even more damage than Mentu had tallied. Neithamun stared through the gloom in the direction of the road, as if Periseneb was going to appear any moment. Her heart was pounding so fast she pressed a hand to her chest. "Is there—is there blood?"

"No, my lady." Mentu ran his hand over the cart's seat. "Nothing." He stared at her, eyes wide. "We should go search for him."

Although what he suggested was exactly what Neithamun wanted to do, she forced herself to take a few deep breaths to fend off panic and regain her common sense. "At night? With Haqaptah's thugs roaming the roads? Not to mention lions and jackals. If an experienced warrior like Periseneb came to grief in broad daylight, what can we hope to accomplish in the dark? We'll search in the morning."

"What if he's been in an accident? What if he's out there, wounded?" The young herdsman's wide eyes reflected his astonishment.

She shook her head. "We can't risk it. I can't take the chance of losing anyone from the estate. If Haqaptah's men or someone else attacked Periseneb, the assailants may still be out there on the road, waiting. We're not soldiers, we can't fight. We'll search in the morning." It hurt her heart to say it, but she added, "He's tough, he'll likely be fine. Maybe the donkey got away from him and he's walking home. You and your sister give the beast a good rubdown, check for injuries, and put him in the barn for the night." Ignoring the incredulous look from Mentu, as well as the mutinous curses he was muttering under his breath, she ascended the stairs. At the top, she paused to issue one more command. "I forbid anyone going to search tonight, do you understand?" Pushing her way through the murmuring crowd of servants and retainers, she said, "Go finish dinner. We can't afford to waste food. I'm sure all will be revealed in the morning."

Scarcely knowing what she talked about, Neithamun forced herself to chat through the rest of dinner, although worry was a knot of pain in her gut and her hands trembled. When she retired to her bedroom, the tears came and she threw herself on the bed. "Please, Great Ones, grant that he's unharmed. Let him return to me unscathed in the morning," she prayed, in between sobs. Eventually, she exhausted all her tears and fell into a light sleep. Somewhere in the middle of the night she woke with a gasp, remembering she hadn't done the tallies for the day. "Set's teeth, I can't believe I forgot." As she sat up, she realized her head was aching. The idea of walking through the dark house to the library to do her accounting was not appealing in the least. And tonight, there'd be no Periseneb to share the burden, make jokes, and speed the task. *He's gotten into my heart and my head.* Nausea assaulted her as she contemplated carrying the full load of Heron Marsh's problems on her own again. Settled on her mattress, adjusting the smooth wood of her carved headrest, Neithamun decided the tallies could wait. *I'll just have to work harder tomorrow.*

In the morning, she could hardly eat. Her nerves were on edge and her stomach clenching at the idea of food. She sat with Khensa and Mentu in the great dining hall, figuring out who she could send as searchers and where the best place to start would be, when she heard Periseneb's customary cheerful whistle. Rising from her chair as the piercing sound was repeated, she abandoned her retainers and ran to the door of the estate house. Standing on the terraced steps, one hand shielding her eyes against the morning sun, she saw him jogging steadily towards the house.

Relieved beyond words, Neithamun flew down the stairs and met him before he could reach the yard proper. Periseneb had to stop to catch her, so great was her momentum. She hugged him as if she never planned to let go. His strong arms holding her and the reassuring solidity of his muscles made her secure, as if nothing could ever harm her. Joy made tears well up in her eyes.

"You're all right, thank the gods." Greatly daring, beside herself with relief, she kissed his cheek and then stepped away, swiping at her eyes hastily. Hands on her hips, she evaluated his appearance from head to toe. "What happened to you? When the donkey trotted into the yard with the broken cart, I—we were so worried."

Rubbing his cheek, Periseneb seemed ill at ease, not meeting her eyes, rolling his shoulders. "I've a lot to tell you, my lady."

"We thought Haqaptah's men must have attacked you—"

"They did, as I drove home from town."

"But, you fought them off, clearly." *What isn't he telling me?* Periseneb's reluctance to look at her was concerning. She noticed new scars on his knee, below the kilt, but how could fresh wounds have healed to scars since yesterday?

"I had help. We have to talk before the others arrive." He took her elbow and steered her toward the house, through the crowd of servants and retainers welcoming him.

"Others?" She stopped walking. "Something tells me you'd better explain now." Remembering the inquisitive crowd, she raised her voice. "All right, he's home safe and we have a day's work to do as usual, so I want each of you to go about your business now."

Periseneb accepted a few more congratulatory remarks as the workers dispersed. Then he followed Neithamun into the house. "We'll go to the library," she said. "I have a notion this discussion should be in private. Are you hungry?"

"No, thank you, I had breakfast already." His words were oddly formal.

Wondering who had fed him, she preceded him into the library and was already seated in the ebony and gold chair when he closed the door and moved to the table. She felt like the lady of the estate in the chair traditionally belonging to the Lords of Heron Marsh, hers now. Not a throne but close enough to give the illusion of control of the situation, despite the knot in her stomach. She spoke hastily, trying to remain haughty. "We should start at the beginning, I imagine. So, you did spend the day in town?"

Periseneb took his usual seat. "Yes, and the situation there is none too good. Your merchant won't sell anything for you because Haqaptah's men administered a serious thrashing to discourage him."

"Oh no!" Hand to her mouth, Neithamun fell against the chair.

As if providing a military report to an officer, Periseneb gave her all the details of what he'd seen and done in town. He took a small pouch from his belt and pushed it across the table to her as he finished describing his day at the market. "Here are the meager profits, my lady."

She wanted to tell him to keep the deben for his troubles, but the estate needed all the money it could get, and apparently most of the cloth had been lost, not to mention the broken beer jugs she'd have to replace. Nodding, she tucked the pouch into her pocket. "So, you headed home?"

"And met an ambush on the way. Haqaptah's thugs, not wearing any masks this time. They meant to kill me," he said. "And would have succeeded except for the intervention of some new friends."

He was so matter of fact, she felt she had to be as well, despite the fear at the news he'd been ambushed. "And who are these friends?"

Rapidly he told her about a small group of refugees from the other end of Shield Nome. "These people had no stake in my fight, didn't have to step in to help me, but chose to take my side. I believe them to be honorable, decent folk." He eyed her and Neithamun had a sinking feeling she knew what he was going to say next. "I've invited them to Heron Marsh."

Even half-expecting the words, she felt her heart stutter a moment in shock, followed by the heat of anger burning through her. She clenched her fists on the edge of the table. "You did what?"

"We need workers to dig the canal from the pond, we can get in a second planting, and we should have trained men standing watch at night—" He spoke fast, his voice pitched persuasively.

Furious, she stood, venting some of her emotion by shoving the chair away. "I can barely feed the people I have now. I've worked myself to the bone trying to save this estate for those who belong here by birthright. How dare you add to my burdens by inviting total strangers under my roof? More people for me to fail if I can't pay the taxes in three weeks?" She couldn't keep her voice from becoming strident and angry as she revealed her worst fear. Afraid she was going to break down, she bit her lip hard and turned away.

She heard the scrape of the stool as he rose and walked to her with a steady tread. She refused to move, flicking tears from her cheeks. He set his large hands on her shoulders and gently tugged at her.

His breath tickled her ear as he spoke in a low voice. "Try not to think of the situation that way."

She jerked her shoulder free, but stayed close to him. Staring at the shelves of scrolls in front of her, she asked, "What other way can I view this? More hungry mouths to feed."

"These are self-reliant people, skilled hunters, who know the demands of running of a major estate. Amethu, their leader, used to be the assistant headman at a large place to the east. Their misfortune may be a gift from the gods for Heron Marsh."

Desire to be persuaded, the need to understand why he'd done this, consumed her. "In what way?"

"Amethu and his men can give us a boost in these last few weeks, enhance our own efforts. You're so focused on paying the taxes, which is important, but I'm trying to build a little for the future as well. Workers like these are priceless and their loyalty to Heron Marsh will be unshakable if you give them a home." He paused, as if hunting for the right words. "You've been so focused on the taxes and the loans and *surviving*, but an estate like Heron Marsh should have hundreds of workers. There shouldn't be fallow fields. The buildings need maintenance. Even here in the house, things are falling apart. Your elderly maids and their granddaughters keep a few rooms clean while the rest molder. Khensa should be overseeing dozens of workers making the estate's signature beer, not doing it virtually by herself. The weavers should be spinning cloth by the hundreds of cubits, not a few paltry lengths at a time. We could be sending the best by ship to other towns, to sell."

She drew a breath to protest his assessment, but Periseneb continued without pause. "I'm not criticizing. I'm merely saying, we need to try to rebuild, not merely scrape by and cover the taxes each year. You'll never truly save the estate until you can climb off the knife's edge of disaster and begin to build."

Suddenly weary, she allowed him to turn her, burying her face against his chest, while he wrapped her in strong arms. "I don't know what to do. I don't want to give false hope. Yet, I can't refute any of the assessments you've made. At least my own people know how desperate the times are. It's not fair to bring others into the quagmire."

He ran his fingers through her hair, which she found soothing. "Amethu and his people know. It's openly spoken of in town, trust me. Haqaptah tried to hire them to help him in his efforts to intimidate and sabotage you and others, but this group had too much honor to participate in underhanded dealings." Periseneb lifted her chin. "At best, they help rebuild the estate. At worst, you give them a place with a roof over their heads for a few weeks before pushing on with their plans to find an oasis in the desolate Red Lands."

"A thin hope on their part, although we might be joining them," she said. "If I can't pay the debts."

There was a knock at the door. Neithamun startled for a moment, but Periseneb held her close. He dropped a kiss on her forehead before releasing her. "It'll be all right," he said, his voice low. "Whatever you decide will be the right choice. And if I must ask your forgiveness later, I swear to do it."

Stepping to the table, she took a deep breath. "Enter," she called to whoever had knocked.

Mentu stuck his head into the room. "Forgive me, my lady, but a crowd of people is coming toward the house."

She nodded. "Yes, we have guests today. I'll be right there."

The boy backed away, eyes wide. "Guests?"

"Have Khensa break out the beer," Neithamun said. "The good beer. Tell her to bring it to the front entry."

She walked toward the door as Mentu ran to do her bidding. Periseneb moved to follow her. "It wasn't your place to invite them here," she said, keeping her eyes averted. The compulsion to re-establish their respective roles forced her to issue the rebuke, although her tongue nearly tripped over the words.

He bowed his head. "I understand. And Amethu understands you may not extend an official invitation to remain. There won't be any trouble if you don't, I promise."

Not so sure, despite his reassurances, Neithamun took her time walking from the library through the house to the front door. She was gathering her wits, weighing the pros and cons of what Periseneb had done. Could she think of anything beyond the oppressive issue of the taxes and the debts? She could hear his steady, measured tread behind her, reassuringly close. *These people saved his life. I owe them for that, if nothing else.*

She walked through a small cluster of gaping servants and out the door to find the newcomers gathered at the foot of the stairs. The man who must be their leader was at the forefront, eyeing her respectfully. For a moment, she said nothing while she counted fifteen armed men, all hard-eyed warriors. She had a difficult time viewing them as estate workers. Without Periseneb to vouch for them, she'd be afraid to have them standing on her land. Then, she saw six women in patched and worn clothes, faces pinched, defiant, standing behind their men. A few children peeked shyly around the edges of their mothers' skirts, eyes wide and bodies too thin. *They're half starved. At least I can keep the people here from going hungry.* "I welcome you to Heron Marsh," she said, knowing what she must do. "I invite you to remain under my roof as long as it is mine to share."

The leader bowed. "We wish to earn our keep, my lady. Lord Periseneb has indicated there might be certain tasks we—all of us—might turn hands to, to earn lodging and food. I will formally pledge our loyalty to you as long as we dwell here."

"We can speak of that later, but the first order of the day is to celebrate Periseneb's rescue and you joining us here. My staff is bringing beer—we must toast the occasion and offer proper thanks to the gods. Afterward, Periseneb can show you to the workers' quarters. Many of the houses are vacant. I give you my permission to choose from among the empty dwellings. Take today to settle in and we can talk of oaths, chores, and work later."

"Well done," Periseneb whispered, squeezing her elbow as the servers passed them, carrying the beer pitchers and mugs to welcome the newcomers as she'd ordered.

Overwhelmed, Neithamun escaped to her own quarters after all the newcomers had been introduced to her, and the proper thanks had been given to the gods. She ordered food brought from the larders and storerooms, so each new household might cook a proper dinner for themselves when evening fell.

Finally free to escape, telling Menwe she wished to be alone, she retreated to her chambers. As she walked through her bedroom, the scent of the lotus reached her and she paused at the vase on her bureau. Touching the vibrant bloom with her finger, she closed her eyes and breathed in the calming perfume. *My entire life has changed since he came.* "Yet, is he the answer to my prayers? Am I doing the right things? Or am I overwhelmed by his strength? Hard to resist his confidence in his recommendations, but are his suggestions the path to follow?"

Only silence answered her questions. Not even a bird song trilled from the garden beyond.

Yet, here was the lotus, where none had been for a hundred years. The flower had to be a sign from the Great Ones. And Periseneb had brought her the flower, had he not?

Lowering her head to sniff the petals for a moment, she closed her eyes and searched her heart for answers.

Sometime later, Menwe knocked timidly at the outer door, tiptoeing into the bedroom. "My lady?"

Holding the lotus, Neithamun strolled from the garden to meet her. "Is something amiss? Am I needed in the barns? Or the weaving chamber?"

"No, all is well. The newcomers are settling into their quarters and our people are going about their daily tasks. Lord Periseneb requests your presence in the library." Menwe paused. "If it's convenient for you, he said."

As she set the lotus in the vase, Neithamun said, "What does he want?"

"I believe he and the new man Amethu want to talk about duties and assignments for tomorrow."

Glancing in the burnished silver mirror, Neithamun straightened her errant hair. No earrings and makeup today. Today was all business. "I'll join them then."

Leaving Menwe to her own assignments, Neithamun marched through the halls to the library. As she approached, she heard the rumble of deep voices as the two men talked. Curious, she crept to the edge of the door to eavesdrop.

"In my opinion, the first priority must be digging the ditch from the pond you described, to have water for the house and the nearest fields without so much daily labor," Amethu said. "We should redirect as many of the estate's workers as we can to assist with the task. Let the fields and weaving go untended for a day or two."

She drew a shaky breath, annoyed the men were disposing *her* people so casually, when neither of them actually had any standing to make decisions about Heron Marsh. Maybe her misgivings weren't so far-fetched after all.

Periseneb's deep tones in response deflated her anger. "Aye, I don't disagree with you, but it's the Lady's choice, not ours. We can only present the arguments. Her word will be the final one."

Stifling a pleased smile, she stepped across the threshold. "Good afternoon." Further reassured by finding the gilded chair had been left empty for her, she took her accustomed seat. "I trust the arrangements and accommodations have been satisfactory for your people, Amethu?"

The two men had risen, bowing slightly as she brushed past. Now they resumed their seats, Amethu nodding. "You've been most generous, Lady Neithamun. We haven't had dwellings to call our own in over a year. My women are busy cleaning and ordering the men about with great happiness. Nothing can erase the events of our past, but there's something reassuring about having a roof and a hearth." He shot a sideways glance at Periseneb. "Even if it be temporary."

"Let's all pray to the Great Ones for aid, and work diligently ourselves to ensure the situation isn't temporary then," she said. "What recommendations do the pair of you have for me?"

Periseneb drew a tablet closer. "We've made a list, but clearly, the first priority is water."

"So, digging a ditch from the pond to the house? And we stop all other work until the task is done?" She enjoyed their open-mouthed surprise, both men at a loss for words. "Agreed. What next?"

Periseneb made a tick mark on his tablet with the quill. "I want to get in a second planting in the eastern field…"

CHAPTER FIVE

Having trouble sleeping, Periseneb made a habit of visiting the library in the wee hours of the night, when he was sure the entire household, including Neithamun, slept. He worked his way through the records, beginning with the day Ra's sun boat at dawn had witnessed his birth and sunset marked his mother's death. He wasn't sure what he was looking for exactly, but the task felt right, as if he needed to read the story told by the crop tallies, the expenditures, the births, and the deaths. Most of the early entries were written in his father's neat hand, or that of the estate's chief scribe. Occasionally, the Lord of Heron Marsh had made some notation himself, the hand writing bold and sloppy, standing out from the hundreds of precise lines his father and the scribe contributed. Periseneb paused at the day he'd left Heron Marsh, but there was no entry at all, not in anyone's hand. Over two hundred years ago, he'd crept away from the overseer's small home under cover of night, knowing his father would disapprove of his plan to join the army. He'd have scoffed openly at the idea of his son doing brave things and coming home a hero with titles and awards from the hand of Pharaoh himself.

With the boundless confidence of youth, Periseneb had been sure of the path he was choosing and the rewards he'd reap. The last thing that ever would have crossed his mind would have been the possibility of never seeing his father again. A major element of his decision had been the burning desire to prove his parent wrong, to demonstrate an overseer's son could rise to be someone of stature.

Rubbing his finger over the blank space on the papyrus, Periseneb was bothered by the lack of entries on the day in question. Two centuries too late, he understood how much his leaving had struck at his father's heart. Merneseneb, who never missed making the day's record in the estate scrolls, not even on the day his wife died, had apparently abandoned all duties for a time in the wake of Periseneb's clandestine departure. *Did he get drunk? Did he try to find me?*

Sipping at the beer he'd brought with him, Periseneb sat back in the chair for a moment. He and his father had had many arguments in this very room, over his desire to become a soldier rather than follow in his father's footsteps. And over his growing fascination with Sitre, daughter of the house. If Merneseneb had had any idea how far mutual attraction had gone, he and his son might have come to blows. But who would suspect the overseer's boy and the heiress to a great estate were sneaking away at every opportunity to lie together? Daring to plan a future together?

We were mad. I was naive to think I could marry so far above my station. Ruefully, he shook his head at the optimism of his youth. Yet, hadn't his service in the army brought rewards? Honors and accolades which failed to do him any good in the end. Murdered through some treachery, an unknown enemy denying him the triumphant homecoming he'd sought, Periseneb died and was left to rot in some unknown grave.

Resting his feet on the stool, Periseneb drank more beer, remembering the first time Sitre had put herself in his path, here in this library. Thinking of her made him uncomfortable, the hair at the back of his neck rising as he recalled what Benerib had said about the woman uttering curses and becoming a ghost. No good would come of allowing his old memories to linger. He trimmed the wick on the oil lamp before pulling the scrolls closer to resume reading.

On the next day, two centuries ago, the entries were doubled, catching up from the omission on the day before. The meticulously neat, detailed notes continued unabated through the months, which became years. Memories assaulted him as he caught glimpses of life unfolding for the people he'd known through the entries set down centuries ago. Periseneb stopped short, rereading the line he'd just read. The notation next to the substantial sum of deben paid out read, "Dowry for Sitre upon her marriage" and the recipient was the eldest son and heir to Lord Haqaptah. Periseneb flipped the papyrus over, double-checking the date. Sitre, the woman for whom he'd given up all vestiges of his normal life to join the army in search of fame and fortune, had married months before he'd set foot in the nome. He shoved the papyrus away from him so violently it fell to the floor, rolling itself into a cylinder with a soft sound.

Benerib had told him this fact, why was the visual confirmation aggravating him so? "What do I care after all these years?" Rising, running his hands through his hair, he paced the length of the table, trying to master his emotions. Stooping, he retrieved the record to read the entry yet again.

Gritting his teeth and wishing he'd brought more beer to steady his nerves, Periseneb unrolled the papyrus and read through the entries again. A few moments later, he froze, eyes locked on an entry in the estate owner's hand, detailing a lavish contribution to the temple and a generous baby gift to celebrate the birth of his first grandson. Six months after the marriage. So Sitre and Haqaptah had been lovers. Or she and someone had been lovers and the baby passed off as Haqaptah's perhaps. He shook his head, remembering what the old servant had told him, how the lusty noblewoman in question had taken men into her bed until she was eighty.

I was well aware I wasn't her first lover. And how many times did she fail to arrive at the appointed time, invariably with some glib excuse for me later, which I was only too happy to accept? Besotted, I was, dazzled by the attentions of the beautiful, noble daughter of the house. The details of Sitre's life weren't adding up to a pretty picture. He rubbed his knuckles, remembering some of the fights he'd had when other workers hinted she might have lain with them a time or two.

What was she going to tell me when we met? How was she going to explain being a married woman with a child?

If only he'd not been killed, he could have been free of her, able to build his own life. Periseneb stared at the library. Heron Marsh might never have been his, but he would have made some piece of land his own, would have met another woman and had a family. He shut his eyes as the picture of Neithamun came unbidden into his mind's eye. A pang of desire shot through his body, stirring his cock. Truth be told, she was the only one he wanted, and she wasn't even born at the time he died. Nor could he have her here, in this time.

Serving a goddess was its own form of torture, less onerous in some aspects than endlessly roaming the wastes of the Afterlife, but more painful in others.

He continued through the scrolls until he reached the entry he'd been dreading more than any details regarding his former lover.

Died this day, Merneseneb, Overseer.

The family tombs were to the west, built into the cliff wall of a deep wadi formation beginning where the Black Lands ended and the desolate Red Lands stretched to the horizon. It took Periseneb half the morning to walk there. The journey reminded him uncomfortably of his wanderings in the gray desert at the fringes of the Afterlife, although this hike was through the fertile Black Lands and in the sunshine. The closer he came to the city of the dead, the heavier his limbs felt. A headache pounded across his head, as if he was wearing his nemes headcloth too tight. He thought of his father, dying with no son to do him honor, no one to make the offerings in the long years after death. Renewed grief and guilt twisted his gut. *I should have come sooner. I should have been here when you died.*

Deadly rage aimed at whoever had murdered him choked Periseneb's throat. Pausing to slake his thirst from the water skin as he passed into the desolate wastes of the Red Lands, he stared at the bleak surroundings. "I *was* coming home to you, Father." *Matters would have been so different once I stood before you as a seasoned soldier, hardly the hot headed boy who fled.*

When he reached the area he sought, he took the leftmost fork in the path, toward the lower cliff wall, where the tombs of particularly favored family retainers were located. From the records, he knew his father had been accorded a place of honor here by the noble family he'd served so faithfully. Less exalted servants were interred in the sandy wastes beyond, in unmarked, shallow graves. In fact, his mother no doubt lay there. The belief his father must have said the proper words for the mother he himself had never known was a small comfort. She would have gained the Afterlife. Perhaps he'd meet her there, if the gods were kind. If he satisfied Ma'at on this strange quest she'd asked him to undertake.

He walked along the wall of burial spots all crowded together, most of the names illegible, scoured away by the sandy desert winds. Occasionally, he'd catch a glimpse of an inscription, a blessing, praise for the dead, part of a name. As the fortunes of Heron Marsh had sunk over the centuries, the tombs had no longer been maintained as custom required.

Finally, he stood before the tomb his father had been granted. A small alcove had been hollowed out of the cliff wall, for the bereaved to make offerings, with the sealed tomb directly behind. Rolling his shoulders and breathing a silent prayer to Ma'at, Periseneb stepped across the threshold. Immediately, he felt a lessening of the tension gripping him so hard since entering the wadi. The air was cooler here. Kneeling in the shaft of sunlight at the entrance, Periseneb unpacked the small sack he'd brought. He lit the tiny oil lamp pilfered from an unoccupied room at the house and rose, examining the walls. The master of the estate had shown his father great honor indeed, ordering one wall painted with scenes of Merneseneb overseeing the harvest and the annual counting of the cattle. Periseneb walked closer, reading the hieroglyphics extolling his father's honesty and dedication to Heron Marsh. The painted scene had been done rapidly, only a bit more detailed than a sketch, but an undeniable mark of esteem from the man he'd served. Raising the oil lamp, Periseneb studied the artist's rendition of his father's face, which was quite true to life, less stylized than the traditional portraits of nobility.

Taking him by surprise, a great sob forced its way from his chest and tears leaked from his eyes. Hastily, he set the lamp on the floor and covered his face with his hands for a moment, trying to regain his composure. He was assaulted by anger and regret for all the things he'd lost—not only his chance to make things right with his father, but the opportunity to enjoy the fruits of his own labors. No wife, no children. Glad there was no one else present, no audience to witness his weakness, he fought the hot tears. Going to his knees, he took several long breaths to regain mastery of his emotions.

Reaching to touch the painted hand of his father, he said, "Forgive me." There was no response, which comforted Periseneb. His father's spirit must be resting happily in the duat, with no further concern for earthly cares. *Not condemned to roam the wastes, as I was.* Giving mental thanks to the lord of Heron Marsh for burying his father with the proper rites, Periseneb wiped his cheeks on his sleeve and took a few deep, calming breaths. Whispering a prayer, he extracted the basket of hard rolls and dried fruit, and the stoppered pitcher of beer from his pack. Rising, he walked to the altar under the spirit door and arranged his offerings there.

"At least they remember how to make the beer properly, Father," he said, smiling a bit as he broke the mug's wax seal to free the delicious aroma for his father's spirit to enjoy. "I wish you were here, although the state of Heron Marsh would distress you. But I'd welcome your advice on trying to set things right. There's so little time."

A breeze unaccountably wafted through the tomb's entrance. The cool caress of air across his brow was like a blessing.

"But you taught me all the things I need to know, didn't you?" He remembered the countless walks he and his father had taken through the fields, the lectures about all subjects having to do with running a major estate, the endless practice in the evenings at scribing. At the time, he'd balked at learning any of the details, but the patient lessons had stuck with him.

He lingered a few moments longer, feeling as if there was more he ought to say, but clearly the spirit of his father wasn't going to be drawn from the happy Afterlife to the offerings. No chance was going to present itself today to make things right with his parent. "Ma'at didn't send me here for such personal reasons," he said to himself, as he stepped from the tiny tomb's entrance and blew out the lamp. "Perhaps, when I finally reach the duat and enjoy the blessed Afterlife, our kas will find each other and I can ask your forgiveness and tell you of my adventures."

Indecisive, he stood in the narrow wadi, a hot breeze plucking at his kilt. Shading his eyes with one hand, he stared down the canyon to the area where the family had its more elaborate tombs. How could he come so close and not pay respects to the other person who'd been so important in his life? Yet he felt no eagerness in his heart, no desire to gaze upon the painted face of the woman who'd inspired him to abandon home and loved ones two centuries ago. If anything, revulsion stirred in his gut. Too much gossip from Benerib? He rubbed his chin, considering all the elderly woman had said.

No, this unease, this reluctance to approach Sitre's last resting place was deeper, imbued in his ka. Goose bumps rose on his flesh, despite the heat of the day. He felt as if some bitter memory lingered in his mind, tantalizingly out of reach. The more he racked his brain, the further the mental picture he was chasing retreated.

He took a drink from the water skin, more to buy himself time than out of any bodily thirst.

Duty was duty. Anything between him and Sitre was in the dusty past.

He walked in the direction of the tombs. Passing the first few family sepulchers, he felt his nerves tingle. It was easy to identify Sitre's, being one of the more recently occupied, a hundred years or so ago. He stood for a moment at the top of the stairs leading into the cavern where she'd been placed with her immediate family. Forcing himself to take the first step into the gloom, he had the fanciful notion that cold air from the grave surrounded him, as if icy fingers stroked his arms and grabbed his ankles.

He remembered the last estate overseer had been found dead at the base of this same staircase, killed in an attempt at tomb robbing. The family was lucky no one had tried robbing them before. On that prosaic thought, Periseneb continued his descent, pausing to relight the oil lamp at the base of the stairs. The corridor was covered in lavish paintings, executed in great detail, unlike the single, rushed wall in his father's tomb. Glancing at the ceiling, he admired an intricate portrait of the goddess Nuit holding up the stars. The gold paint used to depict the stars glittered in the light from his lamp. This work had all been done when Heron Marsh was a great, thriving estate, wealthy and staffed with artists and craftsmen.

Sealed doors on either side of the corridor were inscribed with praise of the tomb's occupants, their piety and their dedication to the principles of ma'at. He didn't focus too closely. It wasn't pleasant to see the graves of those he'd known personally.

Finally he arrived at the one he sought—Sitre, daughter of the house. Odd she hadn't been interred with her husband's people. He remembered Benerib had said there was a feud with her daughters-in-law.

The usual spirit door was built into the wall of the small antechamber to her tomb. A large portrait of Sitre in her youth was surrounded by dancing maidens, birds, and lotus and papyrus flowers. A feast was depicted in lavish detail, off to the side, painted servants hovering eternally to do her bidding and cater to her whims. Periseneb stared at the portrait. The artist had caught something of the essence of the girl he'd known, a hint of expression on her face, perhaps the quirk of an eyebrow. Admiring gods and goddesses were shown in smaller paintings along the border of the chamber, escorting Sitre to the Afterlife, welcoming her to their company.

"Wishful thinking," he said out loud. Based on what he'd been told by the elderly servant, reciting her grandmother's tales of a shrewish, bitter old woman afraid to die, Sitre probably hadn't found much of a welcome in the Afterlife.

There was a rumble underfoot and the earth shifted somewhat. Periseneb kept his balance with an effort, steadying himself with one hand on the wall until the tremor was over. He heard a sharp crack and watched a fissure tear through the central depiction of the woman, in effect severing her head from her body.

"Set's teeth!" He swore as he retreated, stumbling up the stairs and bursting into the hot sunlight. Maybe Ma'at hadn't sent him here to resolve old matters between himself and Sitre, but something uncanny was going on.

He wasted no more time in the city of the dead, but retraced his steps to the estate and matters of the living.

"I need to ask you something," Neithamun said, as she left the dinner table the next evening. "A favor of sorts."

He was surprised, but pleased to be able to oblige her. Neithamun so rarely asked for anything. Stubbornly self-sufficient at all times was the lady of Heron Marsh. "I'm at your service, of course."

"You may be sorry you agreed so fast." The twinkling in her eyes belied the stern warning. "I've been invited to attend a marriage celebration at one of the neighboring estates and stay a few nights. We'd have to travel tomorrow. I'd rather not go, but I think I must. You've shown me I need to refresh my ties with the other neighbors. Even if it means shirking my duties here."

"Have no worries, Amethu will keep things running smoothly. He's proven his abilities over the past week, in my opinion. Which estate are you to visit?"

"Kingfisher, upriver from Haqaptah's." She made a face. "He can't steal their water and the family has too much honor to divert the Nile improperly. I wish Kingfisher was my direct neighbor. The oldest son has returned from Thebes a married man." Her voice took on a soft, wistful tone. "We used to be good friends, in younger days. I don't want to give offense by not meeting his bride."

Her face was set in lines of such sadness that Periseneb had to resist the temptation to fold her into his arms for comforting, although he felt a flash of jealousy at her obvious affection for the man in question. Had she perhaps hoped to be his bride some day? Did she harbor attraction—or more—for him? To distract himself from the direction his mind was roaming, Periseneb opted for practicality. "What will you take for a bride gift?"

Frowning, she tapped her toe on the tile floor as she considered. "I've no deben for a customary gift and no jewels left to give or sell." Her lips quirked a bit in a reluctant smile. "Well, I do have a single pair of my mother's earrings left, but I can't bring myself to part with them. And the stone is cracked on one, rendering the trinkets unfit for a new bride."

"Take a fat calf," he suggested. "I know it's an unusual gift for a noble family, but the animal has high value."

Her face lighting up, eyes sparkling, Neithamun said, "And the fact I can spare such a one will help dispel the rumors the estate is in dire trouble. Although the gossip is true."

"You can tell them since our cattle—*your* cattle are descended from a gift of the goddess Hathor, you felt it was most appropriate for a newly wedded couple. Hathor is the goddess of joy, after all," he pointed out.

"If I say it with a calm demeanor, the couple may even think I believe it, and not laugh," she agreed. "Well, a calf will have to do."

"I'll have Mentu select one of the promising young bulls—but not the best one." He winked. "The boy can groom and cosset the animal tonight and brush its pelt as if we were trying to change a bull into a fine chariot horse. How will you travel tomorrow? You should be carried in a litter befitting your station, but I haven't seen one on the estate."

"I'll use the donkey cart. I don't mind." Neithamun laid a hand on his arm. "I want you to be my escort."

"Well, of course, I wouldn't let you travel alone." Surprise mixed with hurt pricked at him that she felt she had to ask. "I'll bring four of my men, in case we run into ruffians from Haqaptah's crew."

"Thank you, I appreciate the concern." She waved one hand as if to dismiss his remark. Blush rising in her cheeks, she said, "But I meant, not to be my bodyguard. As my—my companion." Words tumbling over themselves, giving him no chance to speak, she explained. "I've no relatives, no one to bear me company at this gathering. I'm not used to social gatherings with my peers any longer." She laughed. "I've been spending too much time with my estate staff. I haven't seen most of these people for years and I'm hoping for a pleasant welcome, since I was invited, but I don't want to be there by myself. I crave a companion for the meals and the ceremonies, someone I can talk to easily." She fussed with the fringe on her sash, glancing at him furtively. "Someone I trust."

Uneasiness over the nature of her request had him shifting from foot to foot as he used to do as a young boy, when his father would challenge him to accomplish something he'd not yet mastered. Annoyed at himself, he straightened his spine and rolled his shoulders. "I've told you, I'm not of noble birth and I can't present myself as something I'm not." He was positive the Great One Ma'at would take exception to his telling any kind of a lie while he was in the Black Lands as her representative.

She laid a hand on his arm and stroked gently. "I'm not asking you to be anyone but yourself, I promise. You're one of Pharaoh's Own and you've been at Court in Thebes. Surely you've been in gatherings of the nobility?"

"Not as a guest." His resistance to her request rose. Should he remain at Heron Marsh and avoid this gathering? That might not be such a bad idea if she was harboring tenderness toward the groom. Reluctance to watch her flirt with, or be sad over, this unknown man made his heart heavy. Yet he couldn't let her travel alone, or with only his makeshift guard force to keep her company.

Neithamun wasn't backing down. Hands on her hips, she tilted her head and set her jaw. "Soldiering is an honorable profession and I'm sure not all the guests will be noble-born."

He foresaw endless complications, but she was so distressed he relented. "All right, I'll accompany you as your guest, if you insist, although your hosts may not appreciate the idea."

"I'll have the servants check in the cedar chests where we stored my uncle's belongings, see if we have any garments left fit to wear," she said. "Your everyday kilt and tunic won't do for this kind of gathering. He was tall and rugged...a soldier, as you are. Broad shouldered." Blushing again, she lowered her eyes.

Not displeased she found him attractive, he was uncomfortable at the idea of wearing someone else's clothes, particularly a nobleman's. The logic was undeniable, however, if he was to mingle with the local nobility as an equal, so he reluctantly agreed. After all, he might learn more about conditions in the nome and about Haqaptah's schemes at this gathering. Squaring his shoulders, he decided he should be there.

Next morning, attired in a fine pleated linen kilt and tunic smelling faintly of cedar, he waited in the courtyard at the foot of the stairs with the four men he'd chosen. Mentu the cowherd and the sturdy young bull selected as the gift stood nearby. The calf was black and white spotted, with stubby horns. The cowherd had brushed the animal's coat until it gleamed and polished the hooves. While they were waiting for Neithamun, giggling maids ornamented the calf with a garland of flowers, accented in front with ribbons tied in an elaborate knot. As Periseneb was giving Amethu some last minute instructions, Neithamun came from the house, accompanied by Khensa and Menwe. The lady was wearing a dress he'd never seen before…crisp white cotton, embroidered with blue lotus flowers and papyrus leaves at the hem, butterflies at the neckline. Her sash was the same blue as the flowers and her wig had turquoise and malachite beads woven into the braids. Unlike most days, today she wore cosmetics, not too showy, but kohl and malachite powder effectively highlighting her expressive brown eyes, while her lips had been reddened.

His breath caught and he was sure his heart stuttered. He found her beautiful in her work clothes, but today she was stunning. *If I'd seen her thus on the day I arrived, I would have known she was a lady of the estate.* As he handed her into the donkey cart, Periseneb said in her ear, "In the glow of your beauty, no one will have eyes for the bride."

Blushing visibly under the makeup, she gave him a pleased glance. "Menwe and the others spent all last week sewing this dress and embroidering the trim, in case I decided to accept the invitation. I have another such dress in the baskets."

"Aye, we surprised her with the new clothes this morning," the maid confirmed, smiling broadly. "Can't have our lady of Heron Marsh going to visit the nobility in her plain blue work shift!" Menwe reached out to tweak a strand of Neithamun's wig so the beads lay flat. "I wish the estate still had the jewels and ornaments she ought to be wearing, but—"

"But it was more important to buy fish meal and have the barn repaired and a scribe's endless tally of other things," Neithamun interrupted with a smile, no hint of impatience in her voice. "We should go. We'll be on the road most of the day as it is and I don't want to be late for the dinner celebrations."

He set out across the estate, skirting the edge of Haqaptah's land without incident, and then making better time on the dusty road running beside the Nile. A quick stop at noonday for bread and cheese, washed down with beer, and then back on the road, arriving at the boundary of the Kingfisher estate in midafternoon. Vaguely uneasy for no reason he could readily discern, Periseneb sent a man running ahead to announce their arrival. By the time the donkey cart made its way up the long track to the house, a small crowd was gathered on the stairs.

Neithamun took one look at the chattering, laughing nobles waiting for her and grabbed his arm, fingers digging into his muscles. "The family didn't expect me to come. Oh, I should have stayed home. What was I thinking?"

He patted her hand and set it in her lap. "You were thinking you'd do your duty as the lady of Heron Marsh and welcome your friend's new bride to the nome. Things will be fine, you'll see." But even he had doubts as they reached the foot of the stairs and he drew the longsuffering donkey to a halt. The expressions on the faces of their hosts varied from frowns to puzzlement. A few of the women were smirking behind their ostrich feather fans, probably at Neithamun's decidedly non-noble mode of travel.

An older man in rich robes and an elaborate wig came forward, his wife beside him. "Lady Neithamun, my house is honored by your unexpected presence at our celebration."

"But—but I was invited," she said, hesitating as she prepared to descend from the cart. Her hand tightened painfully on Periseneb's. "A sealed invitation with the Kingfisher cartouche was brought to the estate last week."

"Of course, now you're here, you're more than welcome," said the lady of the house, brow furrowed, giving her husband a scorching glance. "You must be tired and thirsty, my dear. Pray, come inside and refresh yourself."

"I want no trouble with Haqaptah," the lord of the estate said, loud enough for everyone to hear.

A younger man burst from the door, followed by three women. Periseneb had no doubt this was the son of the house. He clattered down the stairs, brushing past his parents. Shouting, "You did come! I'm so glad." He lifted Neithamun off the ground and enfolded her in a crushing hug.

Periseneb noticed disapproving glances from the bystanders, but a moment later, the young noble had released his flustered childhood friend. He darted up the stairs to take one of the young ladies by the hand, leading her to where Neithamun stood straightening her dress. "Darling, may I present my childhood friend, Lady Neithamun of Heron Marsh? Neity, this is my wife, Lady Tashed, youngest daughter of the High Judge of Thebes. I'm hoping you'll be friends."

"Life, prosperity, health to you." Neithamun inclined her head in greeting. "And blessings on your marriage."

"What a unique dress." His wife's tone indicated unique was perhaps not a good thing. The two women who'd accompanied her onto the broad porch tittered behind their showy ostrich fans.

Although no expert on feminine apparel, Periseneb realized the bride and her companions were dressed in finely pleated, sheer linen gowns, with subtle gold trim, and gemstone collars at the neckline. The new dress of which Neithamun had been so proud was clearly nothing like what the Thebans had on, or even the older women of Kingfisher, although their robes were less sheer.

Apparently sensing the tension in the air, the young noble stared wide-eyed at his parents and then at the other guests clustered on the wide porch. "Is there a problem? Of course I sent an invitation to Heron Marsh when the scribe mentioned none had been directed there. Our families are the oldest of friends. I particularly desired my wife to meet my childhood companion. I want them to be friends."

Periseneb could see Neithamun was consumed by anxiety now, blushing red, running one hand through the beads of her wig. Hoping to take some of the focus from her, he stepped forward, making a slight bow. "I'm Periseneb, late of Pharaoh's Own Guard." How late he wasn't prepared to explain. "I'm a guest at

Heron Marsh, so I felt it only proper to invite myself along, to escort the lady on her journey."

The lord of the estate reciprocated the bow. Voice perfunctory, he intoned, "The guest of my guest is welcome, of course." Dismissing Periseneb and Neithamun with another shake of his head, he took his wife's elbow, shepherding her and the majority of the onlookers inside. "The refreshments and the gaming boards await, my friends. The excitement is over."

Although she followed her father-in-law to the top of the stairs, the new bride and her ladies remained outside.

His son also lingered. "I'm Userkaf." While he and Periseneb shook hands, the heir to the Kingfisher estate glanced with open jealousy at Periseneb's golden falcon badge. "I saw service in the war against the Hyksos, but wasn't privileged to be at Pharaoh's side. Met him at court of course, after he took the throne from the Usurper." He laughed, but his handsome face was sober. "Never had the chance to bring myself enough glory on the battlefield to be invited into the Guard and wear one of those golden falcons. No gold of valor, as long as we're truth-telling. But Pharaoh was well pleased with the sign of loyalty from our family. Later—at dinner perhaps—you must share some stories of your battles with us."

"I wouldn't dream of boring the ladies with such grim tales," Periseneb said with a grin he didn't feel. His Pharaoh had met the Hyksos many a time, but not in any battles this young man had ever heard of.

"We should have a mock skirmish. Or maybe an archery contest!" The other was brimming with energy and ideas. Userkaf's constant motion and stream of excited conversation was jarring to Periseneb. More suggestions came thick and fast. "I doubt I could organize a chariot race on such short notice, but we could have a fishing competition. There are some other guests coming. I'll see what I can plan for tomorrow. Possibly we can hunt. The gazelle herd is plentiful this year."

Neithamun had a wistful, faraway look in her eyes. "You always enjoyed your sports." She glanced at Periseneb. "I used to tag along after him when my family would come for a visit. I carried the arrows, lugged the basket of fish—it was his price for enduring my company."

"Aye, you were such a pest." The cheerful, teasing expression on Userkaf's face belied his words. Reaching out, he patted Neithamun on the cheek, allowing the caress to go on a moment too long for Periseneb's taste. Trailing his hand over her skin suggestively, the other man took her hand. "But you're too much a grown lady now to be given such tasks."

There was the delicate sound of throat clearing from the top of the stairs, where the senior lady of the estate was waiting, having stepped outside to see what was keeping her problematic guest.

Userkaf released his hold on Neithamun, retreating a pace or two.

Periseneb escorted her up the first few stairs, hand at her elbow, sensing resistance in her entire body the further they progressed. He guessed, given half a chance, she'd climb into the cart and drive home, now that she understood her presence wasn't desired by the lord and lady of the estate, no matter what blithe assurances Userkaf uttered. He squeezed her fingers in comradely support before releasing them and giving her a gentle push. "Please, accompany your hostess. I'll see to the bride gift for you."

Taking this remark for his cue, Mentu brought the calf to the fore. The boy stood straight and proud, holding the halter. After a moment, he made a slight adjustment to the floral necklace, now wilting after a day in the sun. As he and Neithamun turned, Periseneb noticed the ribbons were sadly twisted and dusty.

"A cow? For a bride gift?" The new wife's kohl-rimmed eyes opened wide and she exchanged glances with her attendants. The women broke into laughter. The Theban bride pointed at her husband with her plumed fan. "You brought me to the rural hinterlands of Egypt in truth, didn't you?"

But now Neithamun drew herself to her full height and gave them a scornful glance, which warmed Periseneb's heart. This spirited woman was the one he thoroughly enjoyed. "The cattle on my estate are descended directly from the goddess Hathor's herd," she said in a voice as frosty as any other haughty noble's. "No others in this nome are their equal."

"A priceless gift." Userkaf stroked the calf's shiny pelt, as Mentu held the animal in place. "Come see, Tashed," he said to his wife, holding out one hand and beckoning. "Not a cow, but a fine bull. This animal will enhance our herd's bloodlines. Much better than another jeweled collar or an inlaid chair."

Reluctantly, fan clutched to her chest, the wife left her friends and mother-in-law, descending the staircase again as if he was asking her to approach a lion.

Tentatively, she stroked the calf's neck. Fingering the flower garland, she hopped away as the calf swung its head to sniff at her. Rubbing her fingers on her dress, she said, "I didn't realize the full significance of the gift." Speaking to the group waiting on the porch, she said, "You must forgive me, Lady Neithamun. I'm not used to country ways yet."

She was rewarded with a quick kiss from her husband. Neithamun bowed her head, acknowledging the apology.

Userkaf's mother said, "Leave the men to discuss bloodlines and the finer points of cattle. I assure you, ladies, I can provide more suitable topics and activities for us inside, out of the sun." Patting Neithamun's arm, she said, "You must be quite parched after traveling all this way today."

Yielding to their hostess's desire to move into the house, Tashed ascended the steps a second time and the assembled women disappeared inside. Periseneb, his men, and the young lord headed for the enclosure beyond the barn, to let the calf loose and pasture the donkey.

"I appreciate the rare gift from Heron Marsh," Userkaf said, as he and Periseneb strolled a few steps behind Mentu and the others. "My wife meant no offense."

Periseneb kept his opinion to himself. Tashed reminded him of many ladies he'd seen at his pharaoh's court, delivering the most poisonous insults with honeyed voices and sideways glances. "I encouraged Lady Neithamun to accept the invitation. I hope I didn't advise her improperly."

"Things are a bit strained here, I find upon my return home," the noble agreed, watching Mentu remove the flowers and set the calf free to snatch at loose fodder in the enclosed pasture before it trotted over to join the herd at the watering trough. The donkey kicked its heels with an energy the contrary animal hadn't demonstrated all day, and sought shade at the far side of the fenced in space. Forehead wrinkled in a frown, Userkaf regarded Periseneb. "I couldn't believe my family neglected to invite her. Of course, my father doesn't want any unpleasantness with Haqaptah, but the man has no hold over us, unlike he does on poor Neity."

"Will Lord Haqaptah be joining the party?" Periseneb asked, as they strolled toward the house.

"This evening, yes." Userkaf eyed Periseneb for a moment. "Forgive me, but may I ask what your connection to Heron Marsh is? Are you a distant relative of the family? Or perhaps her suitor?"

The questions annoyed Periseneb, setting his protective instincts to high alert. Yet this brash young noble would be here long after he himself had to leave, so best not to be too brusque. He could only hope Userkaf somehow had Neithamun's best interests at heart. "No to both. I'm merely passing through the area on my way elsewhere. I was honored to assist the lady with a difficulty a few days ago, and since I'm not in any rush to reach my destination, I've remained to help for the month."

"Too bad." Userkaf seemed genuinely sorry, eyes hooded and mouth turned down.

Another doubter. Periseneb challenged him. "You're so sure she's not going to be able to pay the taxes? And repay Haqaptah?"

The noble shook his head. "I admire Neity's pride, but a successful outcome is doubtful. From what I understand, Haqaptah has her in a box with no way out, realistically. And the new nomarch is likely to side with him on the issue of the water, no matter the truth of the case, because the hyena spawn already built the dams and his estate is strong. So, even if she's blessed by the Great Ones and manages to pay what she owes this year, he'll triumph in the next year or two. Neity has no reserves and receives no water from the annual inundation... " Userkaf spread his hands as if his case was made.

Periseneb wanted to argue, but since Userkaf had arrived at the same grim conclusion he himself reached whenever he considered the matter, he bit his lip and said nothing.

"I like her," Userkaf said as he started climbing the stairs. "When we were children, I know our fathers talked of a match between us. Of course, nothing came of it. I went off to the wars, her parents died. And when I was in Thebes, I met my Tashed." Eyes sparkling, he apparently recalled some fond personal memory. "But I'll not leave Neity to Haqaptah's merciless schemes, nor the nomarch's uncertain judgment, no matter what my father prefers."

Periseneb was impressed by the man's vehemence, even as his anger stirred at the idea of someone other than himself taking care of her. "You have a plan?"

Nodding, Userkaf grinned. "Actually, this all works out well for me."

Nonplussed by this remark, Periseneb merely stared.

"After the estate is forfeit, to Pharaoh or to Haqaptah, I'm going to offer Neity a place here, with us, as my second wife. I might even talk to her about it tonight, if I can find a private moment. That's part of why I invited her against my father's wishes, to get things settled between us over the next day or two."

Periseneb forced himself to breathe deeply and count to ten before he answered, afraid of what jealousy might lead him to say. This scheme brought forth a torrent of emotions, twisting his gut into a knot. Neithamun would never agree, would she? Her life would be a misery. But really, what were her alternatives? *I won't be here to take care of her.* The knowledge burned. Between the mother-in-law and the first wife, not to mention being used to running an entire estate herself, Neithamun would be unhappy, frustrated, and little better than a servant. Unless she loved this childhood hero and was willing to be second choice. The last thought seared through his mind against his will. "Aren't you concerned your new wife will object?"

Userkaf made a dismissive gesture. "Such arrangements are common in Thebes, more so than here in the provinces. She'll find no fault." He leaned closer. "My Tashed is with child already. It'll be a blessing to her to have Neity to keep her company and take care of the baby. A blessing to me to have another to share my bed when Tashed is too worn with cares and duties."

Uncurling his fingers from the hilt of his belt knife, Periseneb forced himself to say through gritted teeth, "Blessings upon your wife and may the child have an excellent life." He was convinced the future Userkaf was offering—as a second wife, serving as another woman's companion and nursemaid for her child— would be distasteful to Neithamun. Childhood friends or not, how could such a future appeal to one used to being mistress of an entire estate? She deserved to be cherished, loved for herself, the way he—. Periseneb choked off the thought before he could admit too much truth to himself. His emotions didn't matter; he wasn't going to be here for Neithamun. *I have to save Heron Marsh for her, so she can live her own life. And have the freedom to choose whether to take a man into her bed.*

He followed his host into the house and there was no more discussion of the subject, although the conversation weighed on his heart.

CHAPTER SIX

More guests arrived as the afternoon waned. Periseneb and Neithamun accompanied the others to greet each new arrival. He knew she was dreading the moment when Haqaptah would be the latest guest, but her quarrelsome neighbor made no appearance. Periseneb, of course, was among strangers, although he recognized the majority of the estate names, but he was glad to see Neithamun renewing old acquaintances among those least afraid of Haqaptah. She held her head high, pretending not to notice the many in attendance who gave her a wide berth.

As if she had the plague.

In between arrivals, their host entertained the crowd with musicians and rich delicacies served by platoons of servants. Fan bearers stationed at intervals in the spacious hall kept the air moving.

"Kingfisher clearly remains prosperous," Neithamun said to him, as she moved her pawn two spaces on the senet board. "Your move."

After throwing the counting sticks, he studied the array of pawns. Shifting one of his pieces to a shared space sent hers all the way to the beginning. Amused by her muffled groan of consternation, he handed her the black-and-white sticks. Stretching, he glanced at the spacious, beautfully decorated chamber where their hosts had set up the gaming tables. "I can see this estate receives their full allotment of the Nile's bounty each Inundation."

She threw the sticks harder than necessary. "Don't remind me." Biting her lip, she studied her options on the game board. "Even if I'd known Haqaptah was building dams to divert my estate's water, I had no way to stop him. I hope this new nomarch will be forceful about preserving the laws – Pharaoh's and those of the Great Ones."

A herald announced the arrival of new guests. Neithamun took a last bite of honeyed fig, sipped at her beer, and rose to follow the crowd. "Userkaf's parents invited half the nome, I think."

"It's good for you to be seen among the other nobles." Periseneb took her elbow as she moved through the great hall.

"Not in this dress." She glanced at her colorful gown. "Tashed and her companions made it clear how rustic and dowdy I've become. We mustn't tell Menwe—the weavers were so proud to give it to me. And the one I brought for tomorrow's festivities is similar."

A moment later, he took advantage of a convenient nook in the broad hall, pulling her out of the flow of chattering guests.

Brows raised, she gave him a questioning stare.

"I'm no noble, with easy compliments," he said. Frustration at his lack of social graces threatened to freeze his voice, so he swallowed deeply and forged ahead. Gesturing at the crowd thronging the hall, he said, "The other women all look the same. You stand out like the rarest flower in the garden. Or a songbird perhaps, come to rest for a moment in the midst of a flock of common sparrows. I think your peers are jealous. And, if not, they should be." He was embarrassed and a bit surprised at his own vehemence.

A flush rising in her cheeks, she said, "I'd no idea you hid the soul of a poet under a soldier's gruff exterior." Rising on her tiptoes, she kissed his cheek and stepped into the corridor before he could react.

Unsure if he'd conveyed what lay in his heart, he rubbed the spot where her soft lips had brushed his skin. *What am I doing? It's not my place to utter honeyed words to her, no matter how true my sentiments may be.* He leaned his head on the cool granite of the pillar at his side for a moment, seeking to calm his turbulent heart. *No matter how deeply I feel them.* Realizing Neithamun hadn't waited for him, he hastened after her. When he arrived on the porch and took his customary position at her shoulder, he discovered, to his surprise, he did know the latest guest.

It was Hernebti, the high priestess of Isis from the town's temple. She'd arrived in a gilded litter, adorned with black ostrich plumes and carvings of the goddess's signature knot, carried by four burly men, surrounded by guards and attendants and with a cart full of baskets and woven boxes close behind. The newlyweds were fawning over her, Userkaf assisting her from the litter and Tashed helping to brush wrinkles from her finely pleated dress. From the warmth of the greetings between the new bride and Hernebti, Periseneb decided the women must have previous acquaintance in Thebes. He wondered why Isis had sent such a senior priestess to this remote province. But, then again, hadn't the Great One Ma'at sent him to this same locale?

"She's to perform the major blessing tomorrow," someone standing close by remarked. "Userkaf's father made a sizable gift to the temple to secure the favor. He hopes for a grandson."

"He hopes Isis can keep him from being swallowed by the jackals besetting Heron Marsh," another guest said. "Nothing else will, if Haqaptah decides to make schemes in this direction."

"I'm glad I live on the other side of the city, upriver," said the first man, with heartfelt fervency. "I've no dealings with Haqaptah, nothing he covets."

He covets the entire nome. Periseneb shook his head at the naiveté of those surrounding him. Heads in the sand, trying to placate Haqaptah or ignore him, until the jackals came to their door. The new nomarch better be prepared to wage war for this corner of his province. He hoped Haqaptah's plans weren't the problem Ma'at wanted him to solve. With only half of his allotted time remaining, he couldn't identify any path to accomplishing such a deed, short of assassinating the man. But would the goddess of truth, righter of wrongs, want him to kill in cold blood? How could murder win him a spot in the Afterlife?

"I used to want to be a priestess," Neithamun said to Periseneb, interrupting his spiraling self-doubts.

"Truly? For which Great One?"

She waved a hand. "I never felt called to any particular goddess. I was a little girl, you know, trying on different roles that offered more excitement to a child than whatever my mother did daily. I even wanted to be a dancer for a time, after we attended a festival in town and I watched a troop dancing in a parade for the temple. Eventually, I came to realize I'd no sense for music and often fell over my own feet." She laughed. "My mother was horrified when all I could talk of was dancing, but my father told her I'd outgrow the desire for such inappropriate activity. He was right."

She so rarely spoke of her childhood or her mother, he was happy she had good memories. "I don't remember my own mother at all. She died when I was born," he said.

"I'm so sorry." Neithamun's expressive eyes softened.

"I had a close relationship with my father." He stretched the truth a bit, hoping to bring the good cheer back to her face.

Arm in arm with Tashed, the high priestess was ascending the stairs and greeting people in the crowd. Periseneb and Neithamun shifted to make room for the pair of women to pass by, but Hernebti stopped in midstep. Expertly made-up face wreathed in smiles, she said, "Ah, my warrior friend. How nice to see you again. A good omen, to have you here."

As he bowed his head to acknowledge the greeting, he felt Neithamun stiffening beside him. "I'm honored you remember me, my lady."

"One such as you is not soon forgotten." Head tilted, she studied him for a moment. He prayed Hernebti wouldn't make any reference to anything otherworldly she might see or sense about him today. While he was trying to marshal his response, the priestess shifted her focus to Neithamun, standing silent beside him. "You must be the lady of Heron Marsh. I've heard so much about you since I arrived in Khemjefkhu and longed to meet you, but you never come to town, do you?"

Voice taut with wariness, as if she preferred not to speak at all, his companion said, "Yes, I'm Neithamun and no, I don't get away from the estate much these days."

Hernebti's pleasant expression didn't change. "Pity. Well, we must take this chance to become better acquainted over the next day or so." The priestess stared at Neithamun's gown. "The work your estate's weavers do is quite extraordinary, by the way. I wanted to purchase some lengths of the embroidered cotton last week, when your representative was in town, but I missed my chance." She shot a mischievous glance at Periseneb, as if inviting him to share in a little joke. "I quite admire your dress, so colorful." Her tone was warm, not mocking in the least. "We'd nothing like it in Thebes."

Periseneb heard Tashed clear her throat as if to say something, but Neithamun talked right over her. "I'd be happy to send you enough cloth for a dress or two from the next batch we make."

"Oh, lovely, I'd be so appreciative." Hernebti drew Neithamun into the small circle of women. "Please, come with us, if your companion can part with you for a while." One elegant eyebrow raised, she glanced at Periseneb.

"By all means. We can finish our game of senet later," he said.

Nodding to acknowledge his answer, Hernebti walked toward the house, arm in arm with Neithamun, as if they were the best of friends. Glaring at the back of Neithamun's head, Tashed trailed a step behind. Hernebti said, "I've some questions about this area I'm sure you can answer. Local history, local deities, topics of a similar nature. You wanted to know more about the weather, didn't you?" she asked her hostess over her shoulder, as if just remembering her presence. "Since this province is now your home?"

"Yes, of course. I-I have many questions." Tashed's voice faltered.

Periseneb believed her chief curiosity was why the priestess was making such a fuss over Neithamun. He was curious himself, but grateful, since his lady appeared highly pleased over her inclusion in the group, as she'd not been before. *I must remember to thank Hernebti later.*

Haqaptah arrived right after the company had been called to dinner. The food was left to wait as the crowd surged outside to greet this final guest. Periseneb reached the porch in time to see the noble descending from his chariot, handing the reins to the driver and then dusting himself off. Two more chariots full of his mercenaries waited behind.

I hope there's not going to be trouble. Eyeing the burly, heavily armed guards, Periseneb wished he'd brought more than four men, but he'd felt the rest were more badly needed at Heron Marsh. Surely Haqaptah wouldn't create an incident at this high ranking noble's home, would he? Certainly the host and this new guest were exchanging cordial greetings, if a bit overly deferential on the part of the Kingfisher lord.

Neithamun stood beside him, catching her breath as she saw Haqaptah. She reached for his hand and instinctively he curled his fingers around hers. "I was hoping he wouldn't come after all."

"I won't let him cause you a moment of discomfort," Periseneb said, free hand on the hilt of his belt knife. "My word on it."

"Thank you," she murmured. "He probably wanted to make a grand entrance. As if he were in truth the ruler of the nome, instead of subject to Pharaoh's man, like all the rest of us."

Haqaptah was ascending the steps and his grin grew even broader when his gaze fell on Neithamun and Periseneb waiting in the crowd. "Ah, my neighbors, well met. I hope there are no hard feelings over the unfortunate incident with the wandering cattle?"

Not to mention your thugs trying to kill me a few days ago. Periseneb was sure he recognized at least one of the mercenaries as having been among his attackers, albeit a man who'd not been in the forefront. *Afraid of my sword, no doubt.*

"Of course not. I'm sure you've instructed your men on how to treat a lady. And reminded them about the laws concerning stray livestock." Neithamun's voice was polite but pointed.

"Talking livestock already?" Userkaf joined them before Haqaptah could respond to Neithamun's jibe. "Neity gave us a fine young bull as a bride gift," the young nobleman said. "With him to stand at stud in a year, our herd will begin to rival yours, Haqaptah."

"Ah, but none can ever compare to the cattle of Heron Marsh," Haqaptah answered genially. "Or so I'm repeatedly told. We should discuss the finer points of herd management while I'm here. I'm sure Lady Neithamun could instruct us both."

Making her own deliberately staged entrance, a fan bearer at her side as if she were royalty, Lady Tashed stepped from the house, capturing the crowd's attention.

"Ah, here's my wife. You must meet her." Userkaf swept Haqaptah away, as if concerned he and Neithamun shouldn't spend too much time in each other's presence.

Neithamun heaved a sigh, no doubt of relief, and released Periseneb's hand. "He's being unusually pleasant. Perhaps the next few days will go smoothly."

"Too pleasant by half if you ask me. He's up to something." Periseneb eyed the mercenaries in the forecourt, but the men were dispersing, efficiently taking the chariots in the direction of the stables. Kingfisher estate was amply staffed, the way Heron Marsh should be, but would their hosts intervene if Haqaptah attempted something against Neithamun? Or himself? *Probably not.* Yet again, he questioned his own wisdom in encouraging her to travel here from the relative safety of her own lands.

"It doesn't matter what he's scheming," Neithamun said, apparently untroubled by the worries Periseneb was mulling. "Once I've got the deben from the priests of Amun next week for my three bulls, I'll have enough to pay a large chunk of the debts and the taxes. We should be well set then, with the harvest proceeds to erase the total."

And fall right back into difficulties next year, when the life-giving Nile waters don't reach your fields. He didn't want to dampen her more cheerful mood. "I'm going to have a word with my men, make sure everyone stays alert and don't get drawn into altercations with Haqaptah's thugs. Will you excuse me?"

She waved a hand. "By all means. Your priestess friend has been charming to me. We're going to sit together at the banquet and she said to invite you to the table as well."

Deciding it was best not to say anything, given the surprising archness in her tone, he bowed his head and started down the stairs.

Apparently not finished with the topic, she raised her voice. "Didn't you tell me you had no acquaintances in this area?" Neithamun remained where he'd left her.

Is she jealous? Bothered by the idea, he paused on the bottom step, turning slowly on his heel to stare at her. "I told you, we met at the market by chance. I know nothing more of her."

Hands on her hips, Neithamun wasn't finished. "Never spent time with her in Thebes?"

Breaking into laughter by the absurd idea of having met Hernebti in the Thebes of two hundred years ago, he smothered his amusement when he realized how serious Neithamun's face was. Clearly, somehow he'd fallen into the wrong on this issue. Unwilling to let her persist in her misapprehension, Periseneb ascended the stairs three at a time, compelled to set her mind at rest as best he could. Wishing he could explain the priestess's true fascination with him, he settled for saying, "I swear I'm here for you and only you, in all of Shield Nome." Not wanting to see her reaction to this, he left in a hurry. Now he'd probably said too much.

The blessing ceremony was held in the early morning, on the banks of the Nile. Periseneb made sure Neithamun had her shawl, as the breeze from the river was chilly, and they walked together with the crowd of guests from the house. Hernebti and her five attendants were leading the procession, two of her servants carrying a small image of the goddess Isis on a boat woven from reeds. Marching in unison, the temple contingent chanted a lilting song of praise to their deity. The lord and lady of the estate came directly behind, followed by Userkaf and his bride, carrying garlands of flowers. Servants brought fine wine and delicacies for the sacrifice to Isis.

Periseneb's stomach rumbled as the crowd reached the appointed spot and the nobles spread out to watch and listen as Hernebti sang a paean to her goddess. Chuckling, Neithamun poked him in the ribs. "Surely you can wait for breakfast?" she whispered.

He nodded, rubbing his abdomen. The longer he was in the land of the living, the more his appetites grew. Catching a delicious whiff of Neithamun's perfume, he was hungering for more than mere sustenance.

Hernebti's voice was lovely, strong and clear. But as the ceremony progressed, the tattoo on his shoulder first itched, then burned. Perhaps the goddess Isis wasn't pleased to have him standing among her worshippers. Or maybe Ma'at was taking umbrage. He rubbed his shoulder, hoping the pain would subside. He wasn't entitled to be here, partaking of a ceremony meant for the living. Sweat beaded on his brow and his head was spinning.

"Are you all right?" Neithamun was gazing at him, eyes wide with concern. "Old wound bothering you in the morning chill?"

"I can't stay," he said. "I'm sorry." He stepped away, glad she'd insisted on remaining at the fringe of the crowd. People were giving him outraged glances for disturbing the ceremony. "I-I'm sworn to Horus." That much was true, as a warrior he'd given his allegiance to the Falcon God, even if conflicted loyalty to the Falcon God wasn't actually the source of his discomfort. "I'll see you at the house." Cursing at himself for not being able to stay and protect Neithamun, should Haqaptah pick this moment to drop his portrayal of congenial neighbor, he stumbled and barely kept from falling. Even drunk after a night of revelry with his fellow soldiers, he'd never felt so out of control of his limbs. Isis didn't want him to receive her blessing, not even as a mere bystander. *I don't belong here, in the upper world. Even if Ma'at got permission from Osiris for this mission, I'm still a ka out of place.*

Working on the problems of Heron Marsh, spending time with Neithamun—all right, be honest, spending time dreaming of what it might be like to be this man he was pretending to be, free to tell her what she'd come to mean to him—it was perilously easy to forget this life really wasn't his. Were the gods tempting him to test his resolve to win the Afterlife?

Neithamun could never be his to cherish and protect, any more than he could possess Heron Marsh itself. Lurching along the path leading to the house, he tried to control his breathing. Well out of sight of the Nile and no longer able to hear the sacred chants, he perched on a boulder to rest for a moment. Holding his aching head in his hands, he regretted having attended any part of the ceremony and thus angering the Great Ones. *I shouldn't be here at all. What does escorting Neithamun to a celebration have to do with solving any of the problems Ma'at sent me here for?* "Nothing," he said aloud, tasting acid in his throat. Straightening his spine, he was relieved the headache was receding. Rubbing his temples brought a bit of relief, although his thinking went in dismal circles. He should have stayed at Heron Marsh, kept working on the irrigation ditch, preparing for the harvest, anything but this self-indulgent waste of time. Neithamun could never be his to claim. She'd be horrified if she knew who and what he was.

Rising from his temporary seat, he took a cautious step and was relieved the dizziness had subsided. There was no going toward the Nile, so he marched in the direction of the house.

"Periseneb, wait!"

He stopped at the sound of her voice as if he'd been hit by a Hyksos spear. Spinning, he saw Neithamun running along the path, skirts kilted to her knees. His reflexes slammed into battle mode, ready to protect her from whatever danger pursued her. Drawing his belt knife and staring at the empty path behind her, he reached to draw her behind him. "What is it? What's amiss? Has Haqaptah made some assault?"

Staring at his knife, then glancing at his face, she paused a few steps away before he could grab her arm. "No, of course not. I was worried about you. I've never seen a man look so ill. I couldn't stay there and keep my mind on the ceremony when you might be lying here, in need of attention. What's the matter with you today?"

"Old wounds, you guessed it." He replaced the knife in its sheath. "I'll be fine with some beer and maybe a poultice on my shoulder."

"Sit down again and let me see." She reached for his sleeve, but he stepped away.

Steeling his heart against the emotions her presence always brought him, he made his tone curt. "No need, I can take care of myself. You should rejoin your hosts and participate in the rituals."

Glancing over her shoulder for a moment, she shook her head. "I've made the proper appearance. No one is likely to miss me. I'll be happy to stroll with you. We've hardly had any chance to talk since we got here yesterday."

Periseneb stayed silent, lost in his own thoughts, as he walked. He gathered Neithamun was puzzled by his attitude, as she kept giving him sideways looks, but he forced himself to remain aloof, providing one or two word answers to her remarks. When they reached the house, he made a halfhearted excuse about conferring with his men and abandoned her on the steps.

Hernebti and her party left Kingfisher immediately after the lavish, late morning breakfast. Periseneb had no chance to speak with her again, and if truth be told, was actually relieved. She somehow knew entirely too much about him.

True to his word, Userkaf had organized a variety of activities for the rest of the day, beginning with a choice of hunting or fishing. The late afternoon was to feature a mock sword battle and a chariot race, with his father offering a prize to the winner. A troop of dancers and musicians was coming for the evening festivities and then the next day the guests would depart.

At their noisy, convivial table, Neithamun leaned close after the announcement of these events, and said, "I'll back you to win the chariot race any day."

"You'd lose, I'm out of practice." Observing her surprise at his gruff reply, he tried to soften the tone with a small joke. "Getting that thrice damned donkey to go where I desire is no preparation for handling a team of horses."

"The mock battle then?"

"I've fought in too much real combat to relish trading blows with barely trained nobles." He glanced to where Userkaf stood, conferring with his father and Haqaptah.

"Why don't you like him?"

Neithamun's question caught him unawares. Hastily, he schooled his features, trying to erase the distaste he felt for their younger host. "I don't know him well enough to like or dislike him."

"He's competitive with you, however." She toyed with the remnants of her breakfast. "As if all these mock combat drills and races are between you and him. The rest of the guests are his audience."

"If it pleases you, I'll do my best to overshadow his prowess this morning. Shall I hunt or fish, my lady?" Periseneb felt he'd better keep his distance from the sacred Nile, but he was hardly in the mood to hunt gazelles either. So, why not let her choose which she'd rather watch?

"Fishing. I know more about the latter activity, having accompanied Userkaf many a time when we were children."

Her choice and the reason for it didn't please him overmuch, but he had the scribe add his name to the river expedition. Unsurprisingly, Userkaf followed suit. Once he'd walked to the boat landing, he found that the guests were given small reed boats. The fishing was to be done in the marshes, not out in the Nile's main current.

"We're not after Nile perch today," said their host with a laugh. "We're seeking the more delicate species for our table."

At first a few of the married ladies chose to ride along in the boats with their husbands, dutifully admiring their fishing skills, but soon, all of the women had gone ashore and retired to the small tented pavilion where Tashed presided. There the convivial group sat in comfort, sipping beer and nibbling on sweetmeats. As he fished, Periseneb heard periodic laughter from the direction of the pavilion and he hoped Neithamun was having a good time. It was soothing his nerves to be on the water, as long as no one was chanting religious songs, and fishing had been one of his favorite pastimes in life. He sipped the beer he'd been given and decided it was probably time to put in to shore and see how Neithamun was faring. *Show her my impressive catch.* Balancing the long pole to push his reed boat out of the marsh and back to shore, he was pleased with himself.

Once at the dock, he unloaded the line of tilapia and mullet he'd speared, for the scribes to count, and checked cursorily to see if Neithamun was watching.

She was nowhere to be seen. Cursing his inattention, he looked for Userkaf, but the young man was also gone from the fishing expedition. Abandoning his boat and fish without a second thought, he spared a moment to ask a serving girl where Neithamun had gone.

"She's returned to the house, sir. She told my lady Tashed she had a headache and wished to lie down."

Concerned that Haqaptah, who'd chosen the hunting venue, might find her alone, or that Userkaf might seize this opportunity to make his bold proposal, Periseneb jogged away from the river and struck a direct course to the house, rather than taking the scenic but meandering path. When he reached the main building, a servant informed him Neithamun and the young master were in the garden.

Hastening along the corridors as fast as he could, he heard raised voices when he neared the exit to the garden. As he burst into the space, with no clear idea of what he was going to do, but murderous rage in his heart, he heard the sound of a resounding slap, followed immediately by Neithamun's furious voice.

"How *dare* you propose such an arrangement to me?"

"Listen to reason, Neity," Userkaf pleaded. "Haqaptah means to have you and the estate, and I doubt he's planning to offer you marriage. You'll be lucky to be a concubine, if not a slave under his roof. And that soldier you've got hanging around made it clear to me he has no intention of remaining, if you're pinning your hopes on him. My offer is your only choice. Perhaps you need more direct persuasion, a reminder of what we shared before I was called away to war."

Periseneb heard muffled sounds of protest and a scuffle as he bolted past the end of the hedge separating him from the couple. Userkaf had Neithamun locked in his arms, attempting to kiss her, while she struggled to get away. Periseneb grabbed the noble by the shoulders and wrenched him away from her, throwing him to the side. Userkaf kept his balance with difficulty and charged Periseneb, only to be met with a resounding blow to the jaw that sent him sprawling to the ground. In a heartbeat, Periseneb had his opponent pinned, knife at his throat.

"The lady has refused you; accept her answer. Never touch her again, hyena spawn. I *will* kill you."

Userkaf struggled for air, his eyes bulging as he stared at Periseneb.

Neithamun was tugging at his shoulder. "Please, let him go, don't make this situation worse, I beg you. We're guests in this house."

"You being a guest didn't keep him from assaulting you." Pressing the knife a bit harder for a moment, enough to draw a thin line of blood, Periseneb reluctantly released Userkaf and stood. The noble scrabbled in the dirt to put distance between them, then rose to his feet, hand at his neck. Before he could speak, Periseneb said, "We'll be leaving this house within the hour and will make no mention of your ill-advised behavior. I suggest you keep it to yourself as well. Your conduct does you no credit and won't reflect well when your heart is weighed in the balance after death. Try to atone now with silence."

Two Heron Marsh men rushed from the house. "Mentu saw you running and summoned us, thinking there might be trouble," the one in the lead said to Periseneb.

"No trouble." He gave Userkaf a hard stare. "Is there?"

"No." Holding his neck, the noble brushed past the two guards and left the garden without a glance at Neithamun or a word of apology.

Periseneb walked to her. "Are you all right?"

He feared she might be in shock, as she was pale under her makeup and had a subtle trembling running through her frame. He guided her to a nearby bench. "He didn't hurt you, did he?"

She shook her head. "I want to go home," she said in a whisper he could hardly hear. "I never should have come. I never dreamt—"

"Stay here, in the garden. I'll have the men remain with you while I go see to the cart and have the maids collect your things." He beckoned to the two. "You, guard the door and allow no one to enter. And you, stay by Lady Neithamun's side until I return."

His soldiers saluted and took the assigned positions. Periseneb stepped into the house, to find Mentu fidgeting in the hall. The boy straightened as Periseneb approached. "Is my lady all right?"

"Yes. You did the right thing, summoning help." He clapped Mentu on the shoulder. "I'm grateful. Now, go prepare the cart without delay. We want to leave at once."

Mentu ran to obey the orders, nearly knocking over the woman coming down the hall. It was the mistress of Kingfisher, her lips set in a thin line, face grave. Periseneb pre-empted her, speaking first, his anger barely under control. "If you've come to berate Lady Neithamun, I won't allow it. We're departing as soon as I gather her possessions. Your son behaved in an unforgivable manner to a guest under your roof."

The older woman nodded. "I told him his plan was ill conceived, and Neithamun might be slow to see the benefits he felt he was offering. I counseled him to re-establish their friendship during this visit and save the proposal to become his second wife for next month, after Heron Marsh is forfeit, one way or the other. But he was impatient. Is she all right?"

"Shaken. Not physically hurt. Her things?"

"I've set the maids to packing the baskets already. Her possessions will be brought to the side door and placed in the cart shortly. I think it best if Neithamun leaves now, before our other guests are done with the morning's diversions. And before my son has second thoughts or gathers reinforcements."

"If he touches her again without her consent, he dies," Periseneb said.

"You won't need to resort to mortal combat." The older woman tilted her head, staring at him. "If she means that much to you, why haven't you come to some agreement of your own? Userkaf told me he made sure to ask you, in deference to your being one of Pharaoh's Guard and therefore of some account. But you made no claim, he said."

Before Periseneb could answer, Neithamun and the two Heron Marsh men stepped through the doorway. He didn't know if she'd heard what her hostess had said. Head held high, she paused, staring fixedly at a detail of the mural on the far wall, rather than at her hostess. "I must take my leave now, having urgent business at home. Life, prosperity, health to you."

"And the same wishes to you." The woman stepped aside as Neithamun marched past, still not looking at her.

"The cart will be at the side entrance," Periseneb said, hurrying to catch up with Neithamun. "I'm not sure if all is in readiness yet."

"Then I'll commence the journey on foot. I'm not remaining in this house another moment." Jaw clenched, she didn't break stride.

Fortunately, when Neithamun emerged into the bright sunlight, the cart was waiting and servants were setting her baskets into the back. Mentu and the other two Heron Marsh men stood by.

"The servants brought us beer and food to eat along the way," Mentu reported.

"I'm not accepting so much as another crumb of bread from this family, but you may partake." Neithamun stopped beside the cart. "Help me onto the seat and then I want you to drive."

Wide-eyed, the cowherd checked with Periseneb, who could only nod. Neithamun was as upset with him as she'd been with Userkaf, and he couldn't blame her. "Whatever the lady wishes," he said. "Let's move before anyone comes and we're forced into awkward explanations."

He held the donkey's bridle while Neithamun was assisted into the cart. She wrapped herself in her brown cotton shawl, face shadowed. Sitting with her spine straight, she focused on the horizon and didn't say another word. Mentu took his place beside her and flicked the reins to set the donkey in motion. Periseneb and his men deployed around the cart, and so she departed from Kingfisher.

CHAPTER SEVEN

They'd been home from the ill-fated Kingfisher trip for an entire day.

Neithamun retired to her room the moment she'd gotten home and, as yet, hadn't re-emerged.

She didn't make an appearance in the fields, the weaving room, or the brewery. She didn't come to meals.

She didn't come to transcribe the daily tallies. Periseneb and Amethu made quick work of the task, and he sent the other man off to his home in the workers' village. Periseneb sipped his beer and spun the snake game idly after moving his marker one day closer to the end of his sojourn in the Black Lands. Finally, he emptied the mug, placed the mehen board in its hiding place, and left the library.

Pacing through the halls toward Neithamun's chambers, he reminded himself for the thousandth time that matters could be left as they were, unsatisfactory as the situation was. He could accomplish his mission for Ma'at without explaining himself to Neithamun, but he found his aching heart wouldn't allow for such painful discipline. Eternity was too long to carry memories of her etched in sorrow, framed by unspoken words.

He knocked on her door but received no answer. Mind made up, "I'm coming in," he said. Worry sharpening his senses, he entered, closing the portal behind him. No oil lamps or candles were lit, leaving the room dark, but the full moon cast enough light through the open door to the garden to make it plain she wasn't in the chamber. A breeze brought the scent of the enchanted lotus to him, and he followed the sensory note out of the room into the garden, pausing on the threshold as he found Neithamun. Seated on the bench beside the small pond, she held the lush flower in one hand as she gazed across the flowerbeds. The moonlight cast an unearthly silver glow over the scene, and he thought no goddess could be more beautiful.

He hoped the memory of her beauty at this moment would stay with him no matter where his ka was destined to dwell. Drawing a deep breath, he said, "We have to talk."

She remained facing away from him. For another long moment, she kept her silence, twirling the lotus slowly in her hand. When she did speak, her question was direct. "Did you know of Userkaf's plan?"

Only the truth would do here, tempting as it was to prevaricate. Would Ma'at even allow him to lie? No matter. If he planned to avoid a difficult discussion, he shouldn't have sought Neithamun out. Grinding his teeth, he uttered one word. "Yes."

Now she did glance in his direction, head tilted, brow furrowed, as if she'd not expected his answer. "Why didn't you warn me?"

Remembering his blinding anger over the noble's schemes for Neithamun's future, he clenched his fists and gave her the truth again. "It wasn't my place to intervene. I've no right to stand between you and another man's proposal."

She persisted in her questions, voice hard and cold. "Do you think I should have accepted his *generous* offer?"

Hand out, he took a step toward her before he caught himself. "You deserve so much more than being another woman's handmaiden, warming her husband's bed when she doesn't wish to be there."

"Why do you care what happens to me?"

He tried to sidestep. "I'm trying to save the estate for you, so you can have the life you deserve, as the lady of Heron Marsh."

"But why?" She waved her hand as if shooing an annoying fly. "After all, as you constantly remind me, you're merely passing through, amusing yourself for a time with estate management. I mean nothing to you."

"No other woman ever meant half as much to me." Stung by her contemptuous tone, his hot words were spoken before he could stop them. "Why do you think I nearly killed Userkaf when he dared lay hands on you?"

"If I'd said yes to him—"

"I'd have regretted your choice now and into the Afterlife."

She seemed surprised by his vehemence. "Would you have killed him?"

"I would have had to honor your decision, like it or not." Grudgingly, he admitted, "I wouldn't have executed him where he stood if you'd chosen him."

"According to you, I deserve so much more than playing concubine for Userkaf, yet you won't speak for yourself. You offer me nothing?"

He was silent. What could he say? There was precious little he could offer one such as her.

She laid the lotus on the bench and rubbed her forehead, slumping a bit. Covering her eyes, she said, "Until that awful moment when he offered to take me as his second wife, I managed to hide the truth from myself."

"Truth?"

"No one believes I can retain possession of Heron Marsh. No one has confidence in me to solve the problems. I've been fooling myself because I was utterly terrified of the alternatives, for me and for my people. But not even my oldest friend had anything to offer, no suggestion of help, other than making me a second wife and a nursemaid, and condemning me to be a virtual servant, in his bed and out of it." Her voice choked off and he realized she was weeping. Through the tears, she continued. "Do you know how the conversation began, there at Kingfisher? He sought me out and offered to help me with Haqaptah. Being a foolish woman, ever hopeful and believing the best of people, I thought he meant a loan, or to negotiate better terms for me. I was so happy. And then he explained, and when I became angry, he tried—"

Periseneb moved to the bench and sat, pulling her into his arms. She laid her head on his chest as sobs wracked her body. He tightened his embrace, seeking to offer comfort. "I believe in you. I'm trying to help."

"I know." She nodded, hiccupping as the tears ended. "And I appreciate your efforts. But even you don't want to stay."

"What I want doesn't matter." The words felt as though each syllable had been ripped from his heart. "I can't linger at Heron Marsh."

"You say I mean more to you than any other woman, yet in the next breath you refuse to stay with me. I'm confused." Sitting up, she wiped her eyes with her sleeve.

"I'm not." Tilting her chin so he could look full into her eyes, he slowly lowered his lips to hers, giving her time to protest or move, if this wasn't what she wanted. Neithamun closed her eyes as his lips met hers. At first, he kept the caress gentle, fighting his own desires, not wanting to offend or frighten her. She parted her lips under his and he deepened the kiss, his tongue exploring the satin warmth of her mouth, while he held her close. Neithamun settled her arms around his neck and leaned into the kiss, tangling her tongue with his in a sensuous dance. Her breasts pressed against his chest and he felt her nipples pebble with arousal. His cock rose, hard and hot, painfully restrained by the layers of clothing.

Ending the kiss, he nuzzled her soft neck, breathing in the scent of her. "My affection for you has grown every moment I've been at Heron Marsh," he whispered into her ear. "When Userkaf asked if I was your suitor, I wished with all my heart I could have proudly answered yes."

She pulled away as far as his arms would allow her to move. Eyes wide, she said, "What's stopping you? I'm sure I've made my desires obvious. I've done everything but invite you into my bed and might have done that next, had we not gone to Kingfisher." She turned her face to avoid his gaze, her hair falling forward to hide her face. "I feared perhaps you didn't find me attractive enough—"

"I want you," he said. "My body aches for you. Only a soldier's discipline has kept me from seeking the warmth of your embrace. Working beside you daily, sharing meals, doing the tallies at night in the library together, it's been nearly impossible to keep from accepting your unspoken offer. I fantasize about taking you for mine." Oh yes, his fantasies had been explicit. He'd taken many a dip in the pond or the canal to cool his desires after time spent with her.

"But why resist?" Her voice sank so low he could hardly hear the next question. "Do you have a wife waiting somewhere?"

"No, but neither am I free to offer you what you deserve." Holding her on his lap with one arm at her waist, he plucked the lotus from the bench next to them.

She took the blossom from him, and in the moonlight he could see the wistful expression on her face as she studied the intricate arrangement of petals. "Magic," she said before he could respond. "You aren't human, are you?"

"I'm all too human at the moment." The pressure of her soft bottom against his arousal was pleasure and pain mixed together, but he wanted to keep her close to him while they talked. "I serve a Great One, and I've been sent here for exactly thirty days, of which seventeen are left."

Arms twined around his neck, hope giving her voice a lilt, she asked, "Pharaoh sent you?"

He couldn't utter a lie, but neither could he bear to have her recoil from him, which she surely would if he revealed his status as a ghost given temporary life. Swallowing hard, he said, "It doesn't matter who sent me; the fact is, I'll be gone forever at the end of Settlement Day. No matter how things are resolved with Haqaptah and the nomarch, I can't stay. The immutable deadline is why I've driven so hard to make the necessary improvements and brought Amethu and his people in to help. I want you to get through this year's crisis, so you have a good foundation for the future."

"A future you won't be here to see. Or share?"

He shook his head. His throat was too tight with things he wanted to say to allow him to utter any of them. He'd believed exile from the Afterlife was the ultimate punishment, but now his heart told him otherwise. Loss of Neithamun was going to be agony, even if he gained entry to the blessed duat.

There was a small silence. Somewhere outside the walls of the garden, a nightingale warbled, the song bubbly and happy at first, then growing harsh and ending on a piercing note that echoed the pain in his heart. Maybe the bird was speaking for him—he was out of words, plain soldier that he was.

Neithamun laid a soft hand on his cheek, turning his face so she could gaze into his eyes for a moment. "You serve a stern master. How many days did you say are left to us?"

"Seventeen."

"So few." She kissed his neck, soft little caresses whose sensuality shoved his desire higher. He tightened his arms, holding her closer. "I'm a grown woman, capable of making my own decisions." She feathered kisses along his jaw and shifted in his lap, her shapely bottom massaging his cock. He bit his lip as his manhood hardened like a bronze shaft. Next moment she'd slid away, rising to her feet. He groaned in wordless protest. But she had him by the hand and was tugging him to stand. One arm caressing the back of his neck, she kissed him, her tongue aggressively seeking his, while she fumbled with the fastening of his kilt with her free hand.

Hanging onto the shreds of his willpower, he broke off the kiss and folded his much bigger fingers over hers, preventing her from undoing the knot. "I tell you again—I can't stay beyond Settlement Day. There's nothing I want more than to take intimate memories of you with me on my journey, but I have to know you're sure. Do you want to give yourself to a wandering soldier? A man who only offers one brief moment of time?" Despite his aching cock, he had the strength to stop this now, if she said the words.

"We've wasted precious hours of your stay here, not speaking plainly to each other of our desires," she said. "I refuse to squander whatever time remains. If I can only have you in my arms until the new month begins, so be it. Better to have loved once, than to suffer an eternity of regret."

Her words unconsciously echoed his own earlier thoughts so closely that he was taken by surprise. "Do you love me? You've known me such a short time—"

"I speak my truths plainly. You've taken my entire heart and I can't imagine loving anyone the way I love you." Apparently concerned he was hesitating, Neithamun ran her fingers down his side and over his thigh, grasping his hard cock through the layers of his kilt and loincloth. Glancing at him mischievously from under her long lashes, she said, "If you don't allow me to undress you, neither of us will have relief from the sweet agony of desire tonight."

Capturing her lips again, he released his grip on her hand and stroked her breast, cupping the soft flesh and circling the nipple with his palm. Squirming in pleasure, Neithamun had a hard time loosening the knot at his waist, but eventually the kilt came undone and she shoved the fabric aside. She ran her hand under the edge of the loincloth, wrapping her fingers around him, thumb stroking the tip, spreading the silky droplets there until he couldn't stand still under her caresses. Retreating a step for the moment it took him to unwind the cloth, he found her watching him, her gaze intent. More blood rushed to his cock and his impatience grew. Catching her in his arms, he carried her to the bed.

Neithamun touched his shoulder, where the tattoo shone in the moonlight. He shivered as she stroked her hand over the spot. Neithamun pressed a kiss to his skin before leaning against him with a contented smile.

Proceeding inside the bedroom, he set her on the mattress. "Now you have too many clothes on."

"Easily dealt with." Kneeling on the bed, she raised her arms and he pulled the cotton sheath over her head, throwing it to the side.

She wore nothing under the dress. He paused for a moment to admire her ample curves.

Neithamun caught him by the hips, pulling him closer to the bed. His cock jutted and she took him in one hand, the other sliding between his legs to caress his balls, rolling them gently in her fingers, and stroking the sensitive area directly behind. Her fingers caging as much of his girth as she could, she held him in place as she tongued the sensitive head of his cock.

His knees weakened at the sensations.

Neithamun pulled his shaft deep into her mouth.

He fisted his hands in her hair as she pleasured him, trying to keep his hips from bucking as he held off his body's demand for the ultimate release. Every moment was exquisite torture, sensory overload for a man who'd not been touched by a woman—any woman, let alone one he loved—in centuries. Looking at her was as arousing as the physical act she was engaged in. "Enough! By the gods, woman, I'll not be able to wait until I have you under me if you continue this," he groaned.

Giving his cock a final massage, she released him with a satisfied laugh. He sank onto the bed, covering her with his larger frame and scooting them both into the middle of the mattress. Her body was soft and lush under him, warmly inviting. She parted her legs as she reclined and he settled into the vee between her thighs, his cock nudging her curls and the hidden lips beyond. Taking one nipple in his mouth, he caressed her breast with his hand so he could more easily taste and savor the sensations as he explored her body. Alternately suckling and teasing with his tongue, he was pleased by her reaction, unable to stay still, murmuring her delight. Running one hand over her stomach and through the soft curls, he found her wet and ready for him. Inserting first one finger, then another into her channel, he massaged the delicate folds as he switched his attention to the other breast.

"I want you," she said, sounding breathless. "We've waited so long, to delay is torture."

"Sweet pain," he said, working his fingers in and out of the slick folds.

Her hips shifted as she moaned. He brought her to a climax, relishing the sounds of pleasure she made under him. As she breathed deeply, he withdrew his fingers and guided his cock into her, sliding into her warmth with deliberation, so she could become used to him. She was tight, hot, and wet against him, and he couldn't hold off his own release much longer.

Neithamun locked her legs around his body and rocked to pull him further into her soft depths. Shuddering, he began to drive in and out, unable to resist the stimulus she was applying, her inner muscles clenching tight, welcoming his invasion.

"It's all right, let yourself go," she whispered in his ear before she nipped at his shoulder.

Next moment, he was lost in a torrent of pleasure as his seed released into her, joined as one with the woman he loved. Reaching one hand between them, he massaged her and Neithamun screamed his name as she held him desperately tight, arching against him, taking all the pleasure he could provide. His mind blanked under the assault of sensations.

Neithamun lay back as the waves of pleasure receded. She was hot, sweaty, and physically satisfied. Periseneb was an amazing lover. She ran her hands down his spine, enjoying the flexing of his muscles under her touch. Gripping his well-shaped, muscular butt, she relished the sensation of total possession. She was his and he was hers at this moment, which she'd longed for these past two weeks.

He rolled to the side. Wordlessly, she protested as his cock left her body, but he gathered her close, kissing her forehead and then her lips. "We have the entire night," he said. "Give me but a few moments and I'll launch a second campaign."

Laughing at his teasing tone, she snuggled as close as she could get. "I'll meet you halfway, dear heart."

He reached for the light sheet, drawing it over them both. "I don't want you to get chilled."

With his large frame nestled next to her, she had no worries about becoming cold, but she appreciated his care. His attention to details, not only when it came to her comfort, but to everything he was involved in, built her utter confidence in him. A light snore told her he was napping.

He deserved some sleep. The man worked so hard, every day, for an estate that he had no stake in, other than his care for her. Drowsy herself, Neithamun reviewed his words spoken in the garden before adjourning to the bed. Satisfaction at his anger about Userkaf's insulting offer warmed her heart. Did she have to admit to herself that part of inviting him to Kingfisher was to see if she could spur him to some declaration? Her cheeks burned as she reflected on Userkaf's humiliating assumption that she'd be pleased with what he had in mind. She'd never foreseen anything like that happening. But the moment was worth the embarrassment, if it helped Periseneb and her to admit their love for each other.

Raising herself on one elbow, she watched him sleep, admiring his handsome face. He looked younger, less guarded now as he dreamed in her bed. "Seventeen days," she whispered and felt her heart grow heavy. Tears threatened to flood her eyes and she leaned against the carved headboard, hands clasped at her knees, head bowed. *I thought he was the gods' answer to my prayers, the day he rescued Mentu and me, and it seems he may well have been. I was the lucky girl, living a scribe's most fantastic tale, with the handsome stranger come to save my estate, warm my bed, and capture my heart. All has come true, or nearly so, with only the estate hanging in the balance, yet in a little over two weeks I'm to lose him forever? The Great Ones give and they take away just as easily.*

She gave in to the grief, sobbing quietly, trying to stifle the noise with her hand.

"Here now, what's this, did I hurt you?" Periseneb pulled her into his arms, holding her tight. "I know I went too fast, but your touch, the feel of you wrapped around me was amazing. You've got the magic, dear heart."

She shook her head, sniffling. "No, I'm fine, our coupling was wonderful. Better than I'd ever dreamed making love could be."

"Stay here, I'll be right back." He left the bed, returning with the mug of beer from her untouched dinner tray. "A toast is in order," he said, raising the blue faience mug. "Sorry we'll have to drink from the same goblet, my lady, but I think we can successfully make a toast, don't you?"

Neithamun had to grin at his attempt to improve her mood. "What shall we toast to?"

"Us, of course." He took a sip and offered her the cup.

"Probably a good omen this piece of crockery is in the shape of lotus leaves." She drank a swallow or two of the warm beer before returning the remainder to him. Periseneb savored the final droplets and set the mug on the floor. He studied her face for a moment. "Are you having regrets now?" With one finger, he traced the tear track on her cheek. "My worst fear is bringing you sadness, which is why I've fought my desires since the day I arrived."

"*My* worst fear is wasting the time we have by indulging in sadness," she said, capturing his hand and kissing his palm. "Separaation is…hard to contemplate."

"I know." He hugged her to his chest, holding her warm and secure.

"There's no appeal? No way to ask for more time?" She knew the answer, but felt driven to make the plea.

He shook his head, hugging her as if to offer wordless comfort.

She felt his cock rising against her thigh, already hot and hard again so soon. Heat coiled in her loins at this undeniable proof of his desire for her. Reaching with one hand to stroke his shaft, root to tip with a firm grip, she said, "Ready for the next round, my lord?"

He stopped her hand, but didn't remove it from his body. "Are you sure? I don't want to bring you more sorrow."

"I'm sure. We shouldn't waste any of the moments the gods give us. I'll have years enough to lie in this cold bed alone, dreaming of you. Let me store up the good memories, beloved."

"We're thinking the same thing," he answered, easing them both into a reclining position.

She stroked his cheek as she stared into his eyes. "And neither of us will harbor any regret. Promise me."

"I promise. How could I regret being with the woman I love? But the future will be different for you, left here by yourself, when I must travel onward." He smoothed her hair away from her face, pushing the wispy tendrils behind her ears, and then nibbled her sensitive earlobe.

"Too much talking." She captured his lips and rolled her hips against his groin, seeking to distract him. As he came over her, his cock probing her soft flesh, soothing her aching need, Neithamun promised herself she'd fret no more over their parting until the moment arrived. Periseneb could be wrong, after all. Or perhaps if she prayed hard enough, the gods could be swayed. But he was very much here in her bed now, and she was the one wasting time.

A few days of hard work on the estate's many tasks, and nights spent in lovemaking followed, the happiness of being with Neithamun only slightly tainted for Periseneb by the constant knowledge of his limited time. By the fourth day, the estate was in readiness for the exalted guests. The house had been cleaned, Periseneb and the new men had repaired a number of things ignored for far too long, including the doors. Mentu had made sure the three bulls were well groomed. Khensa and the women who weren't cleaning were cooking a huge feast, augmented with freshly killed game Amethu and his hunters had brought in for the occasion.

Neithamun was dressed in her finest gown, wearing her one good wig and her mother's earrings. "I can't believe what a change you've made in the house and the grounds in such a short time," she said to Periseneb. "The priests will be surprised to see how differently we welcome them this year. Last year, we barely had enough food for them and the house was in bad repair, although we tried to hide that under fresh whitewash."

"I couldn't have done it without Amethu and his people." Periseneb clapped his new ally on the shoulder. "What time of day do the priests usually arrive?"

"Mid-morning." Neithamun gazed into the hazy distance, as if hoping to see them coming already. "We do a small blessing ceremony in the family temple before the High Priest and his acolytes inspect the bulls and make their selections." Her face lit up with mischievous good humor. "I receive the deben, which I promptly lock away in a special chest in my room, and then I preside over a lavish banquet, which this year will be even more generous than the estate was able to provide in at least five years. The high priest thanks me, I thank him, and he and his entourage leave early the next morning. Tonight, we'll celebrate the estate having earned enough deben to clear the debts for the year. There'll be no work tomorrow."

"I've a man on guard at the edge of the estate, to give us warning as the priests approach," Amethu said.

Yet, despite all the preparations, no convoy of priests arrived as the day wore on. Noon came and went. Khensa and her assistants replaced the food, clucking at the waste of what had been laid out the first time. Mentu and his sisters regroomed the bulls. Neithamun paced in front of the main door to the house, skirts flaring, while Periseneb stood close by. "Has the delegation ever been late before?" he asked.

She shook her head. "No. " Shielding her eyes with one hand, she stared futilely at the path leading to the road. "I can't imagine what's keeping them."

"Could there be confusion over the day?"

"Not likely. I exchanged notes with the high priest last month, confirming our usual appointment. I had to be sure the deben would come in time for the taxes." Eyes wide, she stopped in mid step and pivoted to stare at him. "You don't think Haqaptah's men have attacked them, do you?"

"Attack the high priest of Amun-Ra in broad daylight? Not likely." Periseneb felt sure. "Even his hyena spawn wouldn't be so bold." He held out a hand. "Come inside, have some beer and something to eat at least. Standing here in the hot sun won't bring them any sooner."

Casting a backward glance at the road, she linked her fingers in his and climbed the stairs. "Surely they'll be here within the hour."

"My lord, one comes!" The guard he'd posted at the estate's border was pelting up the road, shouting.

He and Neithamun turned on the stair. "One?" She stared at Periseneb, her face a study in puzzlement. "Why would the High Priest send one man by himself?"

No good reason came to mind, but numerous disasters did. He hoped he was wrong, saying only, "We'll soon know."

Together, they waited at the top of the stairs as the single arrival completed the drive to the house in a small cart. The man was dressed in ordinary clothing, as befitted a scribe, not a priest. The closer he came to the house, the more uneasy Periseneb grew. The visitor's face was set in grim lines, and he refused to meet anyone's eyes, concentrating on his docile donkey.

"I recognize him," Neithamun said. "He's the scribe who usually accompanies the priests. He handles the papyrus and dispenses the deben when I've transferred ownership of the bulls."

As the driver parked his cart neatly at the base of the stairs, Periseneb met the man, raising one hand in greeting. "On behalf of Lady Neithamun, welcome to Heron Marsh. Do you bring word from the high priest of Amun-Ra?"

Giving him a glance, the scribe climbed from his cart, handing the reins to the hovering Mentu. He patted his donkey on the neck and then rolled his shoulders, as one who must perform an unpleasant task. "Yes, I've been sent to inform the lady—"

Suspecting this wasn't going to be a pleasant conversation, Periseneb interrupted the determined flow of words. "Wait. Let's go inside to the library and speak privately with Lady Neithamun."

The scribe glanced at the servants and guards clustered close by. "Perhaps a discussion in front of fewer ears might be best."

"Bring some beer to the library for our guest," Neithamun said to the cook. Next, she gave orders to her chief cowherd. "See the donkey is taken care of."

"No need. I'll be leaving for town shortly." The scribe glanced at Mentu. "Give him some water and a bit of hay if he'll take it."

Worse and worse. Periseneb's misgivings grew. He and the scribe trailed Neithamun through the house to the library, no one speaking. Amethu came behind, in response to a nod from Periseneb.

Neithamun arrayed herself in the large, gilded chair, her expressionless face betraying nothing. "What word does the high priest send me?"

The scribe sat and sipped at his beer. "There's no good way to say this, so I'll be blunt, my lady. The temple of Amun has no need to purchase bulls from Heron Marsh this year."

She gasped, clutching the edge of the table so hard her knuckles were white. "How can this be? Not a month ago, I exchanged greetings with the high priest, confirming the sale. Does he plan to cancel all sacred celebrations for the next year?"

"No, my lady, observances will continue as decreed by the Great Ones. Your neighbor, Lord Haqaptah, has seen fit to donate five bulls to the temple, to thank the god for the rich bounty of this year's harvest from his fields and orchards. While the animals aren't descended from the herd of the goddess Hathor, each is robust, well formed, and proven at stud—a gift of unparalleled size."

"That sack of hyena droppings," Periseneb swore. "This must be why he was so full of himself and cheerful when we met him at Kingfisher. He was gloating because he'd figured out a way to cut the ground out from under us."

"Yes." Neithamun's face was pale under her makeup, and she seemed to be having difficulty drawing in enough air. She pressed one hand to her chest.

"I'm sorry to be the bearer of such news, my lady." The scribe sounded as if he meant it. "I shouldn't be telling you this, but there were those among the priesthood who argued for purchasing your three bulls in addition. Ultimately, the high priest felt it would be an unwise use of temple resources, when the five bulls came as a gift." He leaned closer. "Please, don't repeat what I've shared."

"No, of course not. I appreciate your telling me." She rose, hands fluttering. "Well, I…I—surely there must be things I have to do now, if you'll excuse me."

Periseneb took her elbow, afraid she might faint. "Amethu will keep you company and escort you to your cart when you're ready to depart," he said to the scribe, giving his assistant a meaningful glance.

Lips tightly compressed, Amethu nodded. "It'll be my honor."

As soon as she was in the hall, Neithamun stopped in her tracks and clutched his arm. "We have to tell my people. This catastrophe affects all of them as much as it devastates me."

He drew her further along the hall, away from the library. "Word is probably flying like a flock of birds over the Nile right now. Your people will have heard that only a scribe arrived, where we'd expected those he serves." Periseneb felt as if he'd been kicked in the gut by the donkey. The tattoos on his shoulder burned. *How can I fail Neithamun now? We were so close to having enough deben for the taxes and the loan.*

"Haqaptah must be laughing himself sick today, knowing his interference has destroyed my hopes." She looked at him, tears of desperation shining in her eyes. "Is there anything you can suggest? Any intervention your mysterious Great One might make? You've brought me a magic lotus and found water where none has been for centuries. Can't you work another miracle?" Biting her lip, Neithamun looked away. "I must sound desperate, even greedy, but this is a disaster."

"I don't know what can be done." But he did know. There was one thing he could ask Ma'at, which might solve the estate's problems. Did he have the courage to face the consequences? "As soon as the scribe has departed, let's assemble the residents of the estate and, as you said, share with them the truth of this disaster. We can tell them I'm working on another plan."

"I don't want to give false hope," she said. "You don't sound too sure about this new idea."

He stared at the cracked, fading fresco on the wall opposite them. "I'll admit this is a last resort, something I'd hoped for my own reasons not to have to do. But I don't want Amethu and his people leaving for the Red Lands prematurely, or your own workers throwing down their tools and deserting." Transferring his gaze to her upturned face, he brushed a kiss across her parted lips and said, "There's one chance remaining, I swear to you. I'm not permitted to utter an untruth."

"Very well then. I'll ask them all to give me a few more days," she said. "My people like you, and more importantly, the majority have come to trust you. As have I."

He felt the burden of Heron Marsh's collective hopes settle on his shoulders like blocks of the pyramid and he prayed to Ma'at he had the answer.

The meeting with the workers and Amethu's people went better than Periseneb had hoped. Neithamun was right—the estate's residents did seem to have confidence in him, and once she announced he had a plan, the muttering stopped and people's expressions became cheerful. Neithamun invited the estate residents to help themselves to the food prepared for the priests, and the evening ended on a positive note.

Periseneb made himself wait until the house had gone quiet and he was sure even Neithamun had done her nightly scribe's work and gone to bed. Then, he left the house and walked in the moonlight toward the small grove of trees sheltering the estate's small shrine.

A sharp challenge halted him in his tracks. "Who goes there?"

Smiling at the efficiency of his watchman, Periseneb identified himself, then asked, "Any disturbances tonight?"

"No, sir, all quiet."

"Let's hope things remain peaceful." He returned the man's salute, even though they were no longer in anyone's army. The ritual was comforting and it felt right. Continuing on his way, a few moments later, Periseneb was entering the shrine, passing between carved pillars inscribed with blessings for any who entered here. The temple didn't belong to a single Great One, but had four smaller rooms, each for a different god or goddess—Thoth, Isis, Renenutet, and Hathor. Periseneb chose to stay in the central chamber, inserting the torch securely in the bronze fixture beside the door before walking into the middle of the space, which was designed to allow the visitor to pray to any member of the Great Ones' pantheon.

Resting one hand on the three remaining tattoos on his shoulder, he said, "I have need of your help, Great One." When he lifted his fingers, he was holding a red feather, new vanes and fronds popping from the quill as it lengthened and took form. A stray breeze snatched it from him and he made a hasty grab, missing it. Taking a single step in pursuit, he stopped abruptly, barely preventing himself from falling over as the goddess Ma'at plucked the drifting pinion from the air and stood in front of him, running the soft fronds through her fingers. Green sparks sizzled along the temple floor and flew erratically through the room, remnants of the power she'd used to respond to his call. Although he'd brought a single torch and the moon had yet to rise, the chamber was now bright as day.

Periseneb knelt, arms crossed over his chest, head bowed. "I'm grateful for your attention, Great One."

"I said I would come if you needed me. Rise and tell me what troubles you tonight."

As he got to his feet, he said, "I fear I'm failing you."

She tucked the feather into her headband. "I'm not displeased, warrior. Much has been accomplished."

"But the estate is still in danger of being forfeited."

"True. Matters are not yet in balance." She made a small gesture, as if weighing two things in her palms. "The outcome I seek remains in doubt, but your path has been a good one. The future contains possibilities, and there is yet time. Why have you summoned me?"

He licked his lips, nausea roiling in his gut. "I want to know where my body lies."

She tilted her head, elegant brows drawn together in a frown on her face. Tapping one toe, she asked, "Are you pursuing my truth or yours?"

"Both, my lady. I've come to realize the two are entwined, which I should have known when you called me forth from the gray wastes to be your champion. My death went against what Shai, god of Fate had foretold for me at birth, didn't it?"

He didn't know if the goddess would answer the question.

Mist flowed into the room from the door, and he smelled the scent of the lotus even more strongly. His entire body tingled for a moment and the breath paused in his lungs. Stuttering, his heart beat in a wild rhythm. Coughing, rubbing his chest, he realized he wasn't in the small rural temple any longer, but stood in some vast hall, grander than any he'd seen in Pharaoh's capital. Colossal columns marched away in both directions, painted in vivid colors, gold accents gleaming, underpinning a ceiling he couldn't see. The floor beneath his humble sandals was tiled, red, black, white, and turquoise squares, some bearing inscriptions changing before his eyes, hieroglyphics flickering too fast to be read. An ebony table stood before him, gilded jackal's heads with ruby eyes and ivory fangs at each corner. He had the uncanny sensation that the eyes watched him. A senet game in progress sat on the tabletop, employing pawns half a cubit high.

One at a time, Ma'at picked up the throwing sticks, beautiful ebony and ivory, inlaid with shining mother of pearl. Rolling the counters in her hands, she said, "Do you remember I told you the first time we met, how even those not in league with the evil one might commit acts furthering his cause?"

"I do."

Throwing the sticks, hardly even glancing at them to add the score before selecting a pawn, she gazed at the game piece between her fingers with downcast eyes and a furrowed brow.

Shivering, he realized the pawn had his features. Sweeping the board with a rapid glance, he recognized Sitre, and maybe a few other faces.

Brows drawn together in a frown, the goddess eyed him, game piece in her hand. "*You* committed no such acts. Yet, you set unfortunate events in motion, which echo through time." Ma'at placed the pawn bearing his likeness off to the side, next to the board. "Your return to Heron Marsh two hundred years ago didn't go as you hoped and expected. Had you lived, nothing would have been as you dreamt."

Swallowing hard, he nodded. "I know that now, my lady. I've read the estate records and talked to the oldest servant at Heron Marsh. I understand many things I didn't grasp in my own lifetime. About my father, about the woman Sitre—"

As if her name was a spell word, the golden scale used for judging hearts suddenly appeared on the table in a blaze of green sparks, next to the senet board. Ma'at set the pawn representing him in one of the cups, which immediately clanked to the tabletop with an ominous thud like the fall of an axe. "Yet in life, you would have had choices, might have taken a path preserving the balance of powers and influences my King Osiris and I sought in this area." She surveyed him for a moment, her brown eyes narrowed, as if seeking a reaction.

Unsure how he was expected to react to the information that he played some role in the skirmishes between deities, he kept himself from staring at the golden scales. Was she already weighing his heart and finding him wanting? With passion scorching his soul, he realized he craved every heartbeat of time he could earn in the upper world. Even the pleasures of the duat didn't outweigh life at Heron Marsh, precious moments lived in Neithamun's company. Thinking of his beloved loosened his tongue to reveal to the goddess what he sought. "Tell me where my body lies, and I may be able to accomplish the balance you seek."

"Proposing a bargain, mortal?" Selecting another pawn, one carved in the shape of a lush female form, Ma'at hesitated. "Are you sure you're ready to face the truths interred with your body? Painful memories currently shielded from the dead will pour into your mind if I agree to your request. Are you strong enough to persevere on your path, *my* path, in the face of what you'll learn?"

Wishing he could see if the face on the pawn was Sitre's or Neithamun's, Periseneb nodded. The challenge was plain in the goddess's tone. Ma'at was testing him, and he couldn't afford to fail if he was going to help Neithamun save the estate. "I'll find the courage, Great One. My heart is resolved."

"Excellent. I chose my champion well, not that I was ever in doubt." She set the pawn in the other golden pan, placing it so Sitre's face was fully in the light. The scales sought equilibrium, swaying until the two cups hung freely in the air, equally balanced.

Annoyance flooded his mind, paired so with Sitre, even if he wasn't sure what the goddess was thinking or how she meant it. *Am I to offset or undo acts committed by Sitre in her lifetime?* He searched his memories, but the events surrounding his death still eluded him. Courage bolstered by the way Ma'at appreciated his plain speaking, he said, "If we're weighing my heart today, I've given it to another, Great One, not the pawn you've chosen."

Nodding, she selected another game piece, holding it out to him. "I know the truth of your heart, warrior. This is the woman of whom you now speak."

He took the pawn, the cool ivory pleasant on his palm. He admired the beautiful rendition of Neithamun's face, her almond-shaped eyes serious, a hint of a smile on her full lips. Boldly, he stepped forward to set the new pawn next to his, on the same side of the balance. Unaccountably, the arms of the scale stayed motionless, although two pieces should have outweighed Sitre's pawn. The process made no sense to him, but he wasn't in the mortal realm now, so the rules were unknown.

Ma'at added her symbol of Truth to the pan holding his heart and the woman he loved. The beam stayed steady. "You've found some answers, my warrior. I'm pleased for you."

He heard scrabbling sounds from deep in the mist and recoiled, reaching for the sword he wasn't wearing. Ammit the Destroyer waddled from the mists, proceeding across the floor, claws clicking on the tiles. Beads of sweat popping out on his brow, he forced himself to stand at parade rest and face the beast as she came nearer. Ammit circled him once, stopping to sniff before moving to sit beside the goddess. He took a shaky breath as the Destroyer lost interest in him. Periseneb was battle tested, knew himself to be far from a coward, yet having Ammit pay him any attention threatened to turn his bones to water. She dealt irrevocable death to a man's ka, if he was judged unfit to enter the Afterlife—there was no appeal from her judgment. *Why did Ma'at summon the beast? Was she warning him not to fail?*

Ma'at plucked the game piece with Sitre's features from the balance and flicked it at the creature.

With a snap of the huge crocodilian jaws, Ammit bit the pawn in two and swallowed as if enjoying some delicacy. Her stubby hippopotamus tail flicked side to side as she made an awkward pivot and retreated into the mists.

Wondering if he understood the significance of what he'd just seen, Periseneb said, "Forgive me, Great One, I know I'm not allowed to know the fate of anyone else's ka but—"

"You've learned on your own that the woman feared the judging of her heart. With good reason." Ma'at shrugged. Retrieving her feather, and placing it firmly into her headband, her manner became businesslike. "Your body lies in a small cave at the edge of the Heron Marsh boundaries, close to the valley of tombs." Waving her elegant hand over the table, Ma'at set loose a shower of green sparks. The scales and senet board were gone, dissolving into dust that blew away under the onslaught of the magic. Forming from thin air, an intricate model of Heron Marsh grew to cover the flat surface, depicting the landscape in exacting detail. Ma'at pointed at the spot where the deep wadis sliced through the terrain, at the boundary of the Black and the Red Lands. "Although you were killed beside the pond, having been lured there by one you trusted, your body was hidden here." She studied him for a moment. "The place is not unfamiliar to you, I think?"

I walked right past it when I visited my father's tomb. He nodded. "I know the area, Great One."

A woman strolled out of the mists, holding a tray with one golden goblet, although by her clothing, multiple gold bangle bracelets, and regal bearing, she was no servant. Her dress was of the finest, sheer linen, a leopard print, accented with golden embroidery. On her head she wore a green crown with seven points. "I've brought the potion you requested, my sister."

By the crown and distinctive garments, Periseneb realized he was in the presence of Sefkhet, Mistress of the House of Books, keeper of all memories. Falling to his knees, he crossed his arms over his chest and bowed his head in respect.

"You may rise." Ma'at waved a casual hand. "My sister has come to assist me with your request to regain the memories of your death."

"Are you sure this is wise?" Sefkhet set the tray on the table and raised one elegant eyebrow, contemplating Periseneb, although he felt the question was directed at her divine sibling.

Ma'at gave her sister a hug. "Who can say? The mortal serving as my warrior in this instance chooses the weapon of memory to fight his battle."

"A double edged blade." Sefkhet toyed with the goblet, spinning it in a slow circle on the tray. Light glinted from the carnelians set into the gold below the fluted rim. Intricate carvings of the goddess inscribing sacred hieroglyphs on scrolls circled the sides, catching his momentary attention.

"I need to know." Nerves raw, Periseneb felt uneasy being discussed by goddesses as if he wasn't standing there with them. Ma'at's pawn he might be, but his status didn't mean he had to remain silent.

"The knowledge can't be taken away again." Sefkhet stared at him, pointing one finger as if to emphasize her point. "If you fail in your duties, and your ka is condemned to roam the wastes, the memories will haunt you."

"I wish to keep all my memories," he answered.

"You wish to remember the woman Neithamun," Ma'at said, index finger raised as if to correct a student.

Head bowed, he acknowledged the hit. "I do, my lady. But I also need to know the circumstances of my death."

Reddened lips thin, Sefkhet shook her head as if his answer displeased her, but made no more objections. Removing a tiny pouch from her scarlet sash, she reached inside the bag and brought out a nearly invisible pinch of golden dust between her fingers. She let the motes drift gently into the liquid in the cup, watching with narrowed eyes as the glistening grains fell from her hand.

Humming a tune almost under her breath, swaying side to side as if beginning a dance, she began to sing louder. Her voice echoed in the chamber as she repeated the chorus of her chant three times. "Water of the blessed Nile, sands of time, whisper to this warrior what he wishes to know." After stirring the mix with an ebony stylus crved in the shape of a heron, she raised the goblet and approached Periseneb.

He eyed her gift with misgiving, as a plume of green mist rose from the drink. Rolling his shoulders, he accepted the goblet from Sefkhet. She rubbed a bit of the golden dust across his forehead, smoothing his hair out of his face before stepping away. The gesture surprised him, as if she meant to be comforting.

Both goddesses watched as he drank. To his surprise and relief, the mixture had a pleasing taste, nothing he could recognize, although he thought perhaps there was honey, maybe mint, and a touch of cinnamon. Despite the steam, the liquid cooled his tongue and as he swallowed the last drops, he felt the cold spreading from his core throughout his entire body. The container became too heavy to hold, dragging his arm toward the floor with its weight, and Sefkhet took it from his numb fingers before he could drop it. Ma'at gripped his elbow with inhuman strength and guided him to a chair placed close to the table.

"Head...spins." Tongue thick, those were the only words he could form. Closing his eyes, he lolled in the seat, not caring if the action was disrespectful. He kept from falling to the floor in disgrace by the black jaguars forming the chair arms.

"Rest. Recover your memories." Ma'at laid one hand on his forehead for a moment, then shifted to pat his shoulder as a comrade might. "We'll keep watch."

Nothing's changed while I was away from home these many years, the woman is still careless of the time of others. He stood in the grove of trees by the pond, his battered leather satchel by his feet. Checking the position of the moon and the stars overhead, he knew Sitre was late, far beyond the time she'd asked him to meet her here. Frustration burned along his nerves. *Why didn't I go straight to my father's house? Why do I humor her wishes, even now?* Reunion with his father was already much delayed. Pharaoh had insisted Periseneb remain at his side for one final campaign, which took far too long, the enemy more wily than expected.

Additional months were required to thoroughly eradicate the threat before Periseneb was released from the army.

But he was home now, or so near as to make little difference.

A chill breeze ruffled the surface of the pond. He heard a fish jump in an attempt to catch some careless night insect. Drawing his cloak more closely about his shoulders, he felt sure he was waiting in vain. Annoyed, he reached for the bundle, ready to swing it to his shoulder and march to his father's home. "I can deal with her and her family in the morning light," he muttered.

"Deal with who, my lion cub?" Sitre's low, vibrant voice cut the night air. Swathed in a cloak, she strolled across the grass toward him, her hips moving sensuously under the fabric. He'd forgotten how she imbued every motion with allure. Opening the cloak to reveal a tight sheath dress that hid nothing from his imagination, even in the moonlight, she said, "Or are you a full grown lion now, a mighty warrior of Pharaoh?" Her tone sounded oddly mocking.

As if stung by a snake, he realized she'd never expected him to amount to anything. *Probably assumed I'd die in my first battle.*

Halting a pace or two away, allowing the cloak to conceal her figure again, she studied him, head tilted. "We've heard nothing of you since you departed so hastily. Until I had your note two days ago, delivered in secret by the messenger you hired."

"You're late," he said, angry at her lack of confidence in him.

"You've been gone from Heron Marsh so long, what are a few more moments?" Sitre's answer was typically unconcerned. "Have you not been filled with anticipation of being in my arms again? Doesn't the wait heighten the desire? As I recall from our previous times here at the pond, you like to be kept in suspense. Up to a point." Her laugh was teasing, intimate. "I'm sure none of the women you bedded in Thebes were as satisfying as the memories of our times together. As proof, here you are! I'm flattered, there's no denying the fact."

Her cloying perfume reached him. The scent made him strangely uneasy. Meeting at the pond seemed like a bad idea now; it summoned too many memories he suddenly wasn't proud of. *Enough talk of the past.* Resisting her charms, Periseneb stayed where he was. "We've much to discuss. It might have been better to wait until tomorrow."

She swayed closer, now standing before him, reaching to touch him. He felt none of the old desire as she twined her arms around his neck, her soft breasts pressing against his chest. An errant memory of some other woman flitted through his mind. A face he couldn't place a name to, yet important to him. Someone else associated with Heron Marsh? But Sitre had been the only woman he'd seriously pursued here on the estate. Wasn't she? His thoughts whirled in a way he was unaccustomed to, threatening to bring on vertigo.

Holding Sitre felt as if he was being disloyal to someone else. His senses and his cock remained unresponsive to her lush charms, even as she ground her hips against him.

The whole meeting felt wrong. Regret for agreeing to this flashed through his mind.

He tried to break her embrace, but she locked her fingers behind his neck, refusing to move away. Subsiding rather than hurt her, he kept his arms at his sides. Sitre pouted, licking her lips in a manner obviously intended to entice him. "What's the matter? You're as nervous as the first time we came to the pond to lie together. I sought to please you by celebrating our reunion here."

"There's something…" He bit his lip. He couldn't explain that he was thinking of another woman, whose name he didn't even recall. But that woman's ghostly image in his mind, the feel of her body under his stood between him and any shred of desire for someone else. "This isn't a good idea. Let me escort you to the house and we can talk in the morning, before we go to see your father." He was on edge, tense, as if going into combat. *What's the matter with me tonight?* Marrying Sitre wouldn't make him happy, but it would preserve his honor. He'd made a promise, and if she'd waited for him, then he would be her husband. Yet, he hesitated. Confusion joined the near-vertigo. He never hesitated, was renowned in Pharaoh's army for charging into situations. *Set's teeth, what's wrong with me tonight?*

"Does your father know you're coming?" She looked over his shoulder into the grove before flicking her gaze back to him.

"Your reply to my note asked me not to tell anyone, and I've gone along with your wishes. I'm going to surprise him when you and I are done talking. When we've decided what steps to take next."

"Talking? Is an exchange of words all you have in mind to do tonight?" Her hand strayed down his abdomen and skimmed his kilt. Her eyes gleamed in the moonlight and her laugh no longer sounded sensual. The tone was cruel, triumphant. She released him, but didn't move away. "Are you regretting your oath? Your message said you were prepared to become my husband. To stand against my father, claim my hand and make us one in the eyes of the Great Ones."

Through gritted teeth, he said, "I'm a man of my word."

"Yes, that's what I was afraid of," she said.

He felt the bite of a knife sliding between his ribs as Sitre stepped away from him, holding a dripping blade.

Puzzled, he hesitated for a fatal moment, unable to believe she'd stabbed him.

He was attacked from behind, another blade slicing between his shoulder blades, the force of the blow bringing him to his knees. He toppled over as the knife wielder thrust again, this time close to the wound Sitre'd inflicted. He couldn't catch his breath, the stars seemed to have fled from the sky as he lay in the cool grass. Pain ran through his entire body and his limbs refused to respond as he tried to rise to defend himself. His arms were as granite, too heavy to obey his mind. He had no sensation in his legs at all.

"Enough," he heard Sitre say. She bent over him, although he could barely see her through the gray veil of pain and weakness blocking his vision. "He'll make no trouble for me now. Who would have known the peasant boy would ever make his way home? And just in time to ruin the achievement of all I've worked so hard for?"

"Indeed, my lady. Not much of a soldier, easy enough for us to take unaware."

Periseneb didn't recognize the voice of his assailant. *Some fool she got to do her bidding.*

"Why couldn't he have died in battle? Or settled down with a soldier's whore in Thebes?" Sitre's voice was taut with petulance, the tone she'd take when a servant didn't move fast enough to do her bidding, or her father denied her some treat she fancied. "But, no, he believed he was going to marry the daughter of the house and sit at my father's right hand in leisure, instead of laboring in the fields where he belongs. Simpleton." She laughed again and the sound was eerie. "Is he dead yet?"

A foot prodded his side where the most serious wounds were, and Periseneb groaned in agony, feebly trying to curl to protect himself.

"Well, no matter. Let's get him loaded into the cart. He'll either die on the way to the cave or soon after we dump him there." Sitre sounded as if she was talking about a stray dog, her voice was so unemotional. "No one the wiser. And you've been well paid to keep your silence."

"Indeed I have, my lady, and grateful for the gold. It'll keep me well on my journey out of the province."

Exerting the final ounces of strength left in his failing body, Periseneb raised himself on one elbow. Sitre's scream of alarm helped him focus on her, although she was nothing to his failing eyes but a misshapen silhouette against the moon's light. He pointed a shaking finger in her direction. "I forgive the man who struck the blows—he's nothing but your tool. But you, Sitre, I curse you. All your dreams will be denied, here at Heron Marsh, and into the Afterlife. Joy shall escape you." Blood gurgled in his throat and he knew he was done for. Swallowing hard, he uttered a final curse in the best voice he could muster. "Ammit the Destroyer will eat your heart for this deed."

There was a crashing blow to his head and the world blacked out.

Awakening with a racing pulse, Periseneb drew a deep breath and realized he was lying on the floor of the family temple. Wisps of green mist were eddying sluggishly away from him, flowing out the open portal of the building to dissipate in the cool morning air with a faint hissing noise. Relieved to be alone, he rolled over and got to his feet. He yanked at his tunic, checking his side, but there were no open wounds, no scars other than those he'd suffered in honorable combat. Apparently, gracious Ma'at had seen fit to spare him those final indignities from his murder when she sent his embodied ka to the upper world.

Nauseous, he staggered from the temple into the small garden alongside the eastern wall, falling to his knees in a flowerbed for a time, racked by dry heaves. His ribs ached and his head pounded, as if he'd been in the fight for his life, instead of reliving memories from two centuries past. Gradually, the pain receded and he got to his feet, straightening his clothing. The horror of his last moments on earth buzzed in his brain. He kept hearing Sitre's laughter. He should have realized what she was capable of and planned accordingly. Instead, he'd offered honor to one who had none to give in exchange. The worst part of the entire experience wasn't the pain or even Sitre's cruel betrayal.

The worst aspect was the sheer waste of his life. If she hadn't wanted to marry him, he'd have been relieved not to fulfill his vow. He would have gladly left her in peace to enjoy the fruits of her scheming, her marriage to Haqaptah. But instead, she had him killed.

Dawn had broken in the present day and the estate workers were going about their morning tasks. Mentu waved as he passed by, whistling cheerfully. Periseneb half lifted his hand in reply, leaning on the nearest column to keep from falling again. Meeting with the Great Ones was never easy on a man; it left him as drained as if he'd been in combat. He took a deep breath, then another as strength flowed to his limbs. Savoring the crisp morning air, Periseneb headed toward the house. Might as well get this over with, see if what he was hoping to find had been placed with his corpse. Perhaps he could have the last laugh over Sitre and her descendants, and claim at least a partial victory.

Having obtained the answer to how and why he'd died, and where his body lay, Periseneb was impatient to complete the investigation. Anxiety over what he might find in the cave, mixed with a sense of time slipping away, kept his gut churning. Only eleven days remained for him to complete his task from Ma'at.

Making a stop at the barn first to grab an empty pack from the storeroom, he proceeded to the kitchen, offering Khensa a polite greeting, although the measured words required will power. He helped himself to a mug of the beer, draining it in one long gulp. He took a few strips of dried meat and a loaf of bread, fresh from the oven, stuffing both into the pack as he left the house. Grabbing a waterskin, he filled it from the newly dug canal and then set off to the west with long strides, not quite running, but anxious to settle the remaining questions of his fate.

"Periseneb, wait!"

The one voice he couldn't ignore—Neithamun. Turning, he saw her running toward him, cotton skirt kilted to her knees to allow her to set a good pace. When she reached him, she skidded to a stop on the loose dirt, braced by the hand he extended to keep her from falling. Protecting Neithamun from even the slightest mishap was second nature to him now.

Taking deep breaths, hands on her hips, she said, "Where are you going?"

"There's something I must do today. I'll be at the table for the evening meal, I promise." Dropping his hand, he turned on his heel and resumed walking. "You should go to the house," he said over his shoulder.

He should have known Neithamun wasn't to be dismissed so lightly. She jogged past him and planted herself in his path, forcing him to halt. "You never came to my bed last night. Mentu said you looked ill this morning, and Khensa sought me out, saying you had such a grim expression, she was afraid you were going into battle of some sort." Staring into his face with her brow furrowed, she said, "I have to agree with her." Eyes widening, she gasped. "You're not leaving me, are you? We have eleven days left by your count."

"No battle. And I'm not leaving." He shook his head. Words were failing him at the moment. Reeling from the memories of his death at the hands of Sitre and her assassin, he couldn't lie to Neithamun, but he couldn't tell her the truth either. Could he?

"Some task you dread?" Neithamun's question was more of a statement. Head tilted, she nodded at her own conclusion. "I'm coming with you."

He retreated a step. "You can't…"

"Yes, I can and I will." Her tone was autocratic, determined. She reached for his hand, twining her soft fingers between his. "You've been shouldering all the burdens of trying to save Heron Marsh these last few weeks, and I'm grateful, but I can't shirk my proper duties any longer. If your errand or task is on behalf of me and my estate, I need to come. I need to do my part. To be a—what's the military term? Shieldmate?" Voice softening, she said, "You don't have to be alone. I'm here for you. To help."

With a groan, he pulled her close, hugging her as if he'd never let her go. She raised her face to his and he kissed her long and hard. "I wish I'd met you in another time and place," he said when the embrace ended. Holding her close, he added, "You're the kind of woman a man dreams of, a true partner."

"Which is what I want to be," she said, resting her head on his chest.

Finger under her chin, he said, "Neithamun, look at me. This isn't going to be a pleasant excursion. I'll understand if you want to change your mind at any point."

She stepped from his grasp and met his gaze. "Surely you've seen by now I don't shirk even the unpleasant tasks. Where are we going?" Her voice was calm, even though she was fidgeting with the amulet on her wrist, worrying the strand of beads.

He shook his head. "Somewhere I'd rather not go, but must." He gazed at the sky for a moment, pondering how much to tell her. She waited patiently for him to reach a decision, so he chose his words with care. "There are secrets about me, things I haven't told you, things I'd hoped you never needed to know. I wanted your memories of me to be good, once I've gone." Swallowing hard, he admitted his deepest misgiving as he brushed a tendril of hair away from her face. "You might even be frightened of me by the time this trip is finished. It would break me to see fear in your face instead of love."

She studied him. "Do you know why I haven't been afraid of you, not one moment since you arrived to rescue Mentu and me?"

"No. At first I wrongly assumed you were naïve, but now I know you have a spine of steel and wits sharper than the tip of a spear."

"Oh, of course you'd expect a country girl to be naïve. Why wouldn't she be, living in a provincial nome, stuck on a rural estate?" Hands on her hips, Neithamun's expression was belligerent for a moment. Then her shoulders slumped and she swallowed hard. "I had the worst nightmares of my entire life the night before you arrived, dreaming of the woman all in black, among other omens. She was standing beside my bed in the final dream, reaching to touch me." Despite the early morning heat as the sun climbed in the sky, Neithamun shivered. Rubbing her arms, she said, "The threat felt so real, so dangerous. I woke screaming, in a cold sweat. I knew the estate and I were in dire peril, but I didn't know what to do, where to seek help." She waved one hand in agitation as he opened his mouth to speak. "Wait, let me finish. So, I sought the peace of the temple and spent the rest of the night praying to the Great Ones for assistance. I fell asleep beside the main altar and Menwe found me there in the morning."

Had her plea set in motion the events bringing me here? "Did you see the Great Ones?"

She brushed her hair out of her eyes. "I don't know. I don't remember anything after reaching the temple and praying. But that afternoon you appeared out of nowhere on Haqaptah's land, saving Mentu and me from whatever foul deeds his thugs were planning, and I was certain you'd come in answer to my prayer. I think I started falling in love with you between one heartbeat and the next. Man, ushabti, or god, I could never be frightened of you. Believe the truth of my vow."

"I can only pray it be so, sweetheart." Periseneb gathered her close for a hug, savoring the sweetness of her body in his arms. He closed his eyes for a moment, trying to fix the memory firmly in his mind. Sefkhet had promised him he would remember Neithamun for all eternity, hadn't she? "I'll love you and only you, in this world and beyond. I swear by my ka."

Arms around his waist, she pressed close, her voice muffled but insistent. "Then allow me to come with you today. We can face whatever it is you're dreading together."

He took her hand in his, although misgivings continued to assail him. Maybe today he'd find out what it was like to have a woman of honor stand beside him. Perhaps she wouldn't recoil in horror, if he had to reveal his nature as a ghost, although that was asking the impossible, given the cursed nature of akhs. "We're heading for the family tombs, to a cave in the rock formations close to the valley where the estate's dead sleep."

He felt a tremor run through her body at his words, but Neithamun didn't say anything, merely nodded her acceptance of the destination. Retrieving his pack from the ground, he offered her half of the loaf of bread, sharing his breakfast as they hiked. While mindful of her shorter stride, he kept a brisk pace on the ancient trail to the west.

"What would you think about promoting Mentu?" Neithamun asked, her voice matter of fact, as if she wasn't in the middle of an unprecedented trek to the tombs and unknown revelations. She took a bite of the bread and chewed before continuing her line of thought. "To work with you and Amethu, learning the estate's business? He's bright—do you think he's too old to become to be a scribe? I taught him a few things, the merest beginning, but he catches on fast."

"An excellent idea." Pleasure over her new attitude in allowing herself to think beyond Settlement Day warmed his heart. "He should be able to achieve proficiency in hieroglyphics and math if he applies himself. Does he wish for such advancement?"

"He came to me, asking to learn, last summer when the tomb-robbing headman died. But we were too mired in problems barely keeping the estate from being forfeit; I had little time to teach him anything." Neithamun smiled ruefully, lips barely curved. "It seemed easier to me to do all the jobs myself. But now I know my plan was flawed and short-sighted."

"Don't reproach yourself. You've done an amazing job with few resources." He passed her the waterskin. "Who would become chief herdsman then?"

"Actually, I want to promote his eldest sister." Before he could say anything, she rushed on with her arguments. "I know it's highly unusual to have a female in charge of the cattle, but she has a way with them—with all the animals on the estate." Neithamun gave him a small poke in the ribs. "Even your least favorite, the donkey, is like a lamb at her bidding."

He chuckled. His dislike for the donkey wasn't any secret. If he'd been staying long term at Heron Marsh, he'd have been acquiring horses and repairing the chariot. "I've seen his sister work her magic on the beast. Nothing about Heron Marsh is ordinary, beginning with the remarkable lady who owns the estate." To accompany the compliment, he bowed his head to her before saying, "If the girl's the best suited to the task, promote her."

Neithamun blushed a bit at his compliment, but she moved on to another issue regarding estate management. He realized she was trying to keep his mind off whatever awaited them in the cave, and warmth flooded his heart anew because this woman cared so much for him. *If I end up condemned to roam the wastes for all time, at least I'll carry the memories of Neithamun's love as armor against the despair.*

They passed the remainder of the trail immersed in discussions of the estate and improvements or changes Neithamun wished to make. She only fell silent as she rounded the final curve and faced the family's valley of tombs shimmering in the heat.

"You don't have to go on. We can find a patch of shade and you can wait for me," he offered, as her steps slowed. "Having you close will be blessing enough. I can ask no more."

Raising her hair off her neck for a moment as a breeze wafted past them, she shook her head. "I said I'd go the entire distance with you, and so I shall. Tell me exactly what we face."

"I'm not sure. I've never been to this cave before. The Great Ones didn't warn me of any perils beyond the pain of memory regained."

She gave him an odd look, but asked no more questions. A few moments later, he stood at the entrance to the cave Ma'at had shown him. Periseneb took the short torch from his pack and lit it by striking sparks with two rocks. He considered offering Neithamun a final chance to remain outside, but one glance at the determined set of her shoulders, her tightly compressed lips and her furrowed brow told him there was no way to dissuade her from accompanying him every step of the way.

Lifting the torch, he marched inside, Neithamun following close behind. The first grisly discovery was only a few feet past the cave's entrance.

A body was sprawled on the rocky floor, partly obscured by a rotting kilt and cloak. Periseneb stopped, nausea sweeping over him. With little more than leathery skin covering bones, the man had been mummified by the desert heat. Casualties in battle were one thing, and he didn't normally fear the dead, but this corpse was part of an unearthly event, tainted by curses and magic.

Neithamun gasped, hiding her face against his chest. He embraced her with his free arm and buried his face in her hair for a moment, breathing deeply of her perfume. Her scent steadied him.

"Are you all right?" he asked her eventually. "There's nothing here to harm you. This is an old tragedy."

She nodded and stepped away as he stuck the torch in a crevice in the rock wall and squatted by the skeleton curled on the floor. To his amazement, this set of bones covered by leathery skin wasn't his. The body was arched, the head thrown back, mouth open in a grotesque silent scream. This man had died in agony. A wineskin lay nearby, uncorked and covered in dust, its contents long ago dissipated. "She poisoned him," he said, understanding dawning. "Probably offered him a final, celebratory drink when their ghastly task here was done. She never meant to let him take his gold and flee." He shivered as he realized the full enormity of Sitre's capacity for evil, plotting two cold blooded deaths in one night.

"What are you talking about? Who is this? And who is the woman you speak of?" Neithamun's voice trembled. She took several steps toward the cave's entrance, glancing longingly at the bright sunshine beyond. "This body must have been here for a long time—how can you know anything about the circumstances?"

"I have to go further," he said, ignoring her questions. So close to what he sought, it was as if he was bound with ropes, inexorably tugged by a captor to his doom. No retreat for him. Grabbing the torch, not looking to see if she followed, he advanced deeper into the cave.

A little patter of rushing footsteps and Neithamun grabbed his tunic in her fist, halting him in midstep. "Don't you dare leave me alone in here." Her voice trembled, but the command was clear.

He paused. "No, I promise you."

Voice sharper than any tone she usually employed with him, she said, "Do you promise me answers as well?"

He rolled his shoulders, being careful to keep the torch well above his head. "I swear by the Great One Ma'at to answer all your questions, once I see what lies beyond."

"All right. Let's get this over with." Releasing the fabric, she gave him a tiny push.

As Periseneb stepped cautiously into the cavern's next open space, he found a second skeleton just beyond the threshold, lying as if casually dumped there. He'd no doubt that was the case. A rotting blue cloak lay partially under the bones. This deep in the cave, no mummification had occurred and there was nothing left of the man he'd been except rags covering a skeleton. *Only bones, thank the gods. What man wants to look upon his own face in death?* Acid in his throat, he planted the torch in the soft soil, braced securely against a rock. Fighting a reluctance to go any further, he gritted his teeth and walked to the bones. He knelt beside the skeleton, anger and unbearable sadness choking him, making his heart stutter in his chest. Without warning, pain knifed through his side where Sitre had stabbed him, the hot sensation surrounding his heart in a web of agony. Clenched fist pressed to his chest, he crumpled to his knees, then onto his side, caught in the force of the memories he'd so recently reacquired. Reality and history fought a battle inside his mind and heart, yielding physical pain at the site of the old, mortal wounds.

With a little cry, Neithamun rushed to his side, calling his name. "What is it? What's happening?" She held him close, stroking his back, her cheek resting on his hair.

He grabbed her arm and hung on tight, unable to speak past the agony and confusion. Visions of the stabbing were like lightning in his mind, harsher than any headache he'd ever felt. Despite the goddess herself having sent him here, it was wrong for a man to find his own corpse.

"An old tragedy, you said, nothing to harm us now," she crooned, voice nearly singsong. "Let the pain go, don't give in. I'm here, let me help."

He closed his eyes, took a deep breath, and concentrated on her voice. He summoned sweet memories of Neithamun and him together, walking the estate, working side-by-side, playing senet…lying in her bed after a night of tender lovemaking. She was right, *this* was his reality now, even if only for thirty precious days. Not Sitre, not the cruel past. Ma'at had given him one chance to bring balance, which was why he was here, in this cursed cave today. He could handle the task—he *had* to. Teeth clenched, he willed his tense muscles to unlock, breathing as deeply as he could manage in order to rise above the pain. He grasped at the shreds of a soldier's discipline to bring his mind and body under his control. There was much yet to be done.

Neithamun's words trailed off as he stirred in her embrace. She rubbed his back one last time. "Are you all right now?" Her voice was a whisper. She kissed his cheek. "Please, say something, I'm frightened for you."

Not for herself, never for herself. Rising to a seated position, he pulled her to him for a moment, kissing her as he held her tight. "You gave me an anchor to cling to, a way to move past the memory. The pain has receded."

"I don't understand any of this, but I'm glad you're feeling better," she said, as he dusted himself off.

He straightened his tunic and the torchlight gleamed on his badge.

Her breath caught in her throat as she looked from him to the skeleton. She reached out to the Pharaoh's badge, still attached to crumbling leather lying across the rib cage of the man on the floor. Not quite touching the emblem, she stared from it to the one on his chest. "The same, it has the same rendition of Horus, with the wedjat eye above." Fingers at her lips as if to silence herself, she whispered, "And the same dent on the left corner."

"Yes, where the badge once deflected a Hyksos sword." He clenched his fist around the falcon on his own chest, needing to anchor himself in the current time, not the past. Acid fears burned through his mind. Would he now dissolve in the presence of his bones, become the ghost he truly was? Could he somehow become a menace to Neithamun? Panic at the possibilities made his voice a harsh croak. "You—you should go now and leave me to finish this."

"I'm not going anywhere, stop trying to talk me into abandoning you. Who is this?" She swung him to face her. "It's you, isn't it? Somehow, this body, it's you. That's how you knew it—he—was here."

"The goddess Ma'at showed me the location last night, but yes, these sad remains are mine." Resigned, arms at his side, he waited for her to recoil in horror. "I'm an *akh*, a ghost, given temporary life by the Great One."

Eyes widening, she took an involuntary step in retreat, a gasp escaping her lips. Then, she shook her head, as if to refute what he'd said. Eyes narrowed, she came to him and stroked his cheek with one hand. Although she trembled, her voice was calm. "I see a man before me, not an akh." She moved her hand to rest in the middle of his chest. "I feel flesh and blood and a beating heart, not the acid form of a wraith." Swallowing hard, she blinked and met his gaze again. When she spoke, her tone was like a student, reasoning through a problem. "One returned to the Black Lands by Ma'at, to serve her, can only be honored, not despised. Whatever you are, whoever you are, you've done me no harm, and sought only to bring good to Heron Marsh." A tremulous smile flickered on her lips. "I could never fear the man I love."

Heart thumping in his chest, he captured her hand and kissed the soft palm. "You bless me with your trust."

Neithamun shifted her position and bent over to pull something out from under her sandal. A cracked and chipped blue faience pendant in the shape of a lotus dangled from a blackened silver chain.

Periseneb touched the necklace with one finger. "I didn't want to believe the truth, didn't remember it until Ma'at and Sefkhet permitted access to my memories, but she betrayed me."

"She?" Forehead wrinkled in confusion, Neithamun stared at the pendant. "A goddess betrayed you?"

He shook his head. *Time for truths, let the counting sticks fall where they may.* "Sitre of Heron Marsh. Your great great aunt." Despite the gasp of astonishment from Neithamun, he continued, determined now to lay out the entire truth for her to pass her own judgment on him. "We were lovers. I gave her this pendant when I departed to enlist in Pharaoh Khakaure Senusret's army. Buying it took all the deben I'd accumulated, and the trinket didn't begin to compare to the least of the jewels in her possession." He laughed a little. "Being a foolish youth, I ran away to make my fortune and win a title and great honors in battle, so she and I could be together openly. I hoped to carve a glorious path in the service of my Pharaoh. Impress her father and claim her hand—to make myself a worthy suitor for the heiress of Heron Marsh, through wealth if not birth."

Neithamun bit her lip. She'd dropped the pendant, wiping her fingers on her skirt. Folding her hands, she said, "If she was the daughter of the house, who were you?"

Teeth clenched, he said, "The overseer's son. Two hundred years ago. If you go back far enough in the records, you can see the day I was born."

Eyebrows raised, she nodded as if reaching some conclusion. "Is the notation of your birth what you were searching for, when I first found you in the library?"

He nodded. "Seeing my name written in the scrolls was an anchor for me in the mad reality of walking the estate as a ghost. I did exist, I was a man, even though it was centuries ago." Reaching for her hand, he said, "I never lied to you or claimed anything other than a common birth."

"I never thought you'd lied to me. Your words always have the ring of truth." Squeezing his hand, she glanced at the dripping cave walls. "There must be more to this tale—I need to hear all of it." With a shiver, Neithamun focused on his face.

"Although this isn't a pleasant spot to talk of your history, I think we must. So, you loved this girl? This ancestress of mine?" Her tone was sad, her eyes hooded.

He shook his head. "No."

She tried to reclaim her hand, her voice harsh. "But, you just said—"

"Let me explain?" Kissing her palm for a moment, he kept possession of her fingers, the touch holding the painful past at bay. "When I grew up at Heron Marsh, I fell under Sitre's spell, as did many others. I was besotted, flattered she chose me." He passed his free hand over his eyes. *I need a drink.* "I was too stupid to realize I was merely the latest in her string of lovers. The idea of winning her was a convenient excuse to fuel my ambitions, gave me the impetus to abandon my home and break my father's heart. But once I was away from here, out in the wider world, free of her influence, I realized I didn't love Sitre. I had friends in the army who were married, and when I spent time in their homes, I saw what love between a man and woman should be. Could be." He took a deep breath, hoping Neithamun heard the truth in his voice. "Yet, I prided myself on my honor, and I'd made promises to Sitre I intended to keep, if she relied upon them. If she... loved me. After a number of years, I sent word to her secretly to tell her I was coming home, and we should talk privately before I met her father." He looked at the pendant, which glowed with an unpleasant blue glare on the cave floor. "In her reply, she begged me to meet her at the pond, in the glade of trees. It was... special to us at one time."

"The pond?" Neithamun's voice was barely a whisper, touched with pain. "No wonder you wouldn't linger there with me."

Saddened to be causing her discomfort, he rushed his next words. "What my heart holds in regard for you is nothing like the emotions she roused." He brushed her cheek with the back of his hand. "I love you."

Eyes closed, brow furrowed, she made a circular motion with her hand. "We can talk about our emotions later. Go on. What happened when you arrived at Heron Marsh?"

"I was hoping she'd found someone else. I wanted freedom from my foolish oath, the ability to live my own life, and find a true love."

Eyes wide open now, Neithamun pointed at the broken pendant. "But you said earlier that she—and that man in entrance, I gather—killed you. Why not tell you she'd changed her mind?"

"She was probably afraid I'd make trouble for her, maybe kill Haqaptah when I found out she'd married him. He was an arrogant hyena, a bully when we were children. Overly conscious of his lofty rank and my lowly one. Insufferable as a youth. She was well aware I hated him, and for good reason." Periseneb rubbed his jaw, remembering some of the more unpleasant incidents, when he'd been forced by circumstance of birth to give way to the young noble.

Recoiling, Neithamun gasped. "Haqaptah?" The name echoed in the cavern, as if a chorus was calling the man.

"The one of my time. I was a hot headed youth, overly reliant on brute strength before the army taught me more effective skills." He wasn't enjoying the memory of himself as a feckless boy. "Or she may have worried I'd create a sandstorm of gossip, sully her name in my anger, make her a laughingstock by openly revealing she'd bedded the servants. I'm sure her proclivities were well known, yet never spoken of. My announcing it publicly would have subjected her to the scorn of all the local nobility. She couldn't bear to be laughed at. Even as a child, the idea of being a source of amusement for someone would send her into a tantrum. No doubt she was sure I was still besotted with her. When all I truly desired was freedom from the foolish promises I'd given as a lovesick boy." Periseneb clenched his fists. "I remember now, all too clearly, how she struck the first blow herself, a knife in the ribs. As I lay dying, she and her henchman were laughing about what a poor soldier I must have been, to be taken so unawares. I was a fool to have trusted her."

Neithamun laid a hand over his fist. "I'm sorry."

He turned his hand to close his fingers over hers, squeezing gently. "I didn't love her. I realized the bitter truth soon enough after leaving home. I didn't even know who she was under the surface beauty. As a boy, I made her a fantasy from a scribe's tale. And she was a real woman." He swallowed hard, vivid memories flooding his mind. "I died cursing her name."

Neithamun stiffened, but didn't withdraw her hand. "A curse?"

He hastened to explain. "Not a curse on Heron Marsh, I'd never commit such a foul act. This is my home. I cursed her, though. With my dying words, I condemned her, said Ammit would eat her heart at the Judging."

Looking at the broken necklace with disgust, Neithamun said, "Which explains why she was so terrified of dying, as the family legends tell. She knew her own guilt."

He nodded. "I pray to the Great Ones my black words didn't affect Heron Marsh itself. But the curse I uttered may have. You and others have told me the pond dried up about two hundred years ago. She killed me there. I've come to believe my murder might be part of why Ma'at chose me to come and right the wrongs."

"Take no blame onto yourself. I think Sitre's evil deeds affected the land, not your words." Neithamun's voice was strong, sure.

He'd failed to consider that possibility.

She was asking more clarifying questions. "And so she and her henchman brought you here? Left you in this cave?"

He nodded. "For two-hundred years, I've been wandering in the outer dark as a shade. No Afterlife for me."

In the torchlight, he saw tears shining in Neithamun's eyes. Voice soft, she said, "We'll perform the rituals, say the spells from the Book of the Dead. I'll have my most trusted servants inter him—you—in the family crypt. If my proposal meets with your approval?"

"Once, your plan would have been my fondest dream, to free me from the gray wastes, to allow my heart to be judged." He looked at the small cave. "I don't know, I honestly don't. Lady Ma'at promised me passage to the Afterlife if I set things right, if I solved the problems. Perhaps it's best to leave things hidden in this cave, undisturbed, and wait for the goddess's judgment."

She shook her head violently. "No, now we're talking about my family's honor. We betrayed you, we owe it to you to make amends." She laughed bitterly. "Although, we'd better do it fast, since Haqaptah will own my family's estate lock, stock, and burial grounds in a few days' time."

"No, he won't. That's why I asked Ma'at to help me find this place." Releasing her hand, Periseneb stood and walked to the torch.

"What do you mean?"

He was searching the cave, torch in hand. "Ah, good, my satchel." He hefted a battered leather sack and brought it to Neithamun. "I was hoping she'd thrown my possessions in here as well, without searching through them. After all, I was only a poor soldier, as far as Sitre knew, and she was probably in a hurry on the night she killed me. I'm sure she wanted to get as far away from the evidence of the crime as possible. Nothing I owned would have been of value to her, or so she'd have believed." He tried to unfasten the rotting drawstring, but the stitching in the satchel's seams fell apart in his hands, spilling the crumbling fabric of his spare garments onto the stone floor, along with several small scrolls, a tablet, and a pouch that thudded dully as it hit the ground. Casting aside the remnants of the satchel, he bent to retrieve the latter, weighing its satisfying bulk for a moment before joining Neithamun. "Hold out your hands."

Swiping her palms on her skirt, she obliged. He upended the small bag and shiny gold objects poured in a flood, overflowing her cupped hands. Her reaction was as dramatic as he'd hoped. Gasping, she caught the treasure, examining the gleaming prizes in the torchlight. Eyes opened wide, she stared at him. "You have *two* necklaces of honor?" Moving to sit cross legged, Neithamun untangled the heavy strands and spread the six fly-shaped pendants out on her lap.

He nodded. "And, ironically, I bear the title of *amkhu*."

"One to be buried at Pharaoh's expense?" Neithamun's eyebrows rose practically to her hairline at the news. "You certainly did come home with enough rank to marry the heiress and take your place at her side. What service did you render your Pharaoh to garner such high honors?"

"It's a long story, one I'd rather not linger in this dank cave to recite. Briefly, I saved the life of my Pharaoh's favorite son in battle, which is what this one is for." He touched one finger to the closest strand of gold. "The second is for distinguished service in the final skirmishes we fought against the Hyksos in my time. I commanded a unit of chariots—the details don't matter now. Although, clearly, we didn't do enough, since your Pharaoh has only recently beaten them from the Black Lands with much difficulty."

She wound the necklaces into a fat coil and tried to hand them to him, but he fended her off. "No. These are for you now, to pay the Heron Marsh debts and taxes."

Shaking her head emphatically, she said, "I can't accept them—the gold belongs to you. The signs of your valor should be buried with—with your bones, to bring you honor in the Afterlife as well."

Overcome by emotion, Periseneb stalked away for a moment. "I'd rather consign them to the Lake of Fire, if you won't accept them." Pacing to where she sat, he said, "Ma'at sent me here to address wrongs, to put matters in balance, as she would say. This is the only way I know how. I've no living relatives, my father died with no heirs. Heron Marsh was *everything* to him."

"And to you?" Voice soft, she said, "I understand so many things now."

Coming to her, he raised her to her feet with his free hand, heedless of the golden necklaces tumbling onto the ground. Holding her tightly by the elbow, he said, "You're all my heart desired and foolishly imagined for a time I'd found with Sitre, before her true nature became clear. She was a mirage, a dangerous chimera. You're the woman I love. If I were free of obligation to Ma'at, my ka would belong to you." Smoothing the hair away from her face, he kissed her forehead. "Let me give you this gift to ensure your future, since I can't be here with you, much as I wish for such a fate."

Mouth pursed, she glanced sideways at him. "To save the estate."

"To save *you*, to ensure you a future of choices. To keep you from ever becoming subject to the likes of Haqaptah or even Userkaf." He was frustrated that she didn't understand his true motivation. The estate was nothing to him without Neithamun.

She couldn't take any more of this. Her mind was reeling at the things Periseneb had shared with her, the idea he was an akh, the ka of a man from two hundred years ago. She didn't know if that bothered her more, or the jealousy over his relationship with her ancestor. She shifted her stance to break free of his hold on her, and he released his grip. The desire to be outside, in the fresh air, was a screaming need in her mind. She glanced at the bones by her feet and her only emotion was sorrow for the life cut short. It was nearly impossible to connect the flesh and blood man in front of her—her lover—with the skeleton. If not for the matching badges, she'd be able to deny the truth. Her throat was dry, but she choked out a question. "Is there anything else we need to do here today, or can we go now?"

He retrieved the two necklaces and scooped up the scrolls and tablet. "Do you see where the bag for these fell? I don't think we should carry gold openly into the house, loyal as your people may be."

Fetching the small sack, she held it open while he awkwardly dropped the strands and the heavy pendants into it, along with the few other items he cared to keep. "We can carry this in your satchel." She paused.

"What?" He was already at the torch, ready to leave.

"Should we at least cover the body? With the remnants of the cloak perhaps?"

Periseneb shook his head, "I think it's best we leave the bones as we found them. The fabric is rotted anyway." Clasping her wrist, he encouraged her to move to the threshold of the chamber.

Compelled to take one more look, she hesitated before stepping into the outer cave. Pulling her hand free from his, she glanced over her shoulder. A scream ripped from her. "The corpse—it's on fire!"

Periseneb shouldered past her and, together, they stared for a moment. The bones and remnants of clothing were engulfed in a rapidly growing blaze, burning soundlessly, in flames of green and orange, golden sparks flying from the conflagration to ignite new fires, despite the absence of conventional fuel.

"How can this be?" she said. A spark landed on her skirt and hastily she beat the tiny pulse of flame out with her hand.

"Flame from the Lake of Fire—run!" Periseneb grabbed her and fled through the narrow passageway, not pausing in the larger outer chamber. Neithamun felt heat at her back as the conflagration pursued them. Periseneb cast aside the torch, scooped her into his arms and sprinted toward the daylight. A mighty gust of scorching wind enveloped them, hurling both outside, to land in a tangle of arms and legs. Dazed by the impact of falling, breath knocked from her lungs, she lay still until he dragged her further from the mouth of the cave. A tongue of the uncanny green flame expanded into the daylight close on their heels, before shrinking inside the cavern. She could see the dancing fire filling the room where she'd been moments before. The deadly play of colors and golden sparks was fascinating, caught the eyes, and captivated.

"We need to get further away," he insisted, trying to help her to her feet.

The ground was quivering underfoot and she heard an ominous rumbling, which broke her concentration on the magical flames. Stumbling, she ran with Periseneb as the ground trembled beneath her sandals until she was some cubits down the trail, where he stopped. Mouth agape in terror and awe, she watched as a landslide blocked the mouth of the cavern under a massive pile of boulders. The dust cloud was shot through with the golden sparks for a moment.

"What happened?" She coughed and he handed her the waterskin.

"I think the gods have no desire for you to provide me with an honorable burial," he said. "I have to win my entry to the Afterlife by fulfilling the conditions Ma'at laid down and in no other manner. So, the Great Ones summoned the Lake of Fire to the cave."

A shiver worked its way through her body. "We could have died in there and no one would know."

He smiled at her, although it seemed he had to work hard to be cheerful. "No, it was a warning only. If the Great Ones had wanted us dead, we would be."

"How can you be so calm? Why aren't you as angry as I am?"

"Angry?" Periseneb's eyebrows lifted, as if her emotion was unwarranted.

Neithamun gestured at the landslide, from which dust continued to rise. "You've been denied an honorable burial. The gods are leaving you no choice but to complete whatever tasks they set if you want to attain the Afterlife." She felt tears burning in her eyes. Brushing a hand across her face, she said, "I could have at least made the situation better for you with the rituals, made sure you had a path."

He took her by the elbow and drew her further away from the cave. "I made a bargain with Ma'at, and I have to keep it. I appreciate what you offered to do for me, but it's outside the boundaries the goddess set."

"Harsh. She sends you back to life with no instructions, no mercy—"

He leaned closer. Voice lowered, he said, "It may well not have been Ma'at who destroyed the bodies and the cave. When we were at Kingfisher, I couldn't stay at the ceremony beside the Nile. I think perhaps Isis and maybe others among the Great Ones disagree with the method Ma'at has chosen to balance the scales. Osiris gave my Great One permission to strike this bargain with me, but I think Isis was displeased to have the natural order of death and judging upset."

She regarded him with shock, speechless. *Disagreements between the gods? His ka treads a dangerous path at Ma'at's bidding. How can he be so calm?*

He tugged her gently along the trail. "I got what I came for. And I can't ever thank you enough for coming with me. Finding my own bones was harder to bear than I expected. The memories were overwhelming."

Neithamun was far from feeling so resigned to the situation, but bit her lip and didn't argue. She walked beside him in silence. Her thoughts were whirling with all he'd revealed about who he was. Glancing at him from under her lashes, she found it impossible to believe he was anything but a man. Yes, she'd seen his skeleton for herself, heard the story, but this person walking beside her, this man she loved with all her heart, couldn't be a ghost. Couldn't be fated to leave her in a few days. As they continued their journey to the house, her mind was occupied by the woman who'd betrayed Periseneb, so long ago. *What did she look like? Have I ever seen a portrait of her in the house?* She took a breath, parted her lips to speak, and then shook her head, angry at herself. *I can't be jealous of someone who had his heart two hundred years ago. He's mine now.* Odd to think she'd never have met Periseneb if Sitre had been true to him, or even reasonable in her dealings.

As if she'd spoken out loud, Periseneb squeezed her hand, looking at her from his greater height. "Are you doing all right? Do you want to stop and rest, have some water?"

Her throat was parched, so she nodded and he led her from the path to sit in the shade of a wizened tamarisk tree. After she slaked her thirst, she handed the waterskin to him and asked, "Why do the gods care if Heron Marsh remains in my hands? How can all this fuss over one small estate in a rural nome be worth a man's ka? How can it warrant disagreements between Great Ones?"

"I think there's more at stake, something to do with Haqaptah and his grander plans, not just what he wants to do with Heron Marsh. There might even be Hyksos' involvement. Ma'at mentioned the Hyksos god one of the times I encountered her." Periseneb's brow was furrowed in a frown as he restored the water to his pack.

Anger flared anew in her heart as she said, "What are you expected to do about the Hyksos? Surely solving potential invasion by an enemy horde is beyond one man's abilities."

"Not a man, a ghost," he answered, voice grim. "But I've no answer for you. I've been trying to figure that part of the puzzle out myself. I'm running out of time, and the only avenue I see is to kill him."

"In cold blood? Where's the honor and balance in such an act? I loathe the man, distant relative or not, but so far he's done nothing to deserve death."

"Exactly." He rubbed his chest as if his heart hurt. "I can't believe Ma'at wants me to become a killer. I slaughtered the enemy in battle—"

"Which is required," she said.

"But the situation is hardly the same. The Hyksos were trying to kill me as well. The fights were fair."

As they resumed walking, she asked, "What's the Afterlife like? Is it as beautiful as the priests and the Book of the Dead say?"

He shot her a sideways glance. "I've never seen it, remember? I was condemned to roam the gray wastes. And those are the home of nightmares—demons, giant snakes, and creatures I've no name for."

She shivered, despite the heat of the day.

When she got to the vicinity of the house, Neithamun was conscious of people staring at them. A few called greetings, which Periseneb answered. Menwe met them at the top of the stairs. "Are you all right?" Hands on her hips, she scrutinized Neithamun. "You look ill, my lady."

She didn't pause, but walked past her maid. "I'm going to my chambers and I'm not to be disturbed."

Menwe gave her an odd look, probably since it was early afternoon and the daily list of outstanding tasks remained long, but said nothing.

Periseneb followed her down the hall.

"Close the door," she said, as he entered her bedroom in her wake. As she heard the portal slide shut, she crossed the chamber to where her father's strongbox waited in the far corner and knelt to open it. Gaily decorated with paintings of life along the Nile, the box appeared to be all of one piece, until examined more closely.

"I remember this." Periseneb squatted next to her, setting the satchel on the floor. "It used to be in the master's chambers."

"Has it been at the house so long? I only knew the box was my grandfather's and then my father's. I had it moved in here when my father died and I became lady of the estate."

He laughed. "I remember when it was built. Kawab, the woodworker, used to make small puzzle boxes in his spare time and the Lord of Heron Marsh commissioned him to create this large one for treasure keeping. I helped carry the box in there the day it was done. I wasn't allowed to stay while treasure was placed inside, but Kawab had already showed me the trick." Reaching past her, he depressed the carving of a fat Nile perch swimming in a school of its identical fellows along the painted Nile bordering the wooden chest. He slid a red snake to the right and glanced at her, one eyebrow raised.

Shivering a bit with the renewed realization Periseneb truly was from an earlier time, Neithamun raised the leftmost blue lotus away from the painted river's surface and spun the wooden flower to the left, a subtle clicking noise filling the air. When the bloom would spin no more, a heron flying high above the peaceful river scene popped out from the surface, balanced on a hidden lever. Periseneb pushed the heron into place and the lid of the box, painted in dark blue with golden stars, silently rose, revealing the gilded, nearly empty interior.

"I wish I had more to give," Periseneb remarked, as he unwrapped the necklaces of valor. "But this should suffice to pay the debts and taxes, and give you a hoard of gold for next year's unknowns."

Heart aching at the idea of a coming year without Periseneb at her side, she accepted the precious golden symbols from his hands and set them into the box, where the fat flies and heavy links gleamed as if molded from liquid gold today instead of centuries past.

"Can you store these as well?" He handed her the various other crumbling scrolls and tablets he'd stored in his pack two hundred years ago. "For safekeeping?"

"Of course. What documents have you here? Your writ of *amkhu?*" She glimpsed a pharaoh's cartouche stamped in red wax on more than one item, but made no attempt to pry by unrolling the papyrus further. Tucking the items next to the golden flies resting on their coiled chains, she depressed the star, which closed the box tight and spun the diadem on Nuit's necklace to set the lock.

"And some other items." He rolled the bag into a ball of fabric and stood, his stance awkward. He shot her an unreadable look. "A few hours of daylight left. I'd better go see what Amethu has the workers doing and contribute to the effort."

She rose, catching his hand and taking the bag away, to drop it on the floor. "No. Please stay." She led him unresisting across the chamber to her bed, where she twined her arms round his neck and, rising on tiptoe, kissed him firmly on the lips. As his arms went around her and he adjusted his hold, she licked her tongue along the seam of his lips, pushing ever so slightly. With an indrawn breath, Periseneb gave her the access she was seeking. She let her tongue explore the warmth of his mouth, twining with his tongue. Grinding her hips against him, she felt his cock rise, pressing hard against her. Still kissing him, she lowered one hand to grasp his manhood through the fabric of the kilt, stroking from root to tip as best she could.

Firmly, Periseneb broke off the kiss, although he didn't move to end the embrace, nuzzling her neck. "What are we doing?" His words whispered next to her ear before he kissed his way along her neck and shoulder.

"You're needed here, in this room," she said. "*I* need you. The estate can take care of itself for the rest of the day." Determined not to cry, trying to focus on the pleasure of the intimacy she sought, she fisted her hands on the hem of his tunic and dragged the garment upward, revealing the hard muscles of his taut abdomen. "I'm claiming you—you're mine, not Sitre's, not Ma'at's. Mine," she repeated.

Obediently, he raised his arms to allow her to remove his shirt, then stood, waiting to see what she'd do next. "Always yours, sweetheart. My heart never truly belonged to any other woman. But the Great One commands me to serve—there's no denying her."

Casting aside the tunic, Neithamun stroked her hand over his chest, lingering on the scars, then touching a fingertip to the tattoo on his shoulder. "Weren't there four feathers?"

"I've used two to request help from the Great One Ma'at."

She pressed a kiss to his skin. "Is that how the magic works?"

"For me, yes."

"She branded you?" The idea sat heavy on Neithamun's heart. *Yet another claim on him, superseding mine.*

"I'm her warrior," was his simple answer. "There's nothing you or I can do about that fact. I'm here by the grace of Ma'at." He lowered his head, seeking her lips. They kissed for a long moment, arms wrapped tightly around each other, the heat of his arousal pressing into her belly. He pulled away slightly. "I'd never have met you if not for Ma'at."

"I'll think of the tattoo as a badge of honor," she said. "Honor is the backbone of your character."

"I'm a man. Well, the re-embodiment of a man." He ran his hands over her breasts, pushing them together, gently massaging the nipples through the cotton dress. "And my heart and ka belong to you now."

"Good," she said, surprising herself with the ferocity in her voice. "It's only the two of us in this room, no gods, no curses, and no complications of any kind." She tilted her head to stare into his eyes, daring him to disagree.

"As it should be," he agreed.

Neithamun slid her hand over his abdomen, past the waistband of his kilt and loincloth, caging his cock with her fingers. Silky soft skin over a hard shaft, his manhood throbbed at her touch. She felt an answering wave of sensation deep within herself. Periseneb stood still while she stroked the length of him and fondled his balls for a moment. Then she withdrew her hand to work on the belt at his waist, playfully slapping his hands away when he tried to help. A moment later, he stood naked before her save for his sandals, which he kicked off before reaching to enfold her in his arms.

Shaking her head, she avoided his embrace, stepping away. One at a time, she removed her sandals and then shimmied out of the dress, dropping the garment to the floor in a heap.

"Beautiful," he said, swallowing hard.

She pushed him to sit on the edge of the bed and as the leather webbing adjusted to his weight, she urged him to the center of the mattress. Already aroused, Neithamun straddled him, guiding his cock into herself with one hand as she lowered herself to sit astride his loins. Holding her firmly by the waist, Periseneb closed his eyes and thrust upward again and again as she rode with his passion. Neithamun watched his face as she clenched her inner muscles to massage his girth. She stroked his well-muscled abdomen before teasing his nipples lightly with her fingernails. Passion mounting, she basked in the intense expression he wore as he strove to please them both.

Suddenly, Periseneb rolled her over, to lie under him, his lips capturing hers, tongue plundering her mouth as she climaxed in a wave of delight, followed a heartbeat later by his release. Neithamun locked her legs around him, driving his cock as deep inside herself as she could and held on while he shuddered and groaned in his pleasure. Her own body rocked with waves of sensation and she tore her lips from his to scream his name as she finished a second time.

"I love you." Periseneb held her close, breathing hard, nuzzling her neck, planting small kisses on her cheeks. "I'm blessed to have the chance to know true love in your arms. The goddesses promised I'd keep the memories of you all my time in the Afterlife, even if I must return to wandering the wastes."

She tucked the cotton sheet closely around herself with one hand. "Will I be able to find you, in the Afterlife?"

He pressed her head to his shoulder, providing her a pillow. With his other arm, he held her close to him, on her side, her legs entwined with his. "I don't know how the Afterlife works inside the duat, beloved, never having set foot there as yet. Surely, if the Great Ones allow me the memories, they'll allow me to find you." He gave her a stern look, eyes narrowed. Shaking a finger, he said, "But not before your appointed time. Swear to me."

"No, I mean in the gray wastes. Would I be able to find you? Is there some landmark we could set, some spot you could wait for me? If—if you fail to please Ma'at?"

He sat upright, eyes wide. "You can't go into the gray wastes. Only the unjudged suffer such a fate."

"I want to be with you." She choked back a sob. "If I'm only to have you for such a short time here, I want to know I can be with you there for all eternity. We can fight demons together."

"I'd never wish such a thing on the woman I loved." He took her by the shoulders. "Swear to me by all the Great Ones, you'll make no effort to avoid your own judgment, no attempt to find my ka if I fail this task." Before she could do more than nod, he crushed her close in a hug. "I shouldn't have told you anything about my fate. My blood runs cold at the idea of you, alone in the wastes."

"Mine runs cold at the idea of us being apart for all time." Stubbornness pushed her to continue the topic. "How am I to bear losing you in a few days, if I don't have the promise we'll be together eventually?"

He twined his fingers in hers and kissed her palm. "I swear, I'll find a way. When I stand before Ma'at for the final time, whether I satisfy her demands or not, I'll press for some promise, some answer for us both." He hesitated. "I could ask Sefkhet to remove your memories of what we meant to each other."

Anger tinged with fright surged through her body. "As well ask her to carve out my heart. I'd always know something, *someone*, was missing. Don't you dare ask her to touch my memories. Swear to me!"

He laid two callused fingers on her lips. "Ssh, don't be alarmed."

Neithamun wasn't to be deterred, pulling his hand away from her face and glaring at him. "Give me your oath you won't ask the goddess for any such thing."

For a heartbeat Periseneb was silent. Jaw set, one muscle throbbing in his cheek, he nodded. "My word as a soldier, then."

She understood his promise was given reluctantly, but he'd honor it. She relaxed against him, caressing his cock with one hand. "Thank you."

He grunted. "I only hope neither of us will regret the decision."

Twined together, each was silent for a few moments. Then, Periseneb said, "You know, when I was under Sefkhet's spell, reliving the hour of my death, something was odd."

Neithamun craved every nugget of information about her beloved, no matter how small. "Tell me."

"When Sitre came to me at the pond, she was her usual seductive self. I…I didn't remember you—"

"Because we hadn't met. I hadn't even been born, my parents hadn't even been born," she said. She ran her hand through her tousled hair. "These concepts are so strange. My head aches trying to sort the events into some sensible tale. I can hardly fault you for not having a memory of me two hundred years ago."

He nodded. "But there was something. I knew I loved another Heron Marsh woman, and though Sitre laid her hands on me, I wasn't tempted by her." He stared into Neithamun's eyes. "This is important, beloved. Even then, even under the spell of the Great Ones, I felt loyalty to you on the deepest levels of my heart. You were there for me."

Neithamun gave voice to what her heart was telling her with each beat. "My fate is joined with yours now, surely the goddess will recognize the truth of it."

"She does."

His voice sounded so positive. Seeking more reassurance, she asked, "How do you know?"

"Before Ma'at and Sefkhet returned my memories last night, there was a kind of judging. Not of my heart," he said hastily, "But the Great One linked you and me and weighed us together in her golden scale."

"I don't understand."

"And I can't explain any better, but we were there together, on her game board." Periseneb chuckled. "Even the Great Ones play senet."

"I don't wish to be anyone's pawn."

In the morning, there was a soft knock at the door and Menwe's voice came through the thin panel. "My lady? I'm sorry to intrude, but we have guests arriving."

Periseneb and Neithamun exchanged surprised glances. He left the bed, scooping up his clothes, and dressing hastily. Neithamun wrapped herself in the sheet and padded to the door, opening it a crack. "Visitors?" Dread crept through her mind with cold tentacles. Could Userkaf be coming to make his case to her again? Who else would visit Heron Marsh for any reason?

Menwe's face was flushed and her eyes sparkled with excitement. "Amethu's man posted at the estate boundary ran all this way to report a priestly delegation is making their way to Heron Marsh."

"Priests?" She looked at Periseneb. "Maybe the High Priest of Amun has changed his mind."

He shrugged. "We'll soon find out." Striding past her, he gave her a gentle swat on the rear. "You'd better put on something more formal than a sheet, beloved." Kissing her cheek, he brushed past Menwe and was gone.

Menwe leaned closer. "Are you all right, my lady?"

"Yes, of course. Come help me get dressed. I'd better have the good wig and makeup if we're going to host exalted personages. If the guests were crossing the estate boundary, we haven't much time."

The maid came into the bedroom, casting a swift glance at the rumpled bed. "I hated to interrupt the pleasant interlude," she said with a giggle. "We were going to bring you breakfast in bed later." She crossed to the baskets and searched for a suitable dress.

Neithamun rinsed her face with water in the basin on the table and patted her skin dry with a length of cotton cloth before swiftly applying her cosmetics. "Time is a precious commodity of which I never have enough," she said over her shoulder. "I'm used to interruptions."

Carrying the dress she'd selected, Menwe joined Neithamun, peering over her shoulder into the mirror. "You—you are happy with him, aren't you? Things are good between you?"

"Why do you ask?" She finished outlining her eyes with the kohl and chose the small bottle of malachite dust next, to add green accents. Fumbling for her favorite makeup brush with the slender, leaf-shaped handle, she worked on her left eyelid.

Menwe pointed at the bed. "I should take the evidence before my eyes as answer, but you seem sad. I apologize for causing an early end to the lovemaking—"

"Stop, please, Menwe." Neithamun dropped the brush and leaned her head against the silver mirror. "I can't cry now," she said with gritted teeth.

Dropping the dress, Menwe hugged Neithamun as she fought to control her breathing. "What is the need for tears, my lady? We've all seen how much he cares for you."

"I can't explain it to you, but Periseneb won't be with me beyond Settlement Day. He loves me—he said so—but he has to leave me then." Hiccupping a bit due to suppressed tears, she held up one hand. "I can't talk about this now. I have to greet our guests properly, whoever may be arriving."

"All right, I won't press you, but at some point I want to hear the whole of this." Menwe moved to retrieve the dress, shaking the folds out with a snap. "How that man could dare to walk away from you—"

Neithamun spun on her heel. "Don't be angry with him—the gods give him no choice. We're caught in something—something even I have trouble believing."

Menwe nodded toward the bedside table where the blue lotus yet bloomed in its vase. "We've all seen the flower, my lady. I think every resident of Heron Marsh has peeked in here at one time or another. The magic gives hope. It's plain unearthly forces are at work here in some fashion." As she assisted Neithamun in donning her dress, the maid continued, voice soft, "We prayed the tale would end with you gaining well-deserved happiness. Not only with the estate saved."

"One can't ask the gods for too much, or your petition is answered with reservations and conditions, I find." Neithamun helped Menwe settle the wig on her head and the two women fussed with refinements for a moment or two. Grasping Menwe's hands in her own, she said, "I'll need you when he leaves, my friend, to help me."

"Anything, you've no need to ask or worry. I'll be here to comfort you."

"I'm so afraid of going on without him, but I must." Neithamun wiped away a tear.

Menwe took the edge of her apron to carefully daub at the green eye shadow, repairing the damage. She handed her mistress the brush with the red ochre for her lips. "Best hurry if you wish to be on the stairs to welcome the guests."

Periseneb emerged onto the steps to find most of the household assembled. Amethu was in charge. "Do we know who's coming?"

His second in command shook his head. "My man said he believes the visitors are the priestess of Isis and her escort."

"Hernebti? I can't imagine why she'd be here." Possibilities ran rampant through his head, with an underpinning thread of concern, lest Neithamun experience jealousy as she had at Kingfisher. *Our time together is so short; I don't want to waste any of it in hurt feelings.*

Sure enough, from the lane leading to the house, he heard trumpets as a procession approached, Hernebti in her elegant litter, surrounded by priests, two priestesses, and a detachment of temple guards.

Neithamun came from the house, striding rapidly to his side and looping her arm through his possessively. "What business can she possibly have with us?" She gave Periseneb a hard stare. "Might this concern what we spoke of earlier today?"

"I don't know," he answered. He leaned closer, his lips close to her ear. "Hernebti suspects something of what you now know from our visit to the cave."

Neithamun's frown was immediate and austere. "How can she possibly—?"

"Apparently, the Great One Isis gave her knowledge. Be assured I've not spoken a word to her about it and I've refused to answer her questions." He squeezed her arm gently. "Only you know my secrets, beloved."

The group came to a halt at the bottom of the stairs. One of the underpriests assisted Hernebti in alighting from her litter as Periseneb and Neithamun descended to meet her.

"Life, prosperity, health to you," Neithamun said. "It's my honor to welcome you to Heron Marsh."

"And my pleasure to be here, although I've come on temple business. I must apologize for arriving with no invitation," the priestess answered. She nodded to Periseneb as he bowed. "Good to see you again, warrior."

"Please, come inside, out of the sun, and have refreshment before we speak of business." Much to Periseneb's relief, Neithamun played the gracious hostess without missing a beat. She and Hernebti ascended the stairs arm in arm, like the best of friends. He and Amethu conferred with the chief underpriest for a few moments, confirming Hernebti's intention to stay the night and journey to Khemjekhu in the morning. Periseneb left his man to deal with Hernebti's guards and servants, while he escorted the party of priests and priestesses inside to join the women.

Neithamun and Hernebti were in the large dining hall, seated at the head of the table. Khensa and her kitchen maids served pitchers of beer and platters of honeyed bread. Bowls of figs, dates, and sweetened nutmeats sat nearby.

"I hope your trip was peaceful?" Neithamun was saying, as the men and women took their places and the maids served beer.

Periseneb tried not to stare as a trio of estate workers brought instruments, arranged themselves in a corner of the room, and played a soft tune. He'd no idea Heron Marsh harbored musicians, but he appreciated whoever had organized the entertainment. As the thought crossed his mind, two of the sturdiest lads from the orchard detail entered the chamber, carrying somewhat moth-eaten ostrich plume fans mounted on ebony staffs. The boys took a spot behind the head table and attempted to create a pleasant breeze for Neithamun and the others. The estate was undeniably threadbare, but at least the proud staff could muster some amenities for unexpected guests.

"A long journey, but thankfully uneventful. I've been sent by the goddess," Hernebti said, picking at the slice of bread. "The Great One Isis desires that the temple acquire a majestic bull for use in processions, and I believe your stock is accounted to be the best in the nome." She paused in the act of raising the bread to her mouth. "Only one, however. I'm sorry to say we can't fully replace the deben I've been told the temple of Amun-Ra ordinarily pays you for three bulls."

Thinking about his gold of valor, now safely lodged in the strong box, Periseneb was undismayed by the smaller purchase Hernebti contemplated. Any extra deben would no doubt come in handy for Neithamun at some point. He was surprised Isis was intervening so directly in Heron Marsh's situation.

"I'll have the chief herdsman bring out our finest animals so you can make your selection," Neithamun was saying. "It'll be an honor to have one of our bulls march in processions for Isis and stand at stud."

The afternoon was passed congenially, as Hernebti and her priests inspected the available bulls and made their selection. Neithamun asked Periseneb to take the deben and lock it in the strong box, after which the best dinner the estate could muster was served. Periseneb tried not to worry overmuch about how deeply the cook must have dipped into the stores to assemble such an elaborate repast, so soon after the cancelled feast for the priests of Amun-Ra. This evening, the estate staff served the dinner, rather than sitting to dine, so the chamber seemed oddly empty to him, with just Hernebti's party, Neithamun, Amethu, and himself.

As the servants removed a rack of gazelle and brought platters of fish, Hernebti said, "I noticed the estate features a family temple. I'd be more than pleased to sing evening services."

Neithamun shot Periseneb a rapid glance, but he kept his face expressionless. "Quite gracious of you," she said. "We've had no formal ceremonies here since my father died. The estate can't afford its own priests currently."

"All the more reason for me to repay your hospitality with a blessing from the goddess." Hernebti took a deep drink from her mug. "The sun will set soon, so we should prepare the temple." She gestured to her priests. "Go, see what's needed for a proper ceremony. I'll join you in a few moments."

"I'll instruct my servants to render assistance and have the staff assemble for this rare occasion." As Neithamun made to rise, Hernebti caught her wrist, her white-knuckled hold strong enough to keep her hostess in her chair.

Hernebti's voice sounded a bit strained. "Oh, you can send someone to handle the arrangements, surely? I would linger over this excellent beer for a bit longer with you. I wish to claim closer acquaintance and ask a few questions about the town and the people, since we had little chance to talk when we met before." She stared at Periseneb with narrowed eyes. "I enjoy chatting with both of you."

Intrigued by her unusual behavior and odd demeanor, Periseneb gestured to Amethu as Neithamun settled into her chair. "You can take care of preparation for the ceremony?"

Eyes watchful, Amethu rose from his own seat and bowed. "It will be my honor."

"Send a runner to let us know the temple is ready and the people are gathered, and we'll be along with the priestess," Periseneb said.

Drumming the fingers of one hand on the table, Hernebti seemed unable to sit still. She said nothing as her companions and the Heron Marsh servants left the room. The moment the last person crossed the threshold, she straightened, pushed her dish away, and said, "We won't have much time without risk of being overheard, and I have to talk to you in private without note being taken. I don't know who I can trust among the local priests."

"Let me be sure none linger in the hall, if the matter is so important." Periseneb marched to the entry and verified no one was in earshot of the chamber before rejoining the two women at the table.

"I've come all the way out here today because I've news I think will be of importance to you, soldier," Hernebti said, her voice low.

"Then the Great One Isis doesn't need a bull?" Neithamun asked. "I can refund the gold—"

"Keep the deben." Shaking her head, the priestess said, "I'm sure she'll be pleased to have the animal in her herd, but no, a purchase was the best excuse I could think of to avoid arousing suspicions. I needed a plausible reason why I'd journey here unexpectedly."

"Best speak plainly to us then," Periseneb said.

"It's about Haqaptah." Hernebti took a deep breath. "If we're interrupted before I can tell you all, we must try to talk privately in the temple after the ceremony."

"I can't attend," Periseneb said. "My presence at any ceremony offends your Great One for reasons I'd rather not explain."

"Always mystery surrounds you." The high priestess eyed him for a moment before nodding. "Well then, I must be quick and blunt. Lady Tashed came to see me three days ago, on the pretext of reviving our friendship from Thebes. Once she was in my personal quarters, she unburdened herself of a terrible secret." Hernebti glanced at Neithamun. "I know you've cause to dislike her, but she's a loyal citizen of Egypt. She not only obeys Pharaoh's law, she's personally acquainted with him through her family."

Neithamun inclined her head, toying with her plate. "I'll accept your word as to her loyalties."

"On the night Tashed spoke of, she overheard her husband, her father-in-law, and others discussing a plot by Haqaptah to kill the nomarch and seize control of the nome." As both Periseneb and Neithamun exclaimed in dismay, the priestess waved her hands for silence. "Apparently, Haqaptah tried to recruit some of the men to join him during his visit, and threatened those who wouldn't. This meeting Tashed spied upon at great risk to herself was when most of the nobles decided to remain neutral and do nothing."

"Neutral?" Periseneb slammed his fist on the table, causing the plates and mugs to jump. "Set's teeth, what's wrong with them? By failing to act, these men are committing treason, not to mention opening the door to the Hyksos. Haqaptah may think he can strike a bargain with the enemy and control them, but he's sadly mistaken."

Hernebti nodded. "I'm relieved you see the matter as I did."

"But what does Tashed expect you to do? Or us?" Neithamun's brow was furrowed. "I've no army to march into the field on Pharaoh's behalf. Are we to send word to the nomarch?" Eyes wide, she shifted her attention from Hernebti to Periseneb. "Why should he believe us?"

"Tashed wished to unburden herself of the secret. My motive is the same. Neither of us is a soldier." Hernebti laid her hand over Periseneb's. "But I think, of all people in this province, you're the right man to tell this news."

"More than you know." His mind was whirling with half-formed plans. This had to be why Ma'at had sent him here. "Have we any details of the plan?"

Hernebti nodded. "Haqaptah intends to ambush the nomarch on his way to Khemjekhu. Tashed said the men spoke of a narrow pass to the east—"

He could visualize the spot, ideal for lying in wait with a force to surprise the unwary. "I know it well. But surely the nomarch travels heavily armed? With troops?"

"Apparently, his custom is to bring only a small contingent of his personal guard, since the Hyksos were defeated and driven out of the province." Hernebti gave the open doorway at the other end of the room a nervous glance before saying, "Tashed heard her father-in-law say Haqaptah has been sending the nomarch honeyed messages, stating how much he admires Pharaoh and supports him."

"What lies," Neithamun said. "The whole territory has heard the stories of how Haqaptah made deals with the Hyksos when the occupying forces were here."

"But the nomarch may not know these things, especially if the local nobles have decided to remain silent and give allegiance to whoever wins." Periseneb hoped Pharaoh's man wasn't so naïve, but this nomarch was unknown to him. "So, Haqaptah kills the nomarch, completes his takeover of power in this part of the province, invites the Hyksos back into Egypt, gives them a base from which to launch attacks, and war begins anew."

"I believe you've identified the substance of the plan." Hernebti nodded.

"What are we going to do?" Neithamun said. "What can we do?"

"My lady, the temple stands ready." Amethu was in the doorway, raising his voice to carry to them at the other end.

A senior priest stood at his shoulder. "The sun sets rapidly at this season."

"Well, we'd best begin the ceremony." Hernebti drained her mug, then stood and smoothed her dress. "Walk with me?" she said to Neithamun.

Periseneb escorted the women to the door, then held Amethu aside at the threshold. "We need to talk, first thing in the morning, after the priestess and her party take their leave."

"Of course." Eyes narrowed, the other man said, "Something weightier than which field to plant next, I gather? Are you coming to the ceremony?"

"I've something to do first. You go ahead." As Amethu obediently took the corridor to the mansion's entrance, Periseneb went to the library. In solitude, he took his hidden mehen board from its secret niche and moved the green malachite ball one space closer to the end of his time at Heron Marsh. So few squares remained, so few hours with Neithamun. At least now, he finally knew what task Ma'at expected him to accomplish, thanks to Hernebti. As the first notes of Hernebti's chant drifted from the temple into the library, he drew a piece of papyrus toward himself and picked up a quill, ready to lay out his strategy for thwarting Haqaptah's attempt to reinstall the Hyksos rule in this province.

In the morning, no sooner had Hernebti's small procession disappeared into the haze, prize bull in tow, than Periseneb and Neithamun closeted themselves in the library with Amethu. It took only a few moments for Periseneb to lay out the details of the plot the priestess had revealed.

Amethu stroked his chin. "Knowing you to be one of Pharaoh's personal guard, I'm assuming you have a plan? Some action which requires my men and me to take up arms again?" His expressionless face gave no hint whether he was willing to commit to the cause.

"I can't give orders, I can only hope you'll choose to stand with me." Periseneb was clear on that point. "First, I need to find out what's going on at Haqaptah's estate. We don't know exactly when the nomarch will be traveling through the dangerous area. We only know he has to be in Khemjekhu on Settlement Day, and I'm assuming he'll arrive a day or two ahead of time. Ideally, I'd like to warn Pharaoh's man, but I may not be able to, depending on what preparations Haqaptah has made. The good thing is the Hyksos seem to be staying out of the affair, waiting to see if the traitor can secure the area for them."

"First things first," Amethu said. "Your Pharaoh gave us mercy, deigned to give us breath, allowed us to return to our homes and families, although it wasn't given to him or us to know the place had been destroyed. I swore allegiance to him and I'm no oathbreaker. Nor are my men."

Neithamun took a deep breath. "Good—"

"But Thebes is many days march from here," Amethu continued, as if she hadn't spoken. "And none of us pledged to bear arms and march on Pharaoh's behalf."

"You could take your people today and leave," Periseneb answered. "Go into the Red Lands and seek an oasis, as you originally planned."

Amethu nodded. "You and your lady have been good to us, given us a home, purpose, and hope for the future." He rose from the chair.

Neithamun stared at him, biting her lip, as if trying to decide what to say. Periseneb left his chair at her side as Amethu walked around the end of the table to face him. The man went down on one knee, fist over his heart, staring at Periseneb. "I pledge my loyalty and that of my people to you, warrior. By the wings of Horus and the jaws of Anubis do I swear to follow you until my dying breath and into the Afterlife, if so ordered. My men shall each do the same. May the sacred Nile, the sun, and the sky serve as my witnesses, and if ever I break this oath, may the gods destroy me."

"I'm honored," Periseneb said, bowing his head. "I accept this pledge in the spirit in which it's offered. May the gods grant you eternal life, prosperity, and health as reward for your loyalty."

Amethu rose. "Since I first beheld you in the marketplace, my lord, I knew you were one to be followed. I assumed it was only our destiny to serve you here, on this estate, but now I understand clearly that my men and I are to fight at your side."

Periseneb clasped the other's shoulder for a moment. "I'm no pharaoh, no high born lord, but I swear to you, I've been sent by the Great One Ma'at to resolve this situation on behalf of Egypt."

"We—we should plan now, shouldn't we?" Neithamun asked after a moment of silence.

The two men glanced at her, Amethu rising to his feet. Periseneb nodded. "I've drawn several battle plans." He walked to the nearest row of baskets and withdrew the charts he'd spent so much time over the night before. He spread them on the library table, Amethu anchoring the curling edges with an inkwell and small slates. The trio bent over the maps he'd created from memory.

Tracing the curve of the road, Amethu said, "Amazing topographical detail."

"I grew up in this region," Periseneb answered. "And I was taught by Pharaoh's best officers to plan a campaign."

"All depends on whether we reach the nomarch before Haqaptah does," Amethu answered. "I see you've prepared alternatives accordingly."

"I'm no soldier, but isn't success or failure also going to depend on how many men Haqaptah has?" Neithamun tapped the spot on the map where her relative's estate lay. "You said he had quite a force of mercenaries."

"Such men are often undependable in battle, lacking the discipline of true soldiers," Amethu said. "If his hired killers are like the bullies we encountered."

"I forgot, you've been on his estate," Periseneb said, lightly smacking his forehead in chagrin. "What did you see there?"

Amethu closed his eyes for a moment, brow furrowed, as he searched his memory. "He has a force of at least five chariots, archers, and probably one-hundred men. Maybe more." Amethu blinked. "I was kept well away from the area where his troops were training, once it became apparent I wasn't joining the ranks. Had I known I was on a spy mission, I'd have paid more attention and been conciliatory for a time."

Periseneb sank into his chair, whistling. "A stronger force than I expected."

Bending over the map again, Amethu studied the terrain. "The nomarch will surely have crack troops with him. Perhaps even some of your caliber."

"I think you're both forgetting something," Neithamun said from her spot in the chair. As the men faced her with wide-eyed surprise, she continued. "Some of the local nobles who are less wary than Kingfisher's lord may well have joined Haqaptah. Tashed didn't know or didn't choose to share the details with Hernebti, so we don't know with certainty. Each traitor would bring a guard force with them. Not as large or as well trained as Haqaptah's, perhaps, but more men to fight, nonetheless."

"Good point." Periseneb rolled his map and tied a string around it. "This province is a nest of snakes." He glanced at Neithamun. "No offense."

She waved a hand dismissively. "I can't disagree."

"First order of business is a surreptitious trip over Haqaptah's borders to see what he's up to and how advanced his preparations may be." Periseneb rose. "I've been there before without getting caught, and can easily repeat the sortie."

"Will you send someone in search of the nomarch, to warn him?" Neithamun asked.

"I'll go myself, once I know what stage the enemy has reached on his planning." Periseneb nodded.

"I'll gather my men now and explain the situation. We'll begin our own preparations to march at your command," Amethu said. "The estate work will have to wait."

"I want to help," Neithamun said. "I'm a loyal citizen of Egypt; my family holds this estate in the name of Pharaoh. Some of my men should go with you." Jaw clenched, eyes alight with courageous passion, she gazed at Periseneb. "I'd go myself, but I've no training with weapons."

Touched by her determination, he reached to squeeze her hand for a moment. Forced to be realistic, he said, "You've hardly any able-bodied male workers on the estate, and your people aren't trained warriors."

"Even one additional man could help." She wasn't giving an inch. "Some of my people are excellent archers…Mentu, for one."

"I'd prefer the few men available stay here to protect Heron Marsh," Periseneb said, equally stubborn.

"We're not in any danger," Neithamun answered. "Haqaptah plans to take my estate through other means than force of arms."

"She's right," Amethu said. "We should at least give the men the chance to join us."

Periseneb knew he'd have to yield the point, but another problem raised its head. "What about weapons? I refuse to lead unarmed men into battle."

"I'll open the armory today and see what's left," Neithamun answered. "The last armorer is long retired, nearly as old as Benerib, but he can render advice.

Most of the things haven't been used in years, but there may be some swords we can sharpen, a few bows, shields—"

"I'll work with the lady to speak to her workers and then examine the contents of this armory, see what can be salvaged for our purpose," Amethu said. "You should lose no time in making the trip to spy out Haqaptah's activities."

But what Periseneb found when he worked his way carefully onto the neighboring estate was alarming in the extreme, as he reported to Neithamun and Amethu a few hours later. Gathered with them again in the library, he laid out the news at once, as Amethu was closing the door, before anyone had sat down. "The place is virtually empty. Haqaptah's gone."

"Gone? You mean he's already taken off to ambush the nomarch?" Neithamun said, sinking into the central chair as if the strength had gone from her legs.

Perching on the end of the library table, Periseneb drained the mug of beer he'd been given and nodded. "The only people left on his estate are women and children. There's no work being done. The chariots are missing, no one is patrolling the fence lines, and his thugs aren't drinking and gaming in front of their barracks."

Rotating the beaded amulet on her wrist, Neithamun frowned. "So, what do we do now?"

Periseneb exchanged glances with Amethu. "March at dawn and hope we can reach the appointed spot before battle has been joined."

"It may already be too late," she said.

Periseneb shook his head. "I don't think so. The timing of the plot is predicated on the nomarch being in town for Settlement Day. I imagine Haqaptah plans to meet with whatever allies he's gathered among the local nobles and then launch a combined attack. Our not having chariots is a blessing in this case, as we can take a more direct route cross country and hope to intercept the nomarch on the road."

"It's all we can do," Amethu agreed.

"How many men have we added from the estate workers?" He didn't have his hopes high for much reinforcement.

Amethu's answer was more encouraging than expected, although the numbers were still pitifully small. "Ten, mostly archers, accustomed to hunting game rather than men. Lady Neithamun's armory had some weapons and shields we could use. I've gotten my own soldiers and the new volunteers organized, and I ran a cursory training this afternoon."

"I'll speak to them myself before we leave at dawn," Periseneb said.

"And I'll be there to give my blessing on behalf of Heron Marsh." Neithamun sounded as if she expected some disagreement, but Periseneb nodded.

"Entirely appropriate. Your words will give the men encouragement."

Amethu rose from his chair. "With your permission, I'm off. I'll alert the troop to be ready to march, and tell them to assemble with their gear in front of the house at dawn." He gave them a lopsided grin. "I know Thuya is waiting for me. My wife hoped we'd never part again, that she'd never see me march to war as I did before, but this is a fight we must wage. She doesn't like it, but she understands."

"Egypt can't bend to the Hyksos' yoke again," Periseneb said. "Nor be subject to their evil gods."

"I hope *our* gods favor this effort," Amethu said. "And lend their aid." Saying no more, he left the library.

"What chance have we, actually?" Neithamun's voice was low, troubled. "I know you've been sent by Ma'at, but even so, you're one man, commanding twenty five other men, some untrained in combat. I watched the drills Amethu ran this afternoon." She shook her head. "Even with the best will in the world, you can't create hardened soldiers from estate workers in one day. You go against who knows what force Haqaptah has mustered. If other nobles have banded with him, he could have hundreds of soldiers."

He held out his hand and she left her chair, coming to sit in his lap, caressing his neck where the muscles were taut, nestling her head against his chest. Hugging her to him, he said, "This coming battle must be the reason the goddess sent me here. She won't abandon me."

"Ma'at isn't a warrior goddess." Neithamun seemed inclined to examine the problems tonight.

"But she chose a warrior for her champion." He infused as much of his own determination into the response as he could, hoping to give his lady encouragement. "I'm well blooded, not only in life but in the gray wastes against demons. Experience no other living man has. Haqaptah doesn't know what he's facing in me."

She traced the symbols on his falcon badge with one finger. An apologetic smile lingered on her lips. "I don't mean to sound as if I doubt you."

"I didn't take it that way," he assured her, dropping a kiss on the top of her head. He let his hand drift down her leg, pulling the hem of her dress up so he could stroke the soft flesh of her inner thigh as he nuzzled her neck. "Shall we go to bed?"

For answer, she slid off his lap. "I should have realized a warrior needs sleep before going to do battle."

Sweeping her into his arms, he said, "*Sleep* is the last thing on my mind tonight."

As he headed for the library door, carrying her effortlessly, Neithamun laughed. "And I feared you'd wish to conserve your strength."

"Skirmishing with you gives me added power for the other kind of combat." He shifted his grip on her somewhat, so his arm brushed the side of one soft breast.

"I know so little of warriors," she said.

"I've no complaints."

She was quiet as they traversed the remaining halls to her chambers, their path lit by hanging oil lamps, but once Periseneb had laid her on her bed, she said, "Will you return to me?"

In the midst of unfastening his kilt, he paused, remembering his vow to speak only truth. He had to clear his throat before he could utter the answer. "I can't promise."

Her face was grave, her eyes wide. "There are days remaining before Settlement Day. Surely Ma'at will let you stay here until then? She gave you a month, didn't she?"

He realized Neithamun was crying, tears slipping down her cheeks. Dropping the kilt to the floor, he sat on the bed and took her into his arms. "We don't know what the Great One will do. If I'm successful and the nomarch is rescued while Haqaptah is defeated, the result may be enough to satisfy Ma'at. She may not feel I need to remain until Settlement Day, knowing you have the gold to pay Heron Marsh's taxes. I don't even know how much Ma'at cares about the estate, separate from the larger issues. She may decide I've already done enough to balance the facts of my death and Sitre's treachery."

Her tears fell harder. He was helpless against his woman's grief, none of his warrior's skills preparing him to relieve her sadness. Since his words appeared to bring little or no comfort to her, he stopped talking and held her close to his chest while she wept. Stroking his hand through her hair, occasionally rubbing her back, he hoped the strength of his embrace would convey wordless comfort.

Taking a deep, shaky breath, Neithamun pushed against his chest a few moments later, and he let her go. She wiped the tears from her face with her hands. Leaving the bed, she went to the table and washed her face with water from the basin. She yanked her dress off over her head and walked naked to the bed. "I'm sorry, even I know weeping is no way to send a warrior off to battle."

Catching her hand, he said, "Never apologize to me for your honest expression of emotion. I treasure the fact of your love." He kissed her palm. "I hate to cause you such pain."

"Better I cry now, in private, than tomorrow morning in front of all." She drew a deep breath and smiled a bit tremulously, leaning close to him. "Didn't you tell me the goddess promised you could keep your memories of us?"

"Yes. I'll treasure each one I've collected in my time here."

"I mean to provide you with something better to remember than a foolish girl's tears." She crawled onto the bed. "Let us stop talking about these things and confine our thoughts to this one room, to us."

"You'll get no argument from me." It was but a moment's delay to remove his loincloth and then he joined her on the bed, taking her into his arms, enjoying the way her soft curves pressed against him as she returned his embrace with unabashed ardor. "Do you know what I wish, more than anything?" he asked when she paused for breath.

"If it's in my power to grant, I will," she said, circling his flat nipple with her finger, then leaning closer to tease the sensitive spot with her tongue.

He had to swallow hard before he could continue. "I wish I was a man of this time; I long to ask you to be my wife. There's nothing the goddess can give me—not even entry into the Afterlife—that would outshine the happiness of being your husband."

She was silent for a moment, but pressed a kiss to the base of his throat. Then she propped herself on one elbow to gaze into his face. "To be your wife is my dearest wish as well. Our hearts are well matched."

"But I'll be leaving you in such a short time—"

"No wife—or husband—has any guarantee how long their life together will be," she said, her voice soft.

"Yes, but a couple can be guaranteed the Afterlife together, and I can't even promise you normal peace of mind about the future the way any mortal man could do. If I fail to accomplish what Ma'at wants—"

"You won't fail." Her voice was confident. "Ask me the question and receive my answer."

"But, what if you find another man, after I—I'm gone? I want you to be happy, to be loved, to have children, if Fate be kind. Not tied to an akh who appeared in your life and then vanished like the morning mist over the Nile."

She tapped him on the chest, not hard, but with purpose. "You're not an akh to me. You're the man I love, will always love. Besides, Fate could grant us a child."

At the idea of becoming a father, his heart skipped several beats. "Are you…?"

She shook her head. "No, but we've one night left, if only you'd stop talking."

Periseneb had the soldier's ability to wake himself at the needed time. Despite having spent most of the night making love to Neithamun, he snapped into full alertness before dawn. Taking a moment to savor the pleasure of his beloved snuggled close to him, warm and soft, he dropped a caress on her shoulder, while stroking his hand down her arm to brush her breast, enjoying the touch of her smooth skin under his palm and the memories of the night. "I have to get dressed now. We'll be leaving soon."

She rolled over to face him and they kissed for a long moment. "We laid out your uniform in your room. I'll meet you on the stairs at dawn, to send you—all of you—off with my blessing." Sitting, she fumbled with the amulet on her wrist.

"I know the goddess Ma'at protects you; I know you're an akh with all the power that suggests, but I want you to wear this." She held the coral and turquoise amulet she never removed. "You may think me foolish, asking a warrior to accept my childhood trinket, but I...I deeply believe you need my protection as well." In the faint light from the oil lamp, he could see the troubled expression on her face, her brow furrowed, her lips tight.

There was only one proper answer. "I'm touched, beloved wife." Savoring the possessive word on his lips, he held out his left arm and she tied the string holding the beads together in a neat knot around his wrist before pressing a kiss onto the spot where his pulse beat.

"My mother gave me this when I was five. I've added beads as I grew older. Heron Marsh has no one patron deity, so there are beads for Sobek, Hathor, Thoth, Renenutet, and Tawaret," Neithamun said, touching her fingertip to each respective carved bead as she named the gods. "All those who affect our daily life here." Forehead wrinkled in concern, as if she'd come to a realization that worried her, she added, "There's no bead for Ma'at."

The semiprecious stones were cool on his skin. "I have her feathers, which should be enough."

"If you...don't come back to me, then I'll be comforted knowing you have my bracelet," she said, hugging him for a moment. Her voice was thick with unshed tears. "Wherever you go."

His heart was full of things he wanted to say, but she laid her fingers on his lips. "Know I love you. If our next meeting is in the Afterlife, so be it. Do what you have to do."

He stared into her eyes for a heartbeat before kissing her and then rolling out of the bed before he could be tempted to do more, drawing the sheets to cover her. "At the stairs then."

Leaving the room, walking away from Neithamun, was the hardest thing he'd ever done. As he closed the door behind him, he heard her sob. The sound hit him like a punch to the gut, but he kept walking. Their last night together had been a precious gift, more memories to store deep in his heart against the coming chill of his inevitable departure for some part of the Afterlife, but the bittersweet interlude was over. Now he had work to do on behalf of Ma'at and Egypt.

He found his original clothing, freshly washed and laid neatly on the bed in the master's chambers, including his breastplate of overlapping layers of brightly colored leather, which someone had painstakingly cleaned and conditioned with precious oils. His sword and shield lay nearby. A new nemes headcloth in blue and gold—Pharaoh's colors—had been set next to the other garments. The dark of night was yielding to the pearl of predawn as he strode through the halls and out the front door, pausing in surprise.

His motley troop of twenty five stood in a neat formation in the area directly below the stairs. Amethu saluted as Periseneb came all the way onto the platform. The entire population of the estate surrounded the warriors, waiting silently in the morning chill. A raggedy cheer started somewhere on the left side of the group and was taken up by other throats, until the sound was deafening, echoing against the walls of the nearby buildings. The soldiers drummed their swords and spears against their shields, adding to the cacophony. He stayed where he was, emotion swelling in his chest at such a sendoff. As the sound began to die, he saluted, fisted hand over his heart, and bowed.

He heard footsteps behind him and swung to see Neithamun emerging from the house, flanked by Menwe, Khensa, and Mentu's younger brother. His lady had taken the time to dress in her best dress, her one elegant wig, and to paint her face as intricately as any court beauty. Her version of armor, he realized, with a flash of understanding. She was as imposing as any queen this morning, taking his breath away.

She kept her face expressionless, but her eyes betrayed the emotion she was bottling up inside. "As the Lady of Heron Marsh, I bestow my blessings upon you, my husband, and upon those of you going forth to do battle for Egypt." As a gasp ran through the crowd at her naming him as husband, she swept the assembled soldiers with her gaze. "May the Great Ones keep you and smite the enemy on your behalf. May the gods give you strength to draw bow and wield sword. May Horus the Falcon speed your triumphant homecoming here when the battle is won." She made a beckoning gesture, and Menwe stepped forward, offering Neithamun a platter bearing the vase holding the magic lotus. Drawing the flower from the water, Neithamun took a half step closer to Periseneb. "I return this symbol of victory to you now, draw upon its magic in battle, as you wielded it here in peace. You brought water to my thirsty estate, worthy men and women to help carry the burdens, and love to my heart and my bed. May this symbol of the gods now give you victory in battle."

Pride warming his heart at her public acknowledgment of their love, he saluted her as deeply as he would have honored Pharaoh, and reached to take the flower from her hand. As their fingers touched, there was a pop of blue and green sparks, and the lotus was no more. The watching crowd gasped. Some people retreated hastily, their steps slowing as others stood fast, including Amethu and the soldiers. Eyes sparkling, Neithamun touched his bicep, below the hem of his sleeve. "The gods have spoken, the magic is yours again."

Glancing to where her fingers rested, he saw there was a brilliant blue lotus tattoo on his bicep. The skin tingled as it had when Ma'at gifted him with her symbol.

"Use the magic well," she said, leaning down from her position a stair above him and kissing his cheek. "Come back to me," she whispered for his ears alone.

There was no time for him to answer her. She moved aside as Khensa and Mentu's sibling came forward. Periseneb realized the boy was holding a cedar staff, taller than himself, from which now unfurled a banner, snapping in the breeze. The Heron Marsh cartouche was emblazoned in white on blue and green.

Neithamun and the boy descended the stairs together, going past him, so he fell in behind them. She stopped in front of Amethu, who saluted. "I entrust you with the insignia of this estate, of my home, and now yours as well. Carry it into the battle, follow Lord Periseneb to victory, and bring glory to Heron Marsh. My blessings upon you—all of you—who fight for Egypt and for us." Her voice carried in the clear morning air and the crowd cheered again, as Amethu accepted the banner from the boy and thanked Neithamun.

Without another word, she spun on her heel and ascended the stairs.

Periseneb took his place at the head of his command, the men forming a column behind him. The crowd parted and he led his troop away from the house, heading for the open countryside and the conflict that awaited. Although Neithamun—his wife, praise the gods—was watching, he didn't seek a final glance. His mind was set on the campaign he'd undertaken, and now was the time to display a soldier's strength and purpose. He had to set the example for his men. The goodbyes had been said and war was at hand.

Two days of hard marching later, Periseneb was aghast at the major battle taking place on the flatland below his perch atop a rise. Judging by the positions of the combatants, he assessed the fight had barely begun. "Set's teeth, I'd hoped we were in time, bringing early warning of danger to the nomarch." When the column reached the other side of the confined area, he'd heard trumpets and the sounds of conflict ahead. He'd climbed the bluff at a driving pace, his men scrambling behind him to remain close. Now, he was staring at a disaster in the making.

"Yet, we saw the tracks of the enemy in the pass as we came through," Amethu answered.

"I'd hoped it was a caravan, bound for the major cities in the east. Apparently, the nomarch decided not to risk the pass at the end of the previous day, since he camped some distance from the entrance. The gods granted one blessing." Periseneb approved. The nomarch had also brought more troops with him than expected. All this was to the good.

Periseneb hadn't been able to find out exactly what military experience Haqaptah could claim, if any. What he was watching now confirmed the man's amateur status. Rather than lying in wait for the nomarch, as Periseneb or any other seasoned commander would have done, springing the trap once Pharaoh's official and his troops were too far into the pass to retreat, Haqaptah and his allies had raced through and onto the plains beyond. Apparently unable to resist the lure of immediate combat, Haqaptah had surprised the nomarch's camp at dawn, before the noble and his soldiers were ready to march.

The nomarch's troops were fighting well, disciplined, but seriously outnumbered.

"I count at least five standards," Amethu said, pointing at the banners waving over different areas of the battlefield, shifting and weaving as the fluid fighting moved.

Having counted the same daunting odds, Periseneb assessed the opposition on the plain in front of them. "One will be Haqaptah's own. So, he gathered more local nobles to his cause than I'd hoped."

Amethu grunted. "The traitors press the nomarch hard on the western flank."

Periseneb glanced at his pitifully small contingent. Were each man from Pharaoh's Own guard, as he was, the reinforcements he brought might make a significant difference, allowing the nomarch to regroup and take the offensive. But nearly half of his troop were unblooded estate workers from Heron Marsh, the rest from a previously defeated force. "We'll charge, taking the enemy by surprise from the rear," he said, raising his voice so all could hear. "Our object is to break through to the nomarch and reinforce his position. It may be that with our help he can retreat to a more advantageous location and organize a more effective defense with his troops." He drew his sword. "Stay close to me, stay focused, strike to kill or disable the opponents and move on. Don't let yourself be surrounded by a pack of the enemy. In the name of Egypt, charge!"

He ran down the slope at a pace barely short of falling, conscious of his men close behind. He waded into the battle, hacking and slicing with his sword, closing his mind to all thoughts except the intent of reaching the nomarch. The enemy forces were confused, taken off balance by an assault from the rear. Periseneb's offensive gave the nomarch's badly outnumbered soldiers a chance to fall back. He heard trumpets and observed chariots moving through the field of battle, as Haqaptah and his fellow nobles rallied their own forces. He was taking losses in his small force and their forward progress stalled as the mercenaries and traitorous locals dug in.

Fending off an attack with his shield and expertly slashing at his opponent across the abdomen with his sword, then back through the neck, he paused for a second to take a breath. Amethu pressed close, shield raised to protect Periseneb's flank. "How are we going to reach the nomarch?" he yelled. "The enemy sees what a small force we are."

Before he could answer, Periseneb had to dive to the side to avoid one of the chariots, driven toward him in a mad rush. *Someone in command must have figured out I'm the leader of this small group.* He rolled, hanging onto his shield and weapon, shaking off the pain of an arrow's feathers stinging his bicep like a glancing slash from a knife. He didn't see Amethu in the dust and confusion, he could only hope his men were alive and continuing to fight. *Lost cause, this is a lost cause; I don't have enough soldiers to turn the tide.*

Silence enveloped a twilight gray world, dim as if the sun had fallen from the sky. For a moment of sheer disbelief, Periseneb feared he'd been re-exiled to the wastelands. Yet, when he glanced left and right, he was standing in the midst of the fierce battle, men and horses frozen as if transformed into granite. He saw arrows suspended in midair, a spear about to strike, a chariot in the midst of toppling—all impossibly motionless. There was no wind, no sound. Only he lived and breathed in this odd place.

Yet he sensed he wasn't alone. Raising his sword and shield instinctively, he spun to find himself facing a troop of warriors led by an officer whose uniform was black and gold. Try as he might, Periseneb couldn't make out the faces of the soldiers, standing at rigid attention. Their leader stepped forward and his face was as inhumanly handsome as any statue to be found in a pharaoh's tomb. Periseneb's attention was caught by the golden insignia the man wore like a crown, holding his nemes headcloth in place. It was the sacred knot of Isis. Glancing at the soldiers again, he realized each man had the same symbol emblazoned in gold on his gleaming ebony black shield.

"You're Ushabti," he said, his dust-choked voice harsh to his own ears.

"Servants of the gods, yes." The man saluted while his soldiers stood rock solid, staring straight ahead. "Captain Intefiqer-Duaen at your service, Lord Periseneb. Isis, queen of the gods, sent me to assist you."

"Isis? Isn't she opposed to my entire existence here?"

A half smile played over Duaen's lips. "She charged me to inform you she's been impressed against her better judgment by you, and will play one turn of the game on your behalf."

"I'm honored by her praise," Periseneb answered, even as he choked on his anger over the idea that this battle was seen by the goddess as a game. Ma'at had warned him repeatedly humans were viewed as pawns in the concerns of their betters. The important thing was that Isis had sent help. He'd no doubt the Ushabti were a deadly fighting force.

"We can be deployed only once," Duaen said. "We've barely another moment or two before time reclaims this place and the battle is joined. What are your orders, Commander? Where do you want us?"

"If you and your warriors can take out the local nobles and their troops on the western flank, my men and I'll continue driving through Haqaptah's main force to reach the nomarch." Gripping his sword, Periseneb felt renewed strength at having reinforcements. "Haqaptah's doom is my mission from Lady Ma'at, and I intend to satisfy her."

As his men marched in silent lockstep away from him, heading west, Duaen hesitated. "My queen charged me to deliver a message as well."

"I welcome the words of the goddess."

"Remember what you are and use it well." Duaen didn't wait to see if what he'd said made any sense to Periseneb, or if there were questions. "We go now to carry out your order." He saluted. "An honor to serve with you."

There was a ground shaking growl of thunder and a flare of intense white light, as if lightning had struck directly in front of Periseneb. For a moment, he was blinded. Blinking hard against the flashes of white in his vision, he searched in vain for the Ushabti captain and his troops. A horn sounded its clarion call from the western side of the battlefield, the notes achingly clear and martial, like none he'd ever heard before. The music lingered on the wind.

As if the summons was a signal for him too, Periseneb felt a moment of overpowering vertigo and ducked from sheer instinct as one of Haqaptah's mercenaries lurched into sudden motion, finishing the downward sweep of his sword, launching a fierce attack meant to cripple and then kill. The sound of battle was raucous and harsh in his ears as he fought his way forward past the man. One precious step at a time, Amethu at his side once more, Periseneb advanced. The combined force of men from the east and the Heron Marsh recruits formed a wedge at his back, and the unit was now unstoppable. Periseneb thrust and parried and hacked his way through the enemy ranks like a man possessed, his only focus on getting to the nomarch before the makeshift defenses collapsed. If the nomarch perished, all was lost.

The flags bearing the insignia of Shield Nome and Pharaoh's cartouche waved defiantly in the distance, marking the nomarch's position.

The mercenaries and rebel troops formed a solid wall in front of him, significantly outnumbering the Heron Marsh contingent. The enemy moved to surround them, which would mean death and defeat. Anger flooded his body with extra energy. He snarled at the soldiers moving toward him, intimidating more than a few to retreat uncertainly.

Taking a deep breath, he searched his mind—what message had Isis sent him? Use what you are. *Well, what I am is a death-dealing akh.*

Standing tall, he dropped his shield and slapped his free hand over the lotus tattoo, feeling his skin tingle. The scent of the flower filled his nostrils, blocking the stench of battle. Power flowed through his tired muscles until he felt as fresh as he'd been before leaving Heron Marsh two days ago. His head buzzed and he shook it once, trying to clear the sound to no avail. His vision sharpened until he could see the tiniest detail of every man in front of him, down to the cracks in their shields and the imperfections in the bronze of their swords. Rolling his shoulders, he realized he loomed over the mortals, able to assess the entire field of battle. The power filled his body like the most potent wine flowing through his gut, and raising his arms to the skies, he guffawed with sheer joy.

This must be what it's like to be a god, bringer of death.

Sword swinging like a scythe, he advanced, slaying five or more men with every blow. Periseneb stalked through the ranks of his enemies like a lion scattering gazelles. Magic flowed from him now, an uncanny weapon of blue and green sparks striking men and killing the targets where they stood, or in mid-flight. No enemy arrow or sword could touch Periseneb as he strode across the field of battle. The force of his magic shunted the weapons aside. Never had he felt like this in battle, never had he slain the enemy in such numbers. He dealt death to three mercenaries preparing to slaughter one of the nomarch's men, lying injured at their feet. His magic sought out the enemies, all of whom he perceived to be marked with flickering black outlines, as if a second sun cast a revolting shadow over them. The nomarch's men and his own Heron Marsh troops were unsullied by the influence of the Hyksos god. Periseneb's magic left them untouched as it sought more targets to kill.

Marching forward, Periseneb laughed with the sheer joy of decimating the opposing forces. In the moment, he didn't care if Amethu and the others followed him, or if the nomarch lived or died. He was supreme, invincible, the champion of a goddess. No mere man could hope to stand against his power. A chariot made a run at him, the horses wide-eyed and sweating. He flung out his hand, as if hurling an invisible dagger, the magic darting through the air like a barrage of arrows, and the men in the chariot fell. The wheels burned with fire from the sparks he was flinging and the team bolted free as the tracings gave way.

The enemy was in full retreat now.

Avid for combat, he sought more victims. Surging through his body like a tidal wave, the power was hungry, demanding to be fed.

The tattoo on his shoulder tingled. Annoyed, he swatted at his skin, as if there was an insect there. He didn't want distractions. He wanted to kill...

As if the thought was cold water thrown in his face, Periseneb took a deep breath and hesitated, surveying the scene. The battle was all but won, the enemy was fleeing. There was no honor in pursuing and striking down those who fled.

It was as if Ma'at whispered in his ear. The tattoos throbbed. A vision of Neithamun crossed his mind and what she'd say to him if he slaughtered those who only wished to surrender. A band of cool sensation circling his wrist caught his attention, even as he slashed through another tangle of mercenaries.

He lifted his wrist for a moment, staring at the amulet his beloved had given him. "Not an akh," he whispered to himself. "She loves a man. An honorable soldier."

As if the words had power of their own, he was rooted in the spot where he stood, unable to take one more step. The magic cascaded from his body, into the earth, as if all his blood was rushing away. He staggered and Amethu rushed to brace him with one arm, while protecting them both with his battered shield.

"Truly, I've never seen anyone fight as you did, my lord. You were possessed." The warrior gave a shaky laugh. "A giant from a scribe's tale, or so you appeared to me in the fever of battle. Fearsome. Are you injured?"

Periseneb shook his head. "No, I'm fine." He glanced at the ragged line of his soldiers and counted only seventeen. Mentu had a wound in his arm, but was otherwise intact. Hoping at least some of the missing men would be found lying injured, not dead, he focused on the priority. "We'll have to search for our comrades later. I must reach the nomarch."

The path to the edge of the nomarch's camp was clear now, and a moment later Periseneb was facing the noble he'd come to rescue. He saluted as if the nomarch was Pharaoh himself, wearing the blue crown of a commander. "Periseneb of Heron Marsh, reporting, my lord."

The nomarch winced, cursing as the physician who was binding up a wound on his bicep tugged the bandage tight. Brow furrowed, he scanned the much-reduced troop standing at attention behind Periseneb. "I was sure you had a much bigger force, an army perhaps. You fought well, all of you. I wouldn't be standing here without your timely intervention."

"It's fortunate the enemy chose to rush your camp, rather than lie in wait above the narrow valley beyond," Periseneb said. "The pass would have been a funnel of death for you and your men."

He stood aside, as several of the nomarch's officers came rushing to report. Behind them were soldiers carrying the torn and soiled banners of the rebellious estates. "I've never seen anything like it," the ranking officer reported, as the troopers dropped the banners on the ground. "Dead men carpet the western flank. Yet we didn't have any new reserves to pour into the battle. How—?"

"I had some unusual allies," Periseneb said, inserting himself into the conference.

The soldier who was reporting gave Periseneb a hard look, doing a doubletake when he noted the golden falcon badge pinned to his chest. According Periseneb more respect, he said, "Men in black and gold? I watched such a force rush the chariots and foot soldiers pinning us down." The officer scratched his head, puzzlement in his voice and wrinkled brow as he continued. "At least, I believed I did, but there's no sign of them now. They were unstoppable, repelling the enemy with ease, slaughtering all the mercenaries in their path, a tightly disciplined unit. Better than our best. Then the wind rose, carrying the sand and dust to obscure my view, and when I cleared my eyes of grit, these allies of yours had left the field. My men and I were able to finish off or capture the remnants of the enemy with no trouble."

"Strange things happen in battle." Periseneb was counting the flags from the rebellious estates. "One's missing. Where's the one for Haqaptah? He's the leader of this entire scheme."

The officers exchanged glances. "We brought all that were captured."

The nomarch pointed at his own officer with the index finger of his good hand. "Retrace your steps on the battlefield, search again for this Haqaptah. Ask the prisoners what became of him. You may promise my mercy to whoever reveals the man's location, and harsh justice to any who seek to hide him."

The officers saluted and hastened to carry out the command.

Leaving the crumpled flags, Periseneb studied the nomarch. "Your face is familiar, my lord."

Laughing, the noble bent over for a moment, twisting his shoulders into an odd alignment, and said in a raspy voice, "Bread for a wounded soldier?" He held out an empty hand, palm up.

Periseneb retreated a step. "*You* were the beggar I rescued from Haqaptah's thugs?"

"Yes, playing the spy was one of my roles for Pharaoh during the years we fought the Usurper and her Hyksos allies. I'm rather good at it, actually." The nomarch's pride was evident as he straightened, regaining proper military posture. "I revert to nefarious activities at times, especially when about to travel to a corner of my province where rumors of incipient trouble run rampant. It's useful to me to observe things from a different perspective than I get as a ruler people toady and lie to."

"Your leg injury was faked?" Periseneb couldn't help but glance at the other's lower extremity, unable to believe the scars and damage he'd seen in the market were an illusion.

"No, the injury is all too true, unfortunately. A wound received in combat at Pharaoh's side. I was blessed to be healed by an extremely skilled physician. But the scars remain." Head tilted, the nomarch made a fist and flexed his arm as the military physician stepped aside. "Excellent field dressing. My thanks." He pointed at Mentu. "Deal with the boy's injury next." Rising from the stool as the doctor moved to obey, he beckoned to Periseneb to follow as he walked deeper into the camp, stopping at a table where beer and mugs had been set out. Pouring himself a serving and taking a long drink, the nomarch turned to Periseneb. "It would appear you and I should be as brothers," the nomarch said, "Both bearing the badge of Pharaoh's Own. We're a close-knit troop, brothers in arms. Yet I know you not." Eyes narrowed, the noble studied Periseneb from head to toe. "You fight as one who is entitled to wear the golden falcon with honor. I owe you my life. Come, have a drink with me. Battle is thirsty work."

With Amethu at his back, Periseneb accepted the offered beer. Setting the mug on the table before he took a sip, Periseneb unfastened his golden falcon and handed it to the nomarch. With a puzzled frown, the noble examined the details on the front, rubbing his thumb over the dent, and then flipped the badge over. He read the cartouche out loud. "Khakaure Senusret?" Giving Periseneb a skeptical glance from narrowed eyes, he snorted. "Impossible. He ruled the Black Lands over two-hundred years ago."

Wiping his upper lip, Periseneb said, "And I fought by his side." Ignoring Amethu's quickly stifled gasp and the skeptical demeanor of the soldiers surrounding the nomarch, he went on. "Please, my lord, I can explain in detail later, but we must find out what's happened to Haqaptah. I can't rest until I know if he lies dead or injured on the field of battle."

"We'll have a report shortly." Nomarch Tiy-Ineb-Menhet handed over the falcon insignia. "So, the gods must have sent you? If you truly fought in the army of a pharaoh long dead."

"Probably stole the badge from a tomb," growled a nearby soldier, who also wore a golden falcon.

Tiy raised a hand to silence his man. "Peace. He fought as one of us would. And his forces saved the day. I'd underestimated the enemy's strength, and he rescued me from my folly."

Hand on the hilt of his sword, Periseneb said, "I serve the goddess Ma'at and cannot lie. Nor would I, not on this subject. The falcon is mine by right of service rendered. To wear Pharaoh's golden badge, to have earned his trust, is the highest honor for a soldier."

"Well said." The nomarch indicated his agreement with the vehement statement.

An officer came running. He saluted as he skidded to a halt. "It is reported by numerous sources how the leader of this rebellion took off in his chariot, fleeing to the west, my lord. He didn't even wait to see the outcome of the battle, but fled as the tide turned with this man's arrival." He gestured to Periseneb.

Tiy raised his eyebrows. "Can we believe this report?"

"The mercenaries who took this Haqaptah's coin were bitter he'd abandoned the field and them."

Periseneb's blood ran cold, thinking of Neithamun and the others at home, defenseless. "If he drove to the west, I'm afraid he's gone in the direction of the Heron Marsh estate as he seeks to escape. I fear what revenge he might take there."

"I see the time for explanations will have to be later," said the nomarch. He yelled for his chariot, his men running to do his bidding. As the officers scattered, he asked Periseneb, "Can you drive a team?"

"Aye. I was commander of one-hundred chariots for Pharaoh, in my day."

"We'll take my chariot and an escort. Be ready to leave in a few moments." Moving aside, Tiy issued rapid orders to the man who'd questioned Periseneb's status.

Realizing he had his own arrangements to make, Periseneb gestured to Amethu. "I need you to stay here, find the rest of our men, and do whatever's needed for the injured and the fallen. Coordinate with the nomarch's commander." He rested his hand on the other man's shoulder. "I give you my word I'll ensure the safety of your wife as soon as I've ensured the wellbeing of my own." It gave him a thrill to refer to Neithamun as his wife, even as the worry hovered in his heart.

Amethu nodded, a muscle in his jaw working. "Thuya is a survivor. And if Haqaptah did venture to Heron Marsh, he's lost his thugs and mercenaries here, so how much damage can one man do? I'll take command of our troop."

Periseneb gave his attention next to Mentu, lingering close by. "Are you able to ride?"

The physician was packing his box of bandages and potions. "I don't advise it. The wound was deep."

The cowherd made a fist with the hand of his good arm. "I'm tough. I've never ridden in a chariot, my lord, but I can hang on, I'm sure. And the injury is well tended."

Accepting the cowherd's self-assessment, Periseneb said, "I want you to come with me, to take charge at the estate, if we find the situation as dire as I fear. I'll have to pursue Haqaptah if he's fled further, so I need someone I can trust to help Neithamun restore order."

Eyes wide, jaw slack, Mentu swallowed hard. "Me?"

"You have the respect of all of Heron Marsh, from the youngest to the oldest. You've got a good head on your shoulders. So, yes, you."

Three chariots came clattering to the front of the tent, the teams of black horses fresh and ready to run. The nomarch finished his beer, gave his second in command a few more rapid fire orders, and then beckoned to Periseneb. "You and I and the boy can ride in my chariot. You'll drive. Let us get to this Heron Marsh or otherwise overtake the traitor at the best speed my horses can manage."

"You go with me yourself, my lord?" Periseneb was surprised. "What of the traitors here?"

"My second in command can deal with matters. We're old hands at mopping up after a battle, having been through years of campaigning together under Pharaoh. He knows what to do. This Haqaptah is the head of the snake, and it's my job to see him dead." Tiy clapped him on the shoulder as he climbed into the chariot, Periseneb taking the reins. "Besides, you tell me you're sent by the goddess Ma'at to restore order, so clearly my duty is to accompany you, man of the past."

For the rest of the day, Periseneb hoped to catch Haqaptah, but the traitor had too much of a head start. "Or else the demons of the Hyksos gods are helping him," the nomarch muttered. Periseneb drove the horses as far and as fast as he dared, the nomarch not protesting the treatment of his teams. Eventually, however, the noble forced even the desperate Periseneb to admit the necessity of camping for the night.

As soon as dawn broke the next morning, the teams were harnessed and the three chariots continued their mad dash toward Heron Marsh. By midmorning, Periseneb had the squad galloping up the road to the house. Periseneb hoped Haqaptah hadn't bothered to stop here, but had made good his escape into the Red Lands. *Where I'll follow him until Ma'at refuses to allow me any more time.* His hopes were dashed as he swept the chariot in a great circle to stop neatly at the foot of the stairs.

Jumping from the vehicle, he scanned the rapidly gathering crowd, but failed to spot Neithamun. He bounded up the stairs, not caring if the nomarch followed or not. Amethu's wife emerged from the doorway, tear tracks on her cheeks.

"What is it? What's happened? Where's my wife?" His questions were sharp and fast, like arrows. He grabbed her by the arm.

"Taken, my lord, by Haqaptah, not two hours ago."

"But unhurt?"

She nodded. "The women of the house tried to protect her. Khensa, Menwe, others. He grabbed Menwe, stabbed her, then threatened to finish the job and kill her if Neithamun failed to come forth. The lady walked from her chamber as calm as you please and ordered him to leave her people alone. He bound her hands and thrust her into his chariot. We—we tried to block the road with our bodies to keep him from leaving." She took a deep breath to steady herself. "We knew you must be on your way, my lord. We hoped to delay him."

"What happened?"

"It was clear he had no compunctions about running us over, and at the last second, we moved aside. Your wife was screaming at us not to sacrifice ourselves."

"Only one chariot?" The nomarch stood at Periseneb's shoulder.

She nodded, eyes wide at the sight of the noble. Belatedly, she bowed to him.

"So, his companions did abandon him, once clear of the pass," said the nomarch. "I thought as much, from the tracks we saw. No matter, my men will hunt them down."

Thuya had her hand on Periseneb's arm. "Please, my lord, what of Amethu?"

"He's fine, came through the battle without a scratch. I left him in charge of our troop at the nomarch's camp. How is Menwe?"

"The wound was savage, a knife slash across the belly. We've tended it as best we can. Will you come see her, my lord?"

"No time. I must be after Haqaptah without delay." But even as he spoke, his conscience pricked him. Menwe was a loyal woman, who had tried her best to save Neithamun. He placed his hand on Mentu's shoulder. Raising his voice, he said, "I'm placing Mentu in charge of the estate in my absence. Obey his orders as you would Lady Neithamun's or mine." Lowering his voice so none could hear but Mentu, he said in a quieter tone, "Best to give everyone the day off, to pray for Neithamun's safe return. If we're not back by tomorrow, then try to get the estate working again."

"I'll send one of my officers to town, to fetch the best physician there," the nomarch said.

"I appreciate the blessing, my lord," Thuya answered before Periseneb could acknowledge the favor.

"Have the horses watered, bring the men beer and bread. We leave in a few moments," Periseneb said. "I'll go see Menwe."

"We laid her in one of the guest bedrooms," Thuya told him, hurrying to keep pace with him. "I fear she won't live long enough to benefit from the nomarch's kind offer of a physician's care. Haqaptah was in a rage and struck to kill. I think if he'd had more time or men with him, he'd have tried to do more damage. But he must have known or feared you were hot on his trail, so he grabbed the lady and left."

Periseneb paused on the threshold of the bedroom where Menwe lay. Blood seeped through the bandages the women had wrapped across her abdomen. Moving to the bed, he leaned over, whispering her name. Menwe moaned and opened her eyes. Seeing him, she grabbed his hand in a surprisingly strong grip. "Have you rescued my lady?"

He squeezed her hand gently, as he sat on the bedside chair Khensa had vacated. "I leave on that mission in a moment. I came to see you, to thank you for trying to protect her."

"What else would I do? She and I are like sisters." She coughed a bit, her free hand going to her stomach as she tried to curl protectively against what was obviously excruciating pain. "I'm dying, my lord. Don't waste time on me, go save Neity."

He was tempted to call for Ma'at and ask her to intervene on Menwe's behalf. But, what if Ma'at's assistance was needed more when he finally confronted Haqaptah? He didn't dare use a marker yet. As the maid slumped onto the headrest, more blood flowing scarlet through her bandages, he laid her limp hand on the mattress and rose. Angry at this senseless attack committed by Haqaptah, he hesitated. There had to be something he could do. A faint hint of the lotus perfume rose to his nostrils, and he stared more closely at his bicep, where

Neithamun had set the magic tattoo, a mere three days ago. Although much faded, he could make out the outline of a few petals. Resting his fingers over the spot, he bowed his head in prayer. "Great Ones, this innocent woman doesn't deserve to die today as another of Haqaptah's victims. If there be any power left in the lotus, any magic at all, I beg you to let me apply it to her healing."

He heard Thuya gasp behind him.

Opening his eyes, he was astonished by faint blue rivulets of sparkling magic ink flowing down his arm. Hastily, he positioned his other hand to catch the liquid. "Get me a mug or a bowl, quickly."

Thuya ran to obey.

A few sparks dripped onto the stained linen, flaring for a moment before disappearing into the fibers of the cloth. But what remained in his hands as Thuya returned with a goblet was no liquid. The perfume became intense as he gazed in astonishment. Five soft, blue lotus petals rested on his palms. The edges of each glittered a bit with residual magic. "I must lay these on the wound," he said, the knowledge coming to him unbidden from some greater power.

Khensa and Amethu's wife removed the soaked bandages gently, while Periseneb kept his eyes on the precious lotus petals, willing them to stay. The wound was deep and shocking to see in a woman's soft belly. Anger choked him as he carefully laid the five petals next to each other along the injury. He hoped this wasn't going to be Menwe's funeral wreath. She relaxed, lines of pain in her face easing, as he added the final petal to his informal dressing. He was aware of the two women chanting a prayer to Sekhmet, the Great One of healing. His own thoughts were for Ma'at, the goddess who'd sent him, although she wasn't known for influence over injuries. All his power came from her, however, and he prayed to be allowed to transfer enough to Menwe to give her a fighting chance at surviving. *She shouldn't pay for her bravery with her life.*

"The wound has stopped bleeding," Khensa whispered, standing at his side.

The lotus petals lay on Menwe's skin like a tight blue bandage. The perfume lingered in the room, although not as strong as it had been. "I can do no more," he said. "Don't let the physician disturb the lotus, if the petals are still present when he arrives."

"No, of course not," Thuya agreed. She drew the sheet up to cover Menwe to the chin, bending close to make sure the injured woman lived. "She breathes more easily, my lord."

His arm was numb. Rubbing his bicep, he turned to leave the room and staggered on the first step away from the bed. Thuya braced him for a moment. "Are you all right?"

Hoping he hadn't seriously weakened himself and risked Neithamun by relinquishing a portion of the store of magic, he nodded. "I have to go."

"My eyes scarcely believe what I saw you do. I have a small healing gift, as I once told you, but the actions you took far exceed anything I can accomplish." The woman released him and stepped closer to the bed. "The servants here say you're a sorcerer, or a Great One in disguise. I think I believe it now."

Mentu was at the threshold. "The nomarch is ready to leave and asks for you."

"Coming." He glanced at Menwe once more. "I don't know if what I tried to do will help or not. We can only hope the Great Ones are merciful."

Then he was striding through the halls to the great door, intent on the pursuit of Haqaptah and the rescue of his wife.

"The man can't be far ahead of us now," the nomarch said, as Periseneb bounded down the stairs and jumped into the chariot beside him.

"But if he reaches the Red Lands, he might have Hyksos allies waiting."

"True. Let us waste no more time. Are you able to drive? You keep rubbing your arm."

"I'm fine. A momentary cramp." He held out his hand and the nomarch passed him the reins.

Calling to the horses and flicking the whip lightly close to the leftmost horse's ear, Periseneb set the chariot in motion, closely followed by the second. Of the third, there was no sign, and he assumed those officers had been dispatched to the city to fetch a doctor, as the nomarch had promised.

At the entrance to the valley where Heron Marsh buried its dead, Haqaptah's chariot had come to a violent halt. One of the horses was down in the traces, apparently dead. The other had broken free and bolted. Of the noble himself, there was also no indication where he might have fled after the crash. A splash of blue cloth against the sandy terrain showed where Neithamun had been flung when the accident occured.

Cursing, heart pounding, Periseneb yanked his team to a halt, flinging the reins to the nomarch even before the wheels had stopped. He leapt from the basket and ran to Neithamun. By the grace of some Great One, she hadn't landed on the rocks, but was curled awkwardly in a sandy area, unconscious, blue dress disheveled and torn. As he cradled her in his arms, calling her name, he discovered her hands were bound tight behind her back. Swearing to gut Haqaptah like a fish if he ever caught the man, Periseneb gently laid her on the sand before drawing his belt knife and freeing her wrists. As he checked her for broken bones or other injuries, he was dimly aware of the nomarch striding to him.

"The horse is dead," Tiy reported. "A trail of blood goes west, which should lead us to Haqaptah. He can't have gotten far in this rough terrain if he's injured. This is your lady of Heron Marsh, I presume? Is she breathing?"

"She lives," Periseneb said. "Maybe she was just stunned. She needs water."

Without a word, the nomarch ran to fetch the waterskin from his chariot. Squatting next to Periseneb as he rinsed Neithamun's face in hopes of awakening her, Tiy said, "I wonder what can have caused the crash?" Rising, he studied the landscape to the west. "Certainly there's no obstacle, nothing but clear road to the Red Lands and his freedom."

At the moment, Periseneb didn't care what had happened to Haqaptah. Under his deliberately gentle touch, Neithamun was stirring. Eyes fluttering, she stared at him for a moment before sitting bolt upright with a scream.

"Shhh, dear heart, you're fine, I've got you." He hugged her tight, not liking the way her pulse raced. "You're safe with me now." He kissed her forehead. "I'm sorry I left you unguarded at the house, easy prey for the cursed hyena bastard to snatch. I should have planned more effectively, should have insisted you take refuge in town, with Hernebti. I hope you can forgive me."

She tugged him closer. "I was terrified when Haqaptah snatched me from my home, but I had no doubt you'd find me." Obeying her unspoken order, he lowered his head to capture her lips. The kiss became less sweet reassurance and more passionate hunger the longer he held her close. Grateful she yet lived, he craved the forgiveness implicit in her passion, rejoiced in having her safe in his arms.

The nomarch, who'd discreetly wandered away to examine the wrecked chariot, cleared his throat. "I've sent my two men to search the area for Haqaptah. Now that we know the lady is safe, the traitor must be our main concern."

With a final caress, Periseneb broke off the kiss. "Can you stand?"

She nodded. "I'm sore all over, but I believe so."

He rose and then lifted her to her feet, taking most of her weight himself until he was sure her legs would hold. She stared beyond him at the nomarch. "Who—"

The noble made her a courtly bow, as if meeting her at a banquet in the palace at Thebes. "Tiy-Ineb-Menhet, ruler of Shield Nome, at your service, my lady."

"Then you were in time to save him?" she asked Periseneb.

"Yes, to my eternal gratitude and some puzzlement, your mysterious husband arrived in the nick of time." Tiy walked to join them. Hands on his hips, he surveyed Neithamun. "Perhaps you should sit on the tail of my chariot? You're pale under those spectacular bruises."

Berating himself for not thinking of allowing her to sit, Periseneb swept his wife into his arms and carried her to the chariot.

She asked the question he'd been dreading. "How is Menwe?"

"I did the best for her that I could, but the wound is grave. A doctor has been sent for."

"At least she lives," Neithamun said, her voice sounding as if she was fighting tears. "She was so brave—reckless to go against Haqaptah on my behalf, but with the heart of a lioness."

Tiy retrieved the waterskin, handing it to her as soon as she was safely seated. After an inarticulate murmur of thanks, Neithamun drank deeply.

"He was taking me to the Hyksos," she said a moment later, giving the water to the nomarch with trembling hands. "He's been working with them for years, he boasted. The enemy was going to make him the ruler of the entire province, if he could first take over our town and the surrounding area."

"A clever plan to use Khemjekhu as a base for launching attacks on the rest of my territory," Tiy said. "Not a bad strategy. Of course, I had a few plans of my own to counter such tactics, not to mention a growing army. Pharaoh has been most generous in supporting me as I consolidate his rule over Shield Nome. But why kidnap you? Was he in love with you?"

"Hardly." She closed her eyes. "For revenge against my—my husband." Blinking away tears, she reached for Periseneb, taking his hand and holding it to her heart. "He said you cost him everything, and it would make him happy to know that even if you ended up with Heron Marsh, you'd never have me. He planned to give me to the Hyksos for their pleasure."

"I feared as much, which is why I came as fast as the nomarch's excellent horses could travel. The man has a twisted mind." Periseneb had another concern. "Sweetheart, what caused the chariot to crash?"

Reaching out to him with both arms, she shivered, closing her eyes. "It was the woman."

Happy to hold her, but disturbed by her shivering, he stroked her hair and was silent.

"Woman?" Tiy glanced at Periseneb with one eyebrow quirked.

Periseneb was sure he knew who Neithamun meant. A chill running down his spine, he asked, "Sitre?"

Neithamun pushed free of his embrace and leaned against the side of the chariot. She lowered her eyes and brushed away tears. "The woman from my nightmares, if she truly is Sitre. She was dressed all in black, her face hidden, the way she appeared in my bedroom the night before you arrived. I pray never to see her again either, even if she did rescue me from Haqaptah."

Periseneb shook his head. "The action isn't like her at all. In life or death, she wouldn't do a good deed for anyone unless it benefitted her in some way." Knowing he owed the patiently waiting nomarch an explanation, he said, "Sitre is an akh." Swallowing hard, he continued. "A ghost tied to this land by the curse of a dying man, two centuries ago."

Tiy stared pointedly at Periseneb's golden falcon badge before glancing away. "There are many mysteries connected to you, shield brother. I hope I'm to have the entire tale before this is all over."

"If I'm able, I promise you a full accounting, my lord." Periseneb had no idea at what point Ma'at would declare his efforts complete and take him to his fate.

Taking the waterskin from where the nomarch had hung it, Neithamun splashed water on her face and wiped running makeup and tears alike off with the edge of her skirt, leaving the fabric smeared with color. "Do you think Menwe will survive?"

"I won't lie, she's in a bad way." Periseneb leaned over, speaking softly. "I gave her what magic was left in the lotus, although I don't know how much help that will be."

Just then there was a shout from the direction of the tombs and he swung to the north to see the two men who'd accompanied them in the other chariot. The soldiers were heading in their direction, carrying a limp figure between them. "Hopefully, Haqaptah's been found."

"Worse for the wear," the nomarch commented. "Why would he run to a spot where there was no good hiding place, or chance of escape?"

Shielding his eyes with one hand, to see the approaching group more clearly, Periseneb frowned. "I don't know, it's a box canyon, with only the family tombs. Easy enough for us to search, with the aid of more troops of course. He's a distant relative, surely he was familiar with the layout of this place."

"Maybe his wits were addled by the crash," Neithamun said. "Mine certainly were."

Raising his voice, the nomarch addressed his oncoming soldiers. "Is the traitor alive?"

"Yes, my lord, but badly injured and unconscious," said one, grappling with his hold on Haqaptah's feet.

"And cold as the grave," yelled the other.

"Cold? In this heat?" The nomarch shrugged. "Dying perhaps."

A moment later, the two men laid their burden in the shadow of the nomarch's chariot. Haqaptah lay as one dead, eyes closed, complexion pasty white.

Uneasy for no reason he could articulate, Periseneb moved between Neithamun and her former captor, while questioning the soldiers. "Where did you find him?"

"In front of the entrance to one of the tombs, about a third of the way up the ceremonial road," said the officer. "He was as you see him." Displaying a dagger and a sword, the man said, "We stripped him of weapons, to be on the safe side."

Thinking uneasily that Sitre's tomb was in the vicinity where Haqaptah had been found, Periseneb squatted next to the unconscious noble and felt his forehead. "Cold as a dead man."

Next moment, Haqaptah's hand braceletted his wrist in an unbreakable grip. Instinctively, Periseneb tried to stand, as the noble, eyes closed, used him as a crutch to rise to his feet as well, standing awkwardly balanced on legs that appeared to be broken. The nomarch and the soldiers made to come to his aid, but Periseneb raised his free hand to hold them off. "Wait. Stay back—something is wrong here."

As if his words had been a signal, Haqaptah's eyes flew open. For a moment, Periseneb saw nothing but solid black—the iris and the white both gone the color of inky night sky—but then the man who held him in an unbreakable grip blinked and the eyes were brown as normal eyes should be. The voice coming from the chalky blue lips, however, was not what he expected. "So, we meet again, my lion?"

Neithamun screamed, hopping off the rear of the chariot and stumbling a few steps. Cursing and making signs against black magic, the nomarch and his men retreated.

The voice was a woman's, low and sultry. Haqaptah's lips were parted, but didn't move in the normal manner of someone who speaks. It was as if he was a puppet, animated by someone else.

Horrified, yet not entirely surprised, Periseneb gasped and tried again to free himself, to no avail. "Sitre?"

Haqaptah raised one limp hand and caressed Periseneb's cheek. In the woman's voice, he said, "Who else?"

"How have you done this thing?" But even as the words left his lips, Periseneb knew the answer.

The ghost inhabiting Haqaptah's body laughed and the sound echoed off the cliffs. "I'm sure you understand, since you're the one who cursed me with his dying breath."

"I didn't curse you to remain here in the Black Lands, haunting the estate," he said, swallowing the bile at the back of his throat. He tugged uselessly at the grip she had on him.

Laughing harder, Sitre-Haqaptah wound his other arm around Periseneb's neck, as if in an embrace. "No, you cursed me to a terrible fate indeed, but I was smart enough to circumvent your intentions. I've never presented myself to the Judging of the Great Ones, and I never will. I've waited through the long years."

Moistening his lips, he asked, "Waited for what?"

"A suitable body to steal. Isn't that what akhs are said to do? Among our other powers? Not all of us are gifted by the Great Ones with a body resembling what we had in life." Sitre-Haqaptah frowned. "But I was sealed in my tomb by the curses and inscriptions at the time of burial, able to roam only in dreams, not to exercise my full powers. My family feared me, as well they should have, and triple-sealed the portal when I was buried." She laughed, the sound giving Periseneb the shivers. "I was trapped in the tomb until her fool of an overseer tried to rob me last year, unsealing the door. I dealt with his impudence. Then I was free to roam in my form as a ka. But it wasn't enough. I want *life*, not just the ability to flit hither and yon and do mischief. For what I crave, I need a vessel, a living body to inhabit."

"But why take Haqaptah?"

"I can only steal the bodies of those who share my bloodline, which he does. And are weak enough, or flawed enough, to obey my summons, which he is, ambitious fool. I thought he'd be a fine vessel for my ka, take me to the Hyksos, where I could learn more black magic, make myself immortal in body as well as ka." Again, the eerie, loose lipped grin. "I'm sure the god of the Hyksos will see my value."

"You won't live to reach the Hyksos," the nomarch said through clenched teeth. He drew his sword.

"This *body* won't live. Unfortunately, the chariot crash caused too many injuries. I was barely able to call him to me in my tomb, and he was dying then. Without your assistance in carrying me to the chariots, I'd have been stymied. His soul has fled to whatever judging he deserves, by those greater than you, petty official." Hobbling a step away from Periseneb, the corpse of Haqaptah waved one hand and the nomarch's sword flew into the brush beside the trail, breaking in two against a boulder. "Mortal weapons don't work against an akh, fools. But my powers will affect you. A plague, I think. Allow me to practice on your companions."

Sitre-Haqaptah made a throwing gesture and red sparks darted from his fingertips to strike the two gaping soldiers. As the men screamed, twisting and clawing at their own extremities, a scarlet rash broke out on every visible inch of skin, spreading like wildfire. Shrieking in agony, first one and then the other collapsed, convulsing in the dust. Their cries grew faint, until both lay still and unbreathing, blood staining the sand.

"Set's teeth, you'll die for this." The nomarch drew his dagger.

Periseneb yanked against the hold keeping him captive, pulling Sitre-Haqaptah off balance on the broken legs. "Sitre, stop."

She kept her grip on him, turning the uncanny black eyes to focus on his face. "Yes, the proper battle is between you and me, isn't it, beloved?"

"I never loved you." His denial was immediate.

"No, perhaps not, but you do love her." The ghastly smile reappeared as the possessed one gestured at Neithamun. "She's an ideal vessel for my ka. No one will suspect anything until it's far too late. I can be the lady of Heron Marsh for all eternity."

Sitre-Haqaptah collapsed into a heap of skin and bones on the ground. Periseneb took a step backward as a dark, viscous cloud of smoke seeped from the corpse's lips and nose. "Take Neithamun and flee," he yelled at the nomarch.

The noble was attempting to extract Neithamun from the danger, but she was fighting him. "I won't leave you," she said, flinging her arm toward Periseneb, as if to yank him to safety.

The cloud was assembling itself into a womanly shape, lazy whorls and tendrils forming a body, flowing hair, and the semblance of a dress. He heard Sitre's voice in his head, low and sensual. *The girl will be mine. There's nothing you can do to stop me. Perhaps you'd like to rule Heron Marsh with me? Wasn't that your original dream? I could be persuaded.*

He swung a fist at the ghost, but his hand passed harmlessly through the cloud, a momentary pain traveling up his arm as the gray miasma touched his skin. The nomarch was dragging Neithamun to the west, but not making much progress. As if in a nightmare, he watched both crumple to the ground.

He may be useful to me, if I can fill his mind with desire for the girl and erase his memories of this incident. A ghostly laugh floated on the air. *If not, he's easily killed.* The silhouette was becoming more solid, parts of Sitre's body and clothing as real as she'd been in life. The face was indistinct, and Periseneb knew once she'd fully materialized, no mortal could stop her from attaining her goals.

The knowledge reverberated in his mind as he sought desperately for some answer, some way to fight an akh and save Neithamun. *But I am not mortal.* He'd been trying to claim the human state, attempting to be the man as he once was, desperate to be a human husband for the woman he loved…except in battle two days before. Isis's Ushabti captain had had to remind him of his true nature. Straightening his spine, he closed his eyes and summoned the magic, the power he had, power no man could wield. He was not human—he was as much of an akh as Sitre, if less evil.

He felt an answering surge of hot tingling through his body as he released his tenacious hold on the human form, relinquished who he'd been in life. Opening his eyes, he took a rapid glance at himself, not surprised to see only a dark cloud of smoke where his body should stand, although he felt as if he yet possessed limbs and organs. Without conscious thought, he flowed across the ground to envelop the nearly finished Sitre, his ghostly essence covering her like a blanket from head to toe. She screamed, red fire blazing from her mouth and eyes, the magic burning a path through him. Clawing at the heavy coils of his akh with her elongated hands, she ripped him into shreds, which he re-formed into a cloud with no effort. Winding one tentacle of smoke around her neck, he constricted the extrusion, while sending another, tipped with a barb worse than any scorpion's, at where he judged her heart to lie.

"Fool! I have no heart, no organs, I've been properly embalmed and buried, remember? Unlike you!" on the last word, Sitre abandoned the battle to give herself human shape and dissolved into a cloud of red and gray mist, escaping his deadly embrace with ease. *I have no vulnerabilities, but you cannot say the same…* She lanced through him with a sword of gray smoke, edged in red, and he recoiled in agony.

How could an akh be subject to so much pain? He almost reverted to human form, trying to absorb the agony she'd inflicted. Surging forward, he made himself a net and enfolded all of Sitre's incorporeal essence. For a moment, the strategy succeeded, but she fought savagely, shoving red sparks into him wherever he touched her. This time, he collapsed to the ground, stunned and human. He rolled onto his back, gasping, as she re-formed herself into the semblance of a woman.

"You can't win this battle, not as a man or an akh," Sitre said, contempt icing her words. "The goddess was a fool to pick you for a champion. I'll let you linger long enough to see me eat the ka of your beloved and take her body. Then I'll send you to the Lake of Fire, and this time you won't be returning to plague me." She straightened the folds of her black dress with a grotesquely feminine gesture and glided over the rough surface of the road, toward the crumpled bodies of Neithamun and Tiy. "Wake up, little girl," she said in a singsong voice. "Time to meet your fate."

Fighting the agony running through his entire body, Periseneb lurched to his feet and staggered after Sitre, stumbling over the ruts. Neithamun stirred and sat, holding her head with both hands for a moment.

"Run," he yelled, but his voice was a mere crow's croak.

Sitre glanced over her shoulder at him, the eyes in her face ghastly red pits. "She can't run from me." She hurled a ball of the red fire at him.

Deliberately falling and rolling away from the weapon, he slapped a hand over the red feather tattoo, strength flowing into his arm, his heart, and then to his legs. Taking a deep breath, he rose. "And you can't escape your fate, bitch."

"Calling the goddess now, are we? Even Ma'at can't match the power I've drawn from you, compounded by the strength of the girl's innocent soul. With all of that to fuel my black magic, I'll make good my transformation."

"Don't be so sure." Periseneb held the red feather in the palm of his hand. With a puff of breath he launched it into the air and said, "I summon Ammit the Destroyer."

Sitre screamed and surged in his direction. "No! Don't you dare—"

"I cursed you to Ammit's care with my dying breath, and now I call her forth to collect you," he said.

Sitre made a desperate grab for the quill, but a stray whiff of wind carried it beyond her clawlike fingers. Falling to the road, Ma'at's token exploded in a cloud of dust shot through with golden trails of light, as if a star had fallen to the ground and burst. In a blink, the cloud reformed into the all too real dread Destroyer. Ten feet long, standing braced on her stubby hippo legs, pink tongue rasping over daggerlike teeth in her crocodile snout, Ammit roared, and the echoes shook the ground.

"No escape now," Periseneb said.

Sitre stumbled away, yelling curses and bits of spells, but Ammit sniffed the air and padded toward her, moving more swiftly than her awkward shape would suggest possible. Periseneb followed the pair. Sitre broke and ran toward her tomb, half smoke, half woman, lifting into the air like some obscene bird. Ammit sprang, bringing Sitre down with her sharp lion claws, pinning the akh to the ground. Pausing for a moment, as if savoring the long delayed victory, she swung her heavy head toward Periseneb. He skidded to a stop, transfixed by the glare from the glowing golden eyes. A nod from the goddess and she opened her jaws, taking Sitre's head and upper torso in one bite, quickly followed by a second gulp, sweeping the entire akh from existence. Periseneb heard a faint scream. Raising her head to the skies, Ammit swallowed and roared in triumph. A flick of the sinuous tongue to clean her teeth and she was gone in a blaze of red sparks, sizzling and dissipating on the hot afternoon breeze.

Periseneb knelt, grateful to have been spared by Ammit, expecting Ma'at to appear and claim him any moment.

He felt a soft hand on his shoulder and Neithamun's voice sounded in his ear. "Are you all right?" She tugged at him. "Say something, please, dear heart."

With a groan, he rose and folded her into his embrace, breathing deeply of her scent.

"Is...is it over?" she asked, voice tremulous.

"I think so. I hope so." He tilted her face to his and kissed her for a long moment.

"Yet, you remain?" Her voice was hopeful.

"Apparently. Maybe Ma'at means to let me have the full thirty days to see you through Settlement Day." He could scarcely believe such generosity from the Great One, but could find no other explanation. "We should see how the nomarch fares."

As they approached, Tiy was leaning on the chariot, racked by dry heaves. Periseneb handed him the waterskin. As he took it, the nomarch said, "I saw it and I don't believe it. Any of it." He gave them an awkward grin. "Certainly, I'm not going to try explaining these events." He stumbled to where the bodies of his two soldiers lay in the dust, kneeling beside them. "Good men, who fought by my side in many a battle." Before he could utter another word, red flames burst from the soil, consuming the bodies.

Periseneb yanked the nomarch away from the fire. "The gods intervene, my lord. I believe the Great Ones want no evidence of what transpired here."

"Have my soldiers been cursed to roam the outer wastes?" Tiy frowned. "How can this be fair or just? Both died in a battle against—well, against great evil."

"I believe if you have the proper ceremonies conducted for them, my lord, the Great Ones will be pleased to receive their kas into the the duat." Periseneb couldn't say why he was so sure of his answer, but the knowledge was in his mind as fact.

"It shall be done." Dusting his hands, the nomarch looked at Periseneb and Neithamun. "What of you? What happens to you now?"

"I'm not sure." He glanced at the one remaining tattoo on his arm. "I still bear the mark of the Great One. Perhaps my fate will be sealed on Settlement Day, as I originally expected."

Neithamun tucked herself into the curve of his arm, tight by his side. "I dread the day."

Tiy bowed to her. "You need have no fear of my judgment, Lady of Heron Marsh. All debt between you and Pharaoh has been paid in full by this day's events, which I'll publicly declare on Settlement Day. And Haqaptah's estate is forfeit, so there'll be no liens against you."

She shook her head mournfully. "Thank you, my lord, but when it comes to the one thing I care most about—my husband's fate—you can't help."

Periseneb heard unshed tears in her voice. He hugged her. "Surely the nomarch's earthly generosity will be echoed by the Great One I serve. She'll judge my heart as worthy and I'll pass safely into the duat." Framing Neithamun's face with his hands, he said, "I've been promised I'll retain my memories of you. I have to wait. I've waited two centuries, I can wait the span of your lifetime for us to be together."

Sobbing, she laid her head on his chest. "And I too will wait out the span of years, but each day will be like the one before - empty and lonely. My heart is yours alone, I'll never marry another, never have children to comfort me."

As he lifted her into the chariot, preparing to make the journey home, he realized her eventual death would leave Heron Marsh with no heir, no member of the family to carry the estate forward. Could he condemn her to live such a lonely life? If part of his mission from Ma'at was to preserve the estate, could he permit Neithamun to mourn him and honor him all her span of years on earth? What kind of selfish being was he?

Periseneb stared unseeing at the stark landscape as the chariot gathered speed, heading east. Perhaps his last task was to ask the Great One to remove not his memories, but Neithamun's. If he truly loved her, didn't he need to set her free of him? And then accept his own sentence of eternity without her?

CHAPTER EIGHT

Khemjekhu had never seen such a Settlement Day in all its history. The herds of cattle from each estate had been paraded before the nomarch under the watchful eyes of his soldiers, and duly counted for taxation. Hernebti had led a joyous celebration from the steps of her Great One's temple through town, and the nomarch had declared a day of feasting and celebration at his own expense.

"Tomorrow, I'll announce my judgment on the estates whose nobles committed treason against Pharaoh and Egypt," he said. "But today, we'll celebrate the defeat of those who conspired against the proper order of things and rejoice in the bounty of the sacred Nile, honoring her. This day is dedicated to the holy purpose, and I'll not interfere with the proper order of things merely to settle the affairs of men. Rest assured, my judgment will be fair and equitable."

After the festivities were well underway, the noble led Periseneb and Neithamun to a private chamber in the house he occupied when in the area. Charging the guards not to allow anyone to disturb them, Tiy closed the doors. "I need wine, and I'm sure you both require some as well." He poured liberally from the gold rimmed pitcher. "This is from Pharaoh's own stock, undoubtedly the best in this nome or any other."

Periseneb took the proffered alabaster cup. "You do us great honor, my lord."

"There'd be no celebration without you. I'd be dead, my army slaughtered. The Hyksos would doubtless be running rampant in the streets today, and Egypt would be facing more years of war. Not to mention the schemes of the creature you destroyed."

Periseneb took a sip and set the cup aside. "My time as Ma'at's warrior is at an end."

"No!" Neithamun's protest was instantaneous. "The day has hours to go."

He shook his head. "I need to settle with the Great One. There's no use in prolonging the agony."

"Then, let us be private." Neithamun glanced at Tiy. "I'm sure the nomarch would lend us a chamber—"

"I want him here, as a witness. To take care of you."

"My word of honor, brother to brother." Tiy bowed. "She shall want for nothing while I live."

"I can take care of myself," she said, scorn in her voice.

Periseneb laid his hand over the remaining red feather. "I'm ready to report to you, Great One, and receive my judgment."

For a moment, nothing happened. Surprised the tattooed emblem hadn't taken form, he prepared to make his request again.

There was the sound of chimes and the scent of the lotus filled the room. Mist swirled about the three of them, and when it cleared, he was standing on the banks of a river, surrounded by green fields and trees laden with lush fruit. Soft green reeds cushioned his feet, and when he glanced down, he realized his battered satchel, sword and shield were stacked neatly next to him. Neithamun and Tiy stood to his left.

Downriver, an elegant boat was drawn up to the shore, gangplank extended to take on more passengers. He heard music and the sound of voices singing, as if a celebration was taking place. The far shore was wreathed in mist, but the duat must be there.

Ma'at stood before him, draped in golden robes, the red ostrich plume gracefully framing her face with its soft fronds. "You've done well, my warrior."

He stood at attention, ignoring Neithamun's quiet sobs, though the sound tore at his heart. "I believe I've accomplished all you sent me to do?"

Ma'at nodded. "Calling Ammit to dispose of the akh rather than me was an inspired move, leading to Sitre's demise and the resolution of the curse you'd uttered. I applaud your ingenuity. Truly, I chose my champion well."

"Yet, I've failed in one regard, my lady." Swallowing hard, he prayed the Great One would be willing to listen to him. "I ask your judgment."

"On what matter?"

"The fate of Heron Marsh."

"Continue." Ma'at gestured with her left hand and a gilded table and chair appeared. She sat, gracefully spreading the folds of her dress in regal fashion.

"My wife has sworn to take no other man to her bed while she waits for her own death. This morning, she told me her womb was empty. I've fathered no child with her in my second time in the Black Lands."

"An akh cannot father a child." The voice of the goddess was cold.

"Leaving the estate with no heir." Before Ma'at could speak, he pointed at Tiy. "Does this concern you?"

"The stability of the nome is already threatened by the five estates I must dispose to new owners tomorrow," Tiy said. "I've no small amount of faith in the Lady Neithamun and her abilities, yet I wish for a strong deputy to leave in charge of the entire area, to hold the western territory of the province for Pharaoh and Egypt. A landowner to rally the other nobles to his standard and command when called upon. A guardian against Hyksos intrusions. A man of military experience who knows the area, which none of my trusted officers do, all being from Thebes or the lower Nile."

"And is there no one in the nome you can name to fill this role?" Periseneb had no idea how long Ma'at would continue to allow the conversation to go on. So far, the Great One was listening with attention, hands folded.

Tiy shook his head. "You know as well as I do, even those who didn't rally to Haqaptah's call failed equally in their duty to Pharaoh. Only Lady Neithamun stepped forward to send me warning and troops in my hour of need. Her death with no heir—at any age—will only weaken the nome further."

"I refuse to marry another and bear him children, just so you can have someone to support you." Neithamun's voice was strong, her declaration contemptuous and haughty. "I love Periseneb."

"Your lineage is important to the fate of all Egypt," Ma'at said, staring at Neithamun. "My sister Sefkhet could remove your memories of Periseneb, carve the love from your heart, and free you to marry again."

Eyes wide, an expression of utter horror on her face, Neithamun shrank back. "My husband has already suggested this horrifying idea to me once, and I rejected it. I beg of you, don't do such a thing."

Ma'at took the feather from her headband.

Periseneb spoke to the nomarch. "Does your Pharaoh honor the will of his predecessors?"

The goddess paused, tilting her head. "Indeed, a fair question."

Tiy licked his lips. "To the extent those wishes are known and can be honored. He won't entertain anything ordered by the Usurper he dethroned."

"No, of course not. But will he honor this?" Periseneb held out the rolled parchment he'd withdrawn from his satchel.

"Your writ of amkhu?" Neithamun asked. "How will the document help us?"

He shook his head. "My status as amkhu wasn't the only favor bestowed upon me by a grateful monarch."

Ma'at held out her hand, and he was forced to give her the scroll. Unrolling it, she scanned the hieroglyphs, which glowed as her gaze passed over them. She studied the cartouche set in red wax at the bottom of the papyrus, touching it with one fingertip. "By order of Pharaoh Khakaure Senusret." Raising her head, she said, "He is long passed into the duat, as was his right, and is well content in the company of his fellow Great Ones." Again, she rubbed a finger over the seal, which blazed with red light. "Yet his earthly command still possesses power. Very well then. It seems you, Periseneb, are to claim any land holding in Shield Nome you desire." She paused, perusing the document again. "Up to and including Heron Marsh itself, for services rendered to Egypt."

"My Pharaoh would honor such a decree." Tiy's answer was prompt.

"Then I claim not Heron Marsh, which has an owner, but the estate of Haqaptah." He spoke boldly. "I will undo the damage he has done to the proper flow of the Nile and will ensure the western territory of the nome remains strong against Hyksos plots. With my wife, we'll hold both estates for the current Pharaoh Nat-re-Akhte."

Ma'at toyed with her feather, running the soft vanes through her fingers.

Neithamun stepped forward, catching his hand. A broad smile on her blushing face, she said, "And will you ensure Heron Marsh has heirs of my lineage?"

"If the gods be kind and bless us with children."

Ma'at tapped her fingers on the table. "So, you wish to be sentenced to live out a human life span, with all the attendant perils and hardships? You forfeit guaranteed entry into the duat?"

"I'll present myself to the judging of my heart as any man does, when the time comes," he said, heart pounding.

The music jangled to a stop mid-chord. The waiting ship unfurled its sails as the gangplank was drawn inboard. The craft nosed into the river, oars dipping into the silvery waters as the boat moved away from them, gliding into the mists.

Ma'at was smiling. "So be it. You've earned your 'sentence,' my warrior, and I wish you well. We'll meet again in due time." She directed her gaze to Neithamun. "School your children thoroughly, ensure each knows their duty to provide proper funeral rites to their parents." She winked. "A duty not to be required of them until the last is well grown, and parents to their own offspring. This, I promise you, in gratitude for the services rendered."

The mists swirled in from the river, and Periseneb held Neithamun tightly as the scent of the lotus overwhelmed him. He felt Tiy grab his shoulder, and then his senses blanked out completely.

When he opened his eyes, he was sprawled in the chair in Tiy's private chamber, Neithamun curled on his lap. The nomarch himself was face down on the table, practically falling from the chair he occupied.

Hand to her hair, Neithamun sat up. Blinking, she took in their surroundings and then swiveled to stare at him, fear in her eyes. "Was our journey real? Or was it a dream induced by the nomarch's wine?"

Forcing himself upright, Tiy groaned. "Thank the gods wine never induced any dream of that nature before. Were it to happen again, I vow I'd have to stop drinking anything but water. Nor have I ever dreamt the same events as my companions. Can there be any doubt the Great One granted your request?" He picked up the scroll lying on the table beside his goblet. "Here's the writ from the hand of your Pharaoh, granting you any estate you desire, which I'm happy to enforce."

"I pray it be so." Neithamun pressed a kiss on his cheek. "I remember she promised we'd have children."

Periseneb had to be sure. Moving Neithamun aside a bit, he rolled up the sleeve of his tunic, to reveal his bicep.

The last red feather tattoo was gone.

"I've come home at last," he said, as he kissed the Lady of Heron Marsh, his beloved wife.